OPERATION
MAYFLY: It was an
order to confirm a suspected
East German rocket site.

THE OPERATIVES:

Taylor: A man with all the right papers and all the wrong luck.

Avery: Young, confused—he lost his doubts slowly, and his scruples too easily.

Leiser: An old pro who wanted desperately to believe it was never too late—but knew differently . . .

"A still more searching, more stripped-down portrait of the spy in action. It goes beyond being a good suspense novel: it is a good novel, period." —*Saturday Review*

"Paradoxical and human . . . A real and moving novel."
—*The Atlantic*

JOHN LE CARRÉ

THE LOOKING GLASS WAR

A DELL BOOK

For James Kennaway

Published by DELL PUBLISHING CO., INC.
750 Third Avenue, New York, N.Y. 10017

Reprinted by arrangement with
Coward-McCann, Inc., New York, N.Y.
First Dell Printing—July, 1966
Printed in U.S.A.

*The carrying of a very heavy weight such as a large
suitcase or trunk, immediately before sending practice,
renders the muscles of the forearm, wrist and fingers
too insensitive to produce good Morse.*

—F. TAIT'S
Complete Morse Instructor, Pitman

FOREWORD

NONE of the characters, clubs, institutions nor intelligence organizations I have described here or elsewhere exists, or has existed to my knowledge in real life. I wish to make that very clear.

My thanks are due to the Radio Society of Great Britain and to Mr. R. E. Molland, to the editors and staff of *Aviation Week and Space Technology*, and to Mr. Ronald Coles, all of whom provided me with valuable technical advice; and to Miss Elizabeth Tollinton for her secretarial help.

I must thank above all my wife for her untiring cooperation.

JOHN LE CARRÉ

Agios Nikolaos, Crete
May, 1964

CONTENTS

ONE   Taylor's Run   9

TWO   Avery's Run   25
        PRELUDE   27
        TAKEOFF   72
        HOMECOMING   102

THREE   Leiser's Run   113
        PRELUDE   115
        TAKEOFF   189
        HOMECOMING   224

ONE

TAYLOR'S
RUN

A fool lies here who tried to hustle the East.

—Kipling

1.

SNOW COVERED THE AIRFIELD.

It had come from the north, in the mist, driven by the night wind, smelling of the sea. There it would stay all winter, threadbare on the gray earth, an icy, sharp dust; not thawing and freezing, but static like a year without seasons. The changing mist, like the smoke of war, would hang over it, swallow up now a hangar, now the radar hut, now the machines; release them piece by piece, drained of color, black carrion on a white desert.

It was a scene of no depth, no recession and no shadows. The land was one with the sky; figures and buildings locked in the cold like bodies in an ice floe.

Beyond the airfield there was nothing; no house, no hill, no road; not even a fence, a tree; only the sky pressing on the dunes, the running fog that lifted on the muddy Baltic shore. Somewhere inland were the mountains.

A group of children in school caps had gathered at the long observation window, chattering in German. Some wore ski clothes. Taylor gazed dully past them, holding a glass in his gloved hand. A boy turned around and stared at him, blushed and whispered to the other children. They fell silent.

He looked at his watch, making a wide arc with his arm, partly to free the sleeve of his overcoat and partly because it was his style; a military man, he wished you to say, decent regiment, decent club, knocked around in the war.

Ten to four. The plane was an hour late. They would

have to announce the reason soon over the loudspeaker. He wondered what they would say: delayed by fog, perhaps; delayed takeoff. They probably didn't even know—and they certainly would not admit—that she was two hundred miles off course, and south of Rostock. He finished his drink, turned to get rid of the empty glass. He had to admit that some of these foreign hooches, drunk in their own country, weren't at all bad. On the spot, with a couple of hours to kill and ten degrees of frost the other side of the window, you could do a lot worse than Steinhäger. He'd make them order it at the Alias Club when he got back. Cause quite a stir.

The loudspeaker was humming; it blared suddenly, faded out and began again, properly tuned. The children stared expectantly at it. First, the announcement in Finnish, then in Swedish, now in English. Northern Air Services regretted the delay to their charter flight two-nine-zero from Düsseldorf. No hint of how long, no hint of why. They probably didn't know themselves.

But Taylor knew. He wondered what would happen if he sauntered over to that pert little hostess in the glass box and told her: two-nine-zero will be a bit of time yet, my dear, she's been blown off course by heavy northerly gales over the Baltic, bearings all to Hades. The girl wouldn't believe him, of course, she'd think he was a crank. Later she'd know better. She'd realize he was something rather unusual, something rather special.

Outside it was already growing dark. Now the ground was lighter than the sky; the swept runways stood out against the snow like dykes, stained with the amber glow of marking lights. In the nearest hangars neon tubes shed a weary pallor over men and airplanes; the foreground beneath him sprang briefly to life as a beam from the control tower flicked across it. A fire engine had pulled away from the workshops on the left and joined the three ambulances already parked short of the center runway. Simultaneously they switched on their blue rotating lights, and stood in line patiently flashing out their warning. The children pointed at them, chattering excitedly.

The girl's voice began again on the loudspeaker, it could only have been a few minutes since the last announcement. Once more the children stopped talking and listened. The arrival of flight two-nine-zero would be delayed at least another hour. Further information would be given as soon as it became available. There was something in the girl's voice, midway between surprise and anxiety, which seemed to communicate itself to the half-dozen people sitting at the other end of the waiting room. An old woman said something to her husband, stood up, took her handbag and joined the group of children. For a time she peered stupidly into the twilight. Finding no comfort there, she turned to Taylor and said in English, "What is become of the Düsseldorf plane?" Her voice had the throaty, indignant lilt of a Dutchwoman. Taylor shook his head. "Probably the snow," he replied. He was a brisk man; it went with his military way.

Pushing open the swing door, Taylor made his way downstairs to the reception hall. Near to the main entrance he recognized the yellow pennant of Northern Air Services. The girl at the desk was very pretty.

"What's happened to the Düsseldorf flight?" His style was confiding; they said he had a knack with little girls.

She smiled and shrugged her shoulders. "I expect it is the snow. We are often having delays in autumn."

"Why don't you ask the boss?" he suggested, indicating with a nod the telephone in front of her.

"They will tell it on the loudspeaker," she said, "as soon as they know."

"Who's the skipper, dear?"

"Please?"

"Who's the skipper, the captain?"

"Captain Lansen."

"Is he any good?"

The girl was shocked. "Captain Lansen is a very experienced pilot."

Taylor looked her over, grinned and said, "He's a very *lucky* pilot anyway, my dear." They said he knew a thing or two, old Taylor did. They said it at the Alias on Friday nights.

Lansen. It was odd to hear a name spoken out like that. In the outfit they simply never did it. They favored circumlocution, cover names, anything but the original: Archie boy, our flying friend, our friend up North, the chappie who takes the snapshots; they would even use the tortuous collection of figures and letters by which he was known on paper; but never in any circumstances the name.

Lansen. Leclerc had shown him a photograph in London: a boyish thirty-five, fair and good-looking. He'd bet those hostesses went mad about him; that's all they were, anyway, cannon fodder for the pilots. No one else got a look in. Taylor ran his right hand quickly over the outside of his overcoat pocket just to make sure the envelope was still there. He'd never carried this sort of money before. Five thousand dollars for one flight; seventeen hundred pounds, tax free, to lose your way over the Baltic. Mind you, Lansen didn't do that every day. This was special. Leclerc had said so. He wondered what she would do if he leaned across the counter and told her who he was; showed her the money in that envelope. He'd never had a girl like that, a real girl, tall and young.

He went upstairs again to the bar. The barman was getting to know him. Taylor pointed to the bottle of Steinhäger on the center shelf and said, "Give me another of those, d'you mind? That's it, the fellow just behind you; some of your local poison."

"It's German," the barman said.

He opened his wallet and took out a banknote. In the cellophane compartment there was a photograph of a girl, perhaps nine years old, wearing glasses and holding a doll. "My daughter," he explained to the barman, and the barman gave a watery smile.

His voice varied a lot, like the voice of a commercial traveler. His phony drawl was more extravagant when he addressed his own class, when it was a matter of emphasizing a distinction which did not exist; or as now, when he was nervous.

He had to admit: he was windy. It was an eerie situation for a man of his experience and age, going over from routine courier work to operational stuff. This was a job for those swine in the Circus, not for his outfit at all. A different kettle of fish altogether, this was, from the ordinary run-of-the-mill stuff he was used to; stuck out on a limb, miles from nowhere. It beat him how they ever came to put an airport in a place like this. He quite liked the foreign trips as a rule: a visit to old Jimmy Gorton in Hamburg, for instance, or a night on the tiles in Madrid. It did him good to get away from Joanie. He'd done the Turkish run a couple of times, though he didn't care for wogs. But even that was a piece of cake compared to this: first-class travel and the bags on the seat beside him, an Allied pass in his pocket; a man had status, doing a job like that; good as the diplomatic boys, or nearly. But this was different, and he didn't like it.

Leclerc had said it was big, and Taylor believed him. They had got him a passport with another name. Malherbe. Pronounced Mallaby, they said. Christ alone knew who'd chosen it. Taylor couldn't even spell it; made a botch of the hotel register when he signed in that morning. The subsistence was fantastic, of course: fifteen quid a day operational expenses, no vouchers asked for. He'd heard the Circus gave seventeen. He could make a good bit on that, buy something for Joanie. She'd probably rather have the money.

He'd told her, of course: he wasn't supposed to, but Leclerc didn't know Joanie. He lit a cigarette, drew from it and held it in the palm of his hand like a sentry smoking on duty. How the hell was he supposed to push off to Scandinavia without telling his wife?

He wondered what those kids were doing, glued to the window all this time. Amazing the way they managed the foreign language. He looked at his watch again, scarcely noticing the time, touched the envelope in his pocket. Better not have another drink; he must keep a clear head. He tried to guess what Joanie was doing now. Probably having a sit-down with a gin and something. A pity she had to work all day.

He suddenly realized that everything had gone silent. The barman was standing still, listening. The old people at the table were listening too, their silly faces turned toward the observation window. Then he heard it quite distinctly, the sound of an aircraft, still far away but approaching the airfield. He made quickly for the window, was halfway there when the loudspeaker began; after the first few words of German the children, like a flock of pigeons, fluttered away to the reception lounge. The party at the table had stood up; the women were reaching for their gloves, the men for their coats and briefcases. At last the announcer gave the English. Lansen was coming in to land.

Taylor stared into the night. There was no sign of the
plane. He waited, his anxiety mounting. It's like the end of
the world, he thought, the end of the bloody world out
there. Supposing Lansen crashed? Supposing they found
the cameras? He wished someone else were handling it:
Woodford, why hadn't Woodford taken it over, or sent
that clever college boy Avery? The wind was stronger; he
could swear it was far stronger; he could tell from the way
it stirred the snow, flinging it over the runway; the way it
tore at the flares; the way it made white columns on the
horizon, dashing them vehemently away like a hated crea-
tion. A gust struck suddenly at the windows in front of
him, making him recoil, and there followed the rattle of
ice grains and the short grunt of the wooden frame. Again
he looked at his watch; it had become a habit with Taylor.
It seemed to help, knowing the time.

Lansen will never make it in this, never.

His heart stood still. Softly at first, then rising swiftly to
a wail, he heard the klaxons, all four together, moaning
out over that godforsaken airfield like the howl of starving
animals. Fire . . . the plane must be on fire. He's on fire
and he's going to try and land . . . He turned frantically,
looking for someone who could tell him.

The barman was standing beside him, polishing a glass,
looking through the window.

"What's going on?" Taylor shouted. "Why are the sirens
going?"

"They always make the sirens in bad weather," he replied. "It is the law."

"Why are they letting him land?" Taylor insisted. "Why
don't they route him further south? It's too small, this
place; why don't they send him somewhere bigger?"

The barman shook his head indifferently. "It's not so
bad," he said indicating the airfield. "Besides, he is very
late. Maybe he has no petrol."

They saw the plane low over the airfield, her lights
alternating above the flares; her spotlight scanned the runway. She was down, safely down, and they heard the roar
of her throttle as she began the long taxi to the reception
point.

The bar had emptied. Taylor was alone. He ordered a

drink. He knew his drill: stay put in the bar, Leclerc had said, Lansen will meet you in the bar. He'll take a bit of time; got to cope with his flight documents, clear his cameras. Taylor heard the children singing downstairs, and a woman leading them. Why the hell did he have to be surrounded by kids and women? He was doing a man's job, wasn't he, with five thousand dollars in his pocket and a phony passport.

"There are no more flights today," the barman said. "They have forbidden all flying now."

Taylor nodded. "I know. It's bloody shocking out there, shocking."

The barman was putting away bottles. "There was no danger," he added soothingly. "Captain Lansen is a very good pilot." He hesitated, not knowing whether to put away the Steinhäger.

"Of course there wasn't any danger," Taylor snapped. "Who said anything about danger?"

"Another drink?" the barman said.

"No, but you have one. Go on, have one yourself."

The barman reluctantly gave himself a drink, locked the bottle away.

"All the same, how do they do it?" Taylor asked. His voice was conciliatory, putting it right with the barman. "They can't see a thing in weather like this, not a damn thing." He smiled knowingly. "You sit there in the nose and you might just as well have your eyes shut for all the good they do. I've seen it," Taylor added, his hands loosely cupped in front of him as though he were at the controls. "I know what I'm talking about . . . and they're the first to catch it, those boys, if something *does* go wrong." He shook his head. "They can keep it," he declared. "They're entitled to every penny they earn. Specially in a kite that size. They're held together with string, those things; string."

The barman nodded distantly, finished his drink, washed up the empty glass, dried it and put it on the shelf under the counter. He unbuttoned his white jacket.

Taylor made no move.

"Well," said the barman with a mirthless smile, "we have to go home now."

"What do you mean, *we?*" Taylor asked, opening his

eyes wide and tilting back his head. "What do you mean?"
He'd take on anyone now; Lansen had landed.

"I have to close the bar."

"Go home indeed. Give us another drink, come on. You
can go home if you like. I happen to live in London." His
tone was challenging, half playful, half resentful, gathering volume. "And since your aircraft companies are un-
able to *get* me to London, or any other damn place until tomorrow morning, it's a bit silly of you to tell me to go
there, isn't it, old boy?" He was still smiling, but it was
the short, angry smile of a nervous man losing his temper.
"And next time you accept a drink from me, chum, I'll
trouble you to have the courtesy—"

The door opened and Lansen came in.

This wasn't the way it was supposed to happen; this
wasn't the way they'd described it at all. Stay in the bar,
Leclerc had said, sit at the corner table, have a drink, put
your hat and coat on the other chair as if you're waiting
for someone. Lansen always has a beer when he clocks in.
He likes the public lounge, it's Lansen's style. There'll be
people milling about, Leclerc said. It's a small place but
there's always something going on at these airports. He'll
look around for somewhere to sit—quite open and above-
board—then he'll come over and ask you if anyone's using
the chair. You'll say you kept it free for a friend but the
friend hadn't turned up; Lansen will ask if he can sit there.
He'll order a beer, then say, "Boy friend or girl friend?"
You'll tell him not to be indelicate, and you'll both laugh a
bit and get talking. Ask the two questions: height and airspeed. Research Section must know the height and airspeed. Leave the money in your overcoat pocket. He'll
pick up your coat, hang his own beside it and help himself
quietly, without any fuss, taking the envelope and dropping
the film into your coat pocket. You finish your drinks,
shake hands, and Bob's your uncle. In the morning you fly
home. Leclerc had made it sound so simple.

Lansen strode across the empty room toward them, a
tall, strong figure in a blue mackintosh and cap. He looked
briefly at Taylor and spoke past him to the barman: "Jens,
give me a beer." Turning to Taylor he said, "What's
yours?"

Taylor smiled thinly. "Some of your local stuff."

"Give him whatever he wants. A double."

The barman briskly buttoned up his jacket, unlocked the cupboard and poured out a large Steinhäger. He gave Lansen a beer from the cooler.

"Are you from Leclerc?" Lansen inquired shortly. Anyone could have heard.

"Yes." He added tamely, far too late, "Leclerc and Company, London."

Lansen picked up his beer and took it to the nearest table. His hand was shaking. They sat down.

"Then you tell me," he said fiercely, "which damn fool gave me those instructions?"

"I don't know." Taylor was taken aback. "I don't even know what your instructions were. It's not my fault. I was sent to collect the film, that's all. It's not even my job, this kind of thing. I'm on the overt side—courier."

Lansen leaned forward, his hand on Taylor's arm. Taylor could feel him trembling. "I was on the overt side too. Until today. There were kids on that plane. Twenty-five German schoolchildren on winter holidays. A whole load of kids."

"Yes." Taylor forced a smile. "Yes, we had the reception committee in the waiting room."

Lansen burst out, "What were we *looking* for, that's what I don't understand. What's so exciting about Rostock?"

"I tell you I've nothing to do with it." He added inconsistently: "Leclerc said it wasn't Rostock but the area south."

"The triangle south: Kalkstadt, Langdorn, Wolken. You don't have to tell me the area."

Taylor looked anxiously toward the barman.

"I don't think we should talk so loud," he said. "That fellow's a bit anti." He drank some Steinhäger.

Lansen made a gesture with his hand as if he were brushing something from in front of his face. "It's finished," he said. "I don't want any more. It's finished. It was O.K. when we just stayed on course photographing whatever there was; but this is too damn much, see? Just too damn, damn much altogether." His accent was thick and clumsy, like an impediment.

"Did you get any pictures?" Taylor asked. He must get the film and go.

Lansen shrugged, put his hand in his raincoat pocket and, to Taylor's horror, extracted a zinc container for thirty-five-millimeter film, handing it to him across the table.

"What was it?" Lansen asked again. "What were they after in such a place? I went under the cloud, circled the whole area. I didn't see any atom bombs."

"Something important, that's all they told me. Something big. It's got to be done, don't you see? You can't make illegal flights over an area like that." Taylor was repeating what someone had said. "It has to be an airline, a registered airline, or nothing. There's no other way."

"Listen. They picked us up as soon as we got into the place. Two MIGs. Where did they come from, that's what I want to know? As soon as I saw them I turned into a cloud; they followed me. I put out a signal, asked for bearings. When we came out of the cloud, there they were again. I thought they'd force me down, order me to land. I tried to jettison the camera but it was stuck. The kids were all crowding the windows, waving at the MIGs. They flew alongside for a time, then peeled off. They came close, very close. It was bloody dangerous for the kids." He hadn't touched his beer. "What the hell did they want?" he asked. "Why didn't they order me down?"

"I told you: it's not my fault. This isn't my kind of work. But whatever London is looking for, they know what they're doing." He seemed to be convincing himself; he needed to believe in London. "They don't waste their time. Or yours, old boy. They know what they're up to." He frowned, to indicate conviction, but Lansen might not have heard.

"They don't believe in unnecessary risks either," Taylor said. "You've done a good job, Lansen. We all have to do our bit . . . take risks. We all do. I did in the war, you know. You're too young to remember the war. This is the same job: we're fighting for the same thing." He suddenly remembered the two questions. "What height were you doing when you took the pictures?"

"It varied. We were down to six thousand feet over Kalkstadt."

"It was Kalkstadt they wanted most," Taylor said with

appreciation. "That's first-class, Lansen, first-class. What was your airspeed?"

"Two hundred . . . two forty. Something like that. There was nothing there, I'm telling you, nothing." He lit a cigarette.

"It's the end now," Lansen repeated, "however big the target is." He stood up. Taylor got up too; he put his right hand in his overcoat pocket. Suddenly his throat went dry: the money, where was the money?

"Try the other pocket," Lansen suggested.

Taylor handed him the envelope. "Will there be trouble about this? About the MIGs, I mean?"

Lansen shrugged. "I doubt it, it hasn't happened to me before. They'll believe me once: they'll believe it was the weather. I went off course about half way. There could have been a fault in the ground control. In the hand-over."

"What about the navigator? What about the rest of the crew? What do they think?"

"That's my business," said Lansen sourly. "You can tell London it's the end."

Taylor looked at him anxiously. "You're just upset," he said, "after the tension."

"Go to hell," said Lansen softly. "Go to bloody hell." He turned away, put a coin on the counter and strode out of the bar, stuffing carelessly into his raincoat pocket the long buff envelope which contained the money.

After a moment Taylor followed him. The barman watched him push his way through the door and disappear down the stairs. A very distasteful man, he reflected; but then he never had liked the English.

Taylor thought at first that he would not take a taxi to the hotel. He could walk it in ten minutes and save a bit of subsistence. The airline girl nodded to him as he passed her on his way to the main entrance. The reception hall was done in teak; blasts of warm air rose from the floor. Taylor stepped outside. Like the thrust of a sword the cold cut through his clothes; like the numbness of an encroaching poison it spread swiftly over his naked face, feeling its way into his shoulders. Changing his mind, he looked around hastily for a taxi. He was drunk. He suddenly realized: the fresh air had made him drunk. The rank was empty. An old Citroën was parked fifty yards up the road, its engine running. He's got the heater on, lucky devil, thought Taylor, and hurried back through the swing doors.

"I want a cab," he said to the girl. "Where can I get one, do you know?" He hoped to God he looked all right. He was mad to have drunk so much. He shouldn't have accepted that drink from Lansen.

She shook her head. "They have taken the children," she said. "Six in each car. That was the last flight today. We don't have many taxis in winter." She smiled. "It's a very *little* airport."

"What's that up the road, that old car? Not a cab, is it?" His voice was indistinct.

She went to the doorway and looked out. She had a careful balancing walk, artless and provocative.

"I don't see any car," she said.

Taylor looked past her. "There was an old Citroën. Lights on. Must have gone. I just wondered." Christ, it went past and he'd never heard it.

"The taxis are all Volvos," the girl remarked. "Perhaps one will come back after he has dropped the children. Why don't you go and have a drink?"

"Bar's closed," Taylor snapped. "Barman's gone home."

"Are you staying at the airport hotel?"

"The Regina, yes. I'm in a hurry, as a matter of fact." It was easier now. "I'm expecting a phone call from London."

She looked doubtfully at his coat; it was of rainproof material in a pebble weave. "You could walk," she suggested. "It is ten minutes, straight down the road. They can send your luggage later."

Taylor looked at his watch, the same wide gesture. "Luggage is already at the hotel. I arrived this morning."

He had that kind of crumpled, worried face which is only a hairsbreadth from the music halls and yet is infinitely sad; a face in which the eyes are paler than their environment, and the contours converge upon the nostrils. Aware of this, perhaps, Taylor had grown a trivial moustache, like a scrawl on a photograph, which made a muddle of his face without concealing its shortcoming. The effect was to inspire disbelief, not because he was a rogue but because he had no talent for deception. Similarly he had tricks of movement crudely copied from some lost original, such as an irritating habit which soldiers have of arching his back suddenly, as if he had discovered himself in an unseemly posture, or he would affect an agitation about the knees and elbows which feebly caricatured an association with horses. Yet the whole was dignified by pain, as if he were holding his little body stiff against a cruel wind.

"If you walk quickly," she said, "it takes less than ten minutes."

Taylor hated waiting. He had a notion that people who waited were people of no substance: it was an affront to be seen waiting. He pursed his lips, shook his head, and with an ill-tempered "Good night, lady," stepped abruptly into the freezing air.

Taylor had never seen such a sky. Limitless, it curved downward to the snowbound fields, its destiny broken here and there by films of mist which frosted the clustered stars and drew a line round the yellow half-moon. Taylor was frightened, like a landsman frightened by the sea. He hastened his uncertain step, swaying as he went.

He had been walking about five minutes when the car caught him up. There was no footpath. He became aware of its headlights first, because the sound of its engine was deadened by the snow, and he only noticed a light ahead of him, not realizing where it came from. It traced its way languidly over the snowfields and for a time he thought it was the beacon from the airport. Then he saw his own shadow shortening on the road, the light became suddenly brighter, and he knew it must be a car. He was walking on the right, stepping briskly along the edge of the icy rubble that lined the road. He observed that the light was unusually yellow and he guessed the headlights were masked according to the French rule. He was rather pleased with this little piece of deduction; the old brain was pretty clear after all.

He didn't look over his shoulder because he was a shy man in his way and did not want to give the impression of asking for a lift. But it did occur to him, a little late perhaps, that on the Continent they actually drove on the right, and that therefore strictly speaking he was walking on the wrong side of the road and ought to do something about it.

The car hit him from behind, breaking his spine. For one dreadful moment Taylor described a classic posture of anguish, his head and shoulders flung violently backward, fingers extended. He made no cry. It was as if his entire body and soul were concentrated in this final attitude of pain, more articulate in death than any sound the living man had made.

The car carried him for a yard or two then threw him aside, dead on the empty road, a stiff, wrecked figure at the fringe of the wilderness. His trilby hat lay beside him. A blast seized it, carrying it across the snow. The shreds of his pebble-weave coat fluttered in the wind, reaching vainly for the zinc capsule as it rolled gently with the camber to lodge for a moment against the frozen bank, then to continue wearily down the slope.

TWO
AVERY'S RUN

There are some things that no one has a right to ask of any white man.

—John Buchan
Mr. Standfast

2.

Prelude

IT WAS THREE in the morning.

Avery put down the telephone, woke Sarah and said, "Taylor's dead." He shouldn't have told her, of course.

"Who's Taylor?"

A bore, he thought; he only remembered him vaguely. A dreary English bore, straight off Brighton Pier.

"A man in courier section," he said. "He was with them in the war. He was rather good."

"That's what you always say. They're all good. How did he die, then? How did he die?" She had sat up in bed.

"Leclerc's waiting to hear." He wished she wouldn't watch him while he dressed.

"And he wants you to help him wait?"

"He wants me to go to the office. He wants me. You don't expect me to turn over and go back to sleep, do you?"

"I was only asking," Sarah said. "You're always so considerate to Leclerc."

"Taylor was an old hand. Leclerc's very worried." He could still hear the triumph in Leclerc's voice: "Come at once, get a taxi; we'll go through the files again."

"Does this often happen? Do people often die?" There was indignation in her voice, as if no one ever told her anything; as if she alone thought it dreadful that Taylor had died.

"You're not to tell anyone," said Avery. It was a way of keeping her from him. "You're not even to say I've gone

out in the middle of the night. Taylor was traveling under
another name." He added, "Someone will have to tell his
wife." He was looking for his glasses.

She got out of bed and put on a dressing gown. "For
God's sake stop talking like a cowboy. The secretaries
know; why can't the wives? Or are they only told when
their husbands die?" She went to the door.

She was of medium height and wore her hair long, a
style at odds with the discipline of her face. There was a
tension in her expression, an anxiety, an incipient discontent, as if tomorrow would only be worse. They had met at
Oxford; she had taken a better degree than Avery. But
somehow marriage had made her childish; dependence had
become an attitude, as if she had given him something ir-
redeemable, and were always asking for it back. Her son
was less her projection than her excuse; a wall against the
world and not a channel to it.

"Where are you going?" Avery asked. She sometimes
did things to spite him, like tearing up a ticket for the con-
cert. She said, "We've got a child, remember?" He noticed
Anthony crying. They must have wakened him.

"I'll ring from the office."

He went to the front door. As she reached the nursery
she looked back and Avery knew she was thinking they
hadn't kissed.

"You should have stuck to publishing," she said.

"You didn't like that any better."

"Why don't they send a car?" she asked. "You said they
had masses of cars."

"It's waiting at the corner."

"Why, for God's sake?"

"More secure," he replied.

"Secure against what?"

"Have you got any money? I seem to have run out."

"What for?"

"Just money, that's all! I can't run around without a
penny in my pocket." She gave him ten shillings from her
bag. Closing the door quickly behind him he went down the
stairs into Prince of Wales Drive.

He passed the ground-floor window and knew without
looking that Mrs. Yates was watching him from behind her

curtain, as she watched everybody night and day, holding her cat for comfort.

It was terribly cold. The wind seemed to come from the river, across the park. He looked up and down the road. It was empty. He should have telephoned the rank at Clapham but he wanted to get out of the flat. Besides, he had told Sarah the car was coming. He walked a hundred yards or so toward the power station, changed his mind and turned back. He was sleepy. It was a curious illusion that even in the street he still heard the telephone ringing. There was a cab that hung round Albert Bridge at all hours; that was the best bet. So he passed the entrance to his part of the Mansions, glanced up at the nursery window, and there was Sarah looking out. She must have been wondering where the car was. She had Anthony in her arms and he knew she was crying because he hadn't kissed her. He took half an hour to find a taxi to Blackfriars Road.

Avery watched the lamps come up the street. He was quite young, belonging to that intermediate class of contemporary Englishmen which must reconcile an Arts degree with an uncertain provenance. He was tall and bookish in appearance, slow-eyed behind his spectacles, with a gently self-effacing manner which endeared him to his elders. The motion of the taxi comforted him, as rocking consoles a child.

He reached St. George's Circus, passed the Eye Hospital and entered Blackfriars Road. Suddenly he was upon the house, but told the driver to drop him at the next corner because Leclerc had said to be careful.

"Just here," he called. "This will do fine."

The Department was housed in a crabbed, sooty villa of a place with a fire extinguisher on the balcony. It was like a house eternally for sale. No one knew why the Ministry put a wall around it; perhaps to protect it from the gaze of the people, like a wall around a cemetery; or the people from the gaze of the dead. Certainly not for the garden's sake, because nothing grew in it but grass which had worn away in patches like the coat of an old mongrel. The front door was painted dark green; it was never opened. By day anonymous vans of the same color occasionally passed down the shabby drive, but they transacted their business in the back yard. The neighbors, if they referred to the place at all, spoke of the Ministry House, which was not accurate, for the Department was a separate entity, and the Ministry its master. The building had that unmistakable air of controlled dilapidation which characterizes government hirings all over the world. For those who worked in it, its mystery was like the mystery of motherhood, its survival like the mystery of England. It shrouded and contained them, cradled them and, with sweet anachronism, gave them the illusion of nourishment.

Avery could remember it when the fog lingered content-edly against its stucco walls, or in the summer, when the sunlight would briefly peer through the mesh curtains of his room, leaving no warmth, revealing no secrets. And he would remember it on that winter dawn, its façade stained black, the streetlights catching the raindrops on the grimy windows. But however he remembered it, it was not as a place where he worked, but where he lived.

Following the path to the back, he rang the bell and waited for Pine to open the door. A light shone in Leclerc's window.

He showed Pine his pass. Perhaps both were reminded of the war: for Avery a vicarious pleasure, while Pine could look back on experience.

"A lovely moon, sir," said Pine.

"Yes." Avery stepped inside. Pine followed him in, lock-ing up behind him.

"Time was, the boys would curse a moon like this."

"Yes indeed." Avery laughed.

"Heard about the Melbourne test, sir? Bradley's out for three."

"Oh dear," said Avery pleasantly. He disliked cricket.

A blue lamp glowed from the hall ceiling like the night light in a Victorian hospital. Avery climbed the staircase; he felt cold and uneasy. Somewhere a bell rang. It was odd how Sarah had not heard the telephone.

Leclerc was waiting for him: "We need a man," he said. He spoke involuntarily, like someone waking. A light shone on the file before him.

He was sleek, small and very bland; a precise cat of a

man, clean-shaven and groomed. His stiff collars were cut away; he favored ties of one color, knowing perhaps that a weak claim was worse than none. His eyes were dark and quick; he smiled as he spoke, yet conveyed no pleasure. His jackets had twin vents, he kept his handkerchief in his sleeve. On Fridays he wore suede shoes, and they said he was going to the country. No one seemed to know where he lived. The room was in half darkness.

"We can't do another overflight. This was the last; they warned me at the Ministry. We'll have to put a man in. I've been going through the old cards, John. There's one called Leiser, a Pole. He would do."

"What happened to Taylor? Who killed him?"

Avery went to the door and switched on the main light. They looked at one another awkwardly. "Sorry. I'm still half asleep," Avery said. They began again, finding the thread.

Leclerc spoke up. "You took a time, John. Something go wrong at home?" He was not born to authority.

"I couldn't get a cab. I phoned the rank at Clapham but they didn't reply. Nor Albert Bridge; nothing there either." He hated to disappoint Leclerc.

"You can charge for it," Leclerc said distantly. "And the phone calls, you realize. Your wife all right?"

"I told you: there was no reply. She's fine."

"She didn't mind?"

"Of course not."

They never talked about Sarah. It was as if they shared a single relationship to Avery's wife, like children who are able to share a toy they no longer care for. Leclerc said, "Well, she's got that son of yours to keep her company."

"Yes, rather."

Leclerc was proud of knowing it was a son and not a daughter.

He took a cigarette from the silver box on his desk. He had told Avery once: the box was a gift, a gift from the war. The man who gave it to him was dead, the occasion for giving it was past; there was no inscription on the lid. Even now, he would say, he was not entirely certain whose side the man had been on, and Avery would laugh to make him happy.

Taking the file from his desk, Leclerc now held it directly under the light as if there were something in it which he must study very closely.

"John."

Avery went to him, trying not to touch his shoulder.

"What do you make of a face like that?"

"I don't know. It's hard to tell from photographs."

It was the head of a boy, round and blank, with long, fair hair swept back.

"Leiser. He *looks* all right, doesn't he? That was twenty years ago, of course," Leclerc said. "We gave him a very high rating." Reluctantly he put it down, struck his lighter and held it to the cigarette. "Well," he said briskly, "we seem to be up against something. I've no idea what happened to Taylor. We have a routine consular report, that's all. A car accident apparently. A few details, nothing informative. The sort of thing that goes out to next of kin. The Foreign Office sent us the teleprint as it came over the wire. They knew it was one of our passports." He pushed a sheet of flimsy paper across the desk. He loved to make you read things while he waited. Avery glanced at it:

"Malherbe? Was that Taylor's cover name?"

"Yes. I'll have to get a couple of cars from the Ministry pool," Leclerc said. "Quite absurd not having our own cars. The Circus has a whole fleet." And then, "Perhaps the Ministry will believe me now. Perhaps they'll finally accept we're still an operational department."

"Did Taylor collect the film?" Avery asked. "Do we know whether he got it?"

"*I've* no inventory of his possessions," Leclerc replied indignantly. "At the moment, all his effects are impounded by the Finnish police. Perhaps the film is among them. It's a small place and I imagine they like to stick to the letter of the law." And casually, so that Avery knew it mattered, "The Foreign Office is afraid there may be a muddle."

"Oh dear," said Avery automatically. It was their practice in the Department: antique and understated.

Leclerc looked directly at him now, taking interest. "The Resident Clerk at the Foreign Office spoke to the Assistant half an hour ago. They refuse to involve themselves. They say we're a clandestine service and must do it our own way. Somebody's got to go out there as next of kin; that is the course they favor. To claim the body and effects and get them back here. I want you to go."

Avery was suddenly aware of the pictures round the room, of the boys who had fought in the war. They hung in two rows of six, either side of the model of a Wellington bomber, rather a dusty one, painted black with no insignia. Most of the photographs had been taken out of doors. Avery could see the hangars behind, and between the young, smiling faces the half-hidden fuselages of parked aircraft.

Beneath each photograph were signatures, already brown and faded, some fluent and racy, others—they must have been the other-ranks—self-conscious and elaborate, as if the writers had come unnaturally to fame. There were no surnames, but sobriquets from children's magazines: Jacko, Shorty, Pip and Lucky Joe. Only the Mae West was uniform, the long hair and the sunny, boyish smile. They seemed to like having their photographs taken, as if being together were an occasion for laughter which might not be repeated. The men in front were crouching comfortably, like men used to crouching in gun turrets, and those behind had put their arms carelessly over one another's shoulders. There was no affectation but a spontaneous goodwill which does not seem to survive war or photographs.

One face was common to every picture, right to the end: the face of a slim, bright-eyed man in a duffle coat and corduroy trousers. He wore no life jacket and stood a little apart from the men as if he were somehow extra. He was smaller than the rest, older. His features were formed; he had a purpose about him which the others lacked. He might have been their schoolmaster. Avery had once looked for his signature to see if it had altered in the nineteen years, but Leclerc had not signed his name. He was still very like his photographs: a shade more set around the jaw perhaps, a shade less hair.

"But that would be an operational job," said Avery uncertainly.

"Of course. We're an operational department, you know." A little buck of the head. "You are entitled to operational subsistence. All you have to do is collect Taylor's stuff. You're to bring back everything except the film,

which you deliver to an address in Helsinki. You'll be instructed about that separately. You come back and you can
help me with Leiser—"

"Couldn't the Circus take it on? I mean, couldn't they
do it more simply?"

This smile came slowly. "I'm afraid that wouldn't answer at all. It's our show, John: the commitment is within
our competence. A military target. I would be shirking our
responsibility if I gave it to the Circus. Their charter is political, exclusively political."

His small hand ran over his hair, a short, concise movement, tense and controlled. "So it's our problem. Thus far,
the Ministry approves my reading"—a favorite expression
—"I can send someone else if you prefer—Woodford or
one of the older men. I thought you'd enjoy it. It's an important job, you know; something new for you to tackle."

"Of course. I'd like to go . . . if you trust me."

Leclerc enjoyed that. Now he pushed a piece of blue
draft paper into Avery's hand. It was covered with Leclerc's own writing, boyish and rounded. He had written
"Ephemeral" at the top and underlined it. In the left-hand
margin were his initials, all four, and beneath them the
word *Unclassified*. Once more Avery began reading.

"If you follow it carefully," Leclerc said, "you'll see that
we don't specifically state that you *are* next of kin; we just
quote from Taylor's application form. That's as far as the
Foreign Office people are prepared to go. They've agreed
to send this to the local consulate via Helsinki."

Avery read:

> Following from Consular Department. Your Tele-
> print re Malherbe. John Somerton Avery, holder of
> British passport no ——, half brother of deceased,
> is named in Malherbe's passport application as next
> of kin. Avery informed and proposes fly out today
> take over body and effects. NAS flight 201 via Ham-
> burg, ETA 1820 local time. Please provide usual
> facilities and assistance.

"I didn't know your passport number," Leclerc said.
"The plane leaves at three this afternoon. It's only a small
place; I imagine the Consul will meet you at the airport.

There's a flight from Hamburg every other day. If you don't have to go to Helsinki you can take the same plane back."

"Couldn't I be his brother?" Avery asked lamely. "Half brother looks fishy."

"There's no time to rig the passport. The Foreign Office is being very sticky about passports. We had a lot of trouble about Taylor's." He had returned to the file. "A *lot* of trouble. It would mean calling *you* Malherbe as well, you see. I don't think they'd like that." He spoke without attention, paying out rope.

The room was very cold.

Avery said, "What about our Scandinavian friend"—Leclerc looked uncomprehending—"Lansen. Shouldn't someone contact him?"

"I'm attending to that." Leclerc, hating questions, replied cautiously as if he might be quoted.

"And Taylor's wife?" It seemed pedantic to say widow. "Are you attending to her?"

"I thought we'd go around first thing in the morning. She doesn't have a telephone. Telegrams are so cryptic."

"We?" said Avery. "Do we both need to go?"

"You're my aide, aren't you?" Leclerc said.

It was too quiet. Avery longed for the sound of traffic and the buzz of telephones. By day they had people about them, the tramp of messengers, the drone of registry trolleys. He had the feeling, when alone with Leclerc, that the third person was missing. No one else made him so conscious of behavior, no one else had such a disintegrating effect on conversation. He wished Leclerc would give him something else to read.

"Have you heard anything about Taylor's wife?" Leclerc asked. "Is she a secure sort of person?"

Seeing that Avery did not understand, he continued:

"She could make it awkward for us, you know. If she decided to. We shall have to tread carefully."

"What will you say to her?"

"We shall play it by ear. The way we did in the war. She won't know, you see. She won't even know he was abroad."

"He might have told her."

"Not Taylor. Taylor's an old hand. He had his instructions and knew the rules. She must have a pension, that's most important. Active service." He made another brisk, finite gesture with his hand.

"And the staff; what will you tell them?"

"I shall hold a meeting this morning for Heads of Sections. As for the rest of the Department, we shall say it was an accident."

"Perhaps it was," Avery suggested.

Leclerc was smiling again; an iron bar of a smile, like an affliction.

"In which case we shall have told the truth; and have more chance of getting that film."

There was still no traffic in the street outside. Avery felt hungry. Leclerc glanced at his watch.

"You were looking at Gorton's report," Avery said.

He shook his head, wistfully touched a file, revisiting a favorite album. "There's nothing there. I've read it over and over again. I've had the other photographs blown up to every conceivable size. Haldane's people have been on them night and day. We just can't get any further."

Sarah was right: to help him wait.

Leclerc said—it seemed suddenly the point of their meeting—"I've arranged for you to have a short talk with George Smiley at the Circus after this morning's conference. You've heard of him?"

"No," Avery lied. This was delicate ground.

"He used to be one of their best men. Typical of the Circus in some ways, of the better kind. He resigns, you know, and comes back. His conscience. One never knows whether he's there or not. He's a bit past it now. They say he drinks a good deal. Smiley has the North European desk. He can brief you about dropping the film. Our own courier service is disbanded, so there's no other way: the F.O. doesn't want to know us; after Taylor's death I can't allow you to run around with the thing in your pocket. How much do you know about the Circus?" He might have been asking about women, wary, an older man without experience.

"A bit," said Avery. "The usual gossip."

Leclerc stood up and went to the window. "They're a curious crowd. Some good, of course. Smiley was good. But they're cheats," he broke out suddenly. "That's an odd word, I know, to use about a sister service, John. Lying's second nature to them. Half of them don't know any longer when they're telling the truth." He was inclining his head studiously this way and that to catch sight of whatever moved in the waking street below. "What wretched weather. There was a lot of rivalry during the war, you know."

"I heard."

"That's all over now. I don't grudge them their work. They've more money and more staff than we have. They do a bigger job. However, I doubt whether they do a better one. Nothing can touch our Research Section, for example. Nothing." Avery suddenly had the feeling that Leclerc had revealed something intimate, a failed marriage or a discreditable act, and that now it was all right.

"When you see Smiley, he may ask you about the operation. I don't want you to tell him *anything*, do you see, except that you are going to Finland and you may be handling a film for urgent dispatch to London. If he presses you, suggest it is a training matter. That's all you're authorized to say. The background, Gorton's report, future operations—none of that concerns them in the least. A training matter."

"I realize that. But he'll know about Taylor, won't he, if the F.O. knows?"

"Leave that to me. And don't be misled into believing the Circus has a monopoly of agent running. We have the same right. We just don't unnecessarily." He had restated his text.

Avery watched Leclerc's slim back against the lightening sky outside; a man excluded, a man without a card, he thought.

"Could we light the fire?" he asked, and went into the corridor where Pine had a cupboard for mops and brushes. There was kindling wood and some old newspapers. He came back and knelt in front of the fireplace, keeping the best pieces of cinder and coaxing the ash through the grate, just as he would in the flat at Christmas. "I wonder if it was really wise to let them meet at the airport," he asked.

"It was urgent. After Jimmy Gorton's report, it was very urgent. It still is. We haven't a moment to lose."

Avery held a match to the newspaper and watched it

burn. As the wood caught, the smoke began to roll gently into his face, causing his eyes to water behind his glasses. "How could they know Lansen's destination?"

"It was a scheduled flight. He had to get clearance in advance."

Tossing more coal on to the fire, Avery got up and rinsed his hands at the basin in the corner, drying them on his handkerchief.

"I keep asking Pine to put me out a towel," said Leclerc. "They haven't enough to do, that's half the trouble."

"Never mind." Avery put the wet handkerchief in his pocket. It felt cold against his thigh. "Perhaps they will have now," he added without irony.

"I thought I'd get Pine to make me up a bed here. A sort of ops room." Leclerc spoke cautiously, as if Avery might deprive him of the pleasure. "You can ring me here tonight from Finland. If you've got the film, just say the deal's come off."

"And if not?"

"Say the deal's off."

"It sounds rather alike," Avery objected. "If the line's bad, I mean. 'Off' and 'Come off.' "

"Then say they're not interested. Say something negative. You know what I mean."

Avery picked up the empty scuttle. "I'll give this to Pine."

He passed the duty room. An Air Force clerk was half asleep beside the telephones. He made his way down the wooden staircase to the front door.

"The Boss wants some coal, Pine." The porter stood up, as he always did when anyone spoke to him, at attention by his bed in a barrack room.

"I'm sorry, sir. Can't leave the door."

"For God's sake, I'll look after the door. We're freezing up there."

Pine took the scuttle, buttoned his tunic and disappeared down the passage. He didn't whistle these days.

"And a bed made up in his room," Avery continued when Pine returned. "Perhaps you'd tell the duty clerk when he wakes up. Oh, and a towel. He must have a towel by his basin."

"Yes, sir. Wonderful to see the old Department on the march again."

"Where can we get breakfast around here? Is there anywhere nearby?"

"There's the Cadena," Pine replied doubtfully. "But I don't know whether it would do for the Boss, sir. We had the canteen in the old days. Slingers and wadge."

It was quarter to seven. "When does the Cadena open?"

"Couldn't say, sir."

"Tell me, do you know Mr. Taylor at all?" He nearly said "did."

"Oh yes, sir."

"Have you met his wife?"

"No, sir."

"What's she like? Have you any idea? Heard anything?"

"Couldn't say, I'm sure, sir. Very sad business indeed, sir."

Avery looked at him in astonishment. Leclerc must have told him, he thought, and went upstairs. Sooner or later he would have to telephone Sarah.

3.

THEY BREAKFASTED somewhere. Leclerc refused to go into the Cadena and they walked interminably until they found another café, worse than the Cadena and more expensive.

"I can't remember him," Leclerc said. "That's the absurd thing. He's a trained radio operator apparently. Or was in those days."

Avery thought he was talking about Taylor. "How old did you say he was?"

"Forty, something over. That's a good age. A Danzig Pole. They speak German, you know. Not as mad as the pure Slav. After the war he drifted for a couple of years, pulled himself together and bought a garage. He must have made a nice bit."

"Then I don't suppose he'll—"

"Nonsense. He'll be grateful, or should be."

Leclerc paid the bill and kept it. As they left the restaurant he said something about subsistence, and putting in a bill to Accounts. "You can claim for night duty as well, you know. Or time in lieu." They walked down the road. "Your air ticket is booked. Carol did it from her flat. We'd better give you an advance for expenses. There'll be the business of having his body sent and that kind of thing. I understand it can be very costly. You'd better have him flown. We'll do a postmortem privately over here."

"I've never seen a dead man before," Avery said.

They were standing on a street corner in Kennington,

looking for a taxi; a gasworks on one side of the road, nothing on the other: the sort of place they could wait all day.

"John, you've to keep very quiet about that side of it; about putting a man in. No one's to know, not even in the Department, no one at all. I thought we'd call him Mayfly. Leiser, I mean. We'll call him Mayfly."

"All right."

"It's very delicate; a question of timing. I've no doubt there'll be opposition, within the Department as well as outside."

"What about my cover and that kind of thing?" Avery asked. "I'm not quite . . ." A taxi with its flag up passed them without stopping.

"Bloody man," Leclerc snapped. "Why didn't he pick us up?"

"He lives out here, I expect. He's making for the West End. About cover," he prompted.

"You're traveling under your own name. I don't see that there's any problem. You can use your own address. Call yourself a publisher. After all you *were* one. The Consul will show you the ropes. What are you worried about?"

"Well—just the details."

Leclerc, coming out of his reverie, smiled. "I'll tell you something about cover; something you'll learn for yourself. Never volunteer information. People don't *expect* you to explain yourself. After all, what is there to explain? The ground's prepared; the Consul will have our teleprint. Show your passport and play the rest by ear."

"I'll try," said Avery.

"You'll succeed," Leclerc rejoined with feeling, and they both grinned shyly.

"How far is it to the town?" Avery asked. "From the airport."

"About three miles. It feeds the main ski resorts. Heaven knows what the Consul does all day."

"And to Helsinki?"

"I told you. A hundred miles. Perhaps more."

Avery proposed they take a bus but Leclerc wouldn't queue so they remained standing at the corner. He began talking about official cars again. "It's utterly absurd," he said. "In the old days we had a pool of our own, now we have two vans and the Treasury won't let us pay the drivers overtime. How can I run the Department under those conditions?"

In the end they walked. Leclerc had the address in his head; he made a point of remembering such things. It was awkward for Avery to walk beside him for long, because Leclerc adjusted his pace to that of the taller man. Avery tried to keep himself in check, but sometimes he forgot and Leclerc would stretch uncomfortably beside him, thrusting upward with each stride. A fine rain was falling. It was still very cold.

There were times when Avery felt for Leclerc a deep, protective love. Leclerc had that indefinable quality of arousing guilt, as if his companion but poorly replaced a departed friend. Somebody had been there, and gone; perhaps a whole world, a generation; somebody had made him and disowned him, so that while at one moment Avery could hate him for his transparent manipulation, detest his prinking gestures as a child detests the affectations of a parent, at the next he ran to protect him, responsible and deeply caring. Beyond all the vicissitudes of their relationship, he was somehow grateful that Leclerc had engendered him; and thus they created that strong love which only exists between the weak; each became the stage to which the other related his actions.

"It would be a good thing," Leclerc said suddenly, "if you shared the handling of Mayfly."

"I'd like to."

"When you get back."

They had found the address on the map. Thirty-four Roxburgh Gardens; it was off Kennington High Street. The road soon became dingier, the houses more crowded. Gaslights burned yellow and flat like paper moons.

"In the war they gave us a hostel for the staff."

"Perhaps they will again," Avery suggested.

"It's twenty years since I did an errand like this."

"Did you go alone then?" Avery asked, and wished at once that he had not. It was so easy to inflict pain on Leclerc.

"It was simpler in those days. We could say they'd died for their country. We didn't have to tell them the details; they didn't expect that." So it *was* we, thought Avery.

Some other boy, one of those laughing faces on the wall.

"They died every day then, the pilots. We did reconnaissance, you know, as well as special operation. . . . I'm ashamed sometimes: I can't even remember their names. They were so young, some of them."

There passed across Avery's mind a tragic procession of horror-struck faces: mothers and fathers, girl friends and wives, and he tried to visualize Leclerc standing among them, naïve yet footsure, like a politician at the scene of a disaster.

They stood at the top of a rise. It was a wretched place. The road led downward into a line of dingy, eyeless houses; above them rose a single block of flats—Roxburgh Gardens. A string of lights shone on the glazed tiles, dividing and redividing the whole structure into cells. It was a large building, very ugly in its way, the beginning of a new world, and at its feet lay the black rubble of the old: crumbling, oily houses haunted by sad faces which moved through the rain like driftwood in a forgotten harbor.

Leclerc's frail fists were clenched; he stood very still.

"There?" he said. "Taylor lived there?"

"What's wrong? It's part of a scheme, redevelopment . . ."

Then Avery understood. Leclerc was ashamed. Taylor had disgracefully deceived him. This was not the society they protected, these slums with their Babel's Tower: they had no place in Leclerc's scheme of things. To think that a member of Leclerc's staff should daily trudge from the breath and stink of such a place to the sanctuary of the Department: had he no money, no pension? Had he not a little bit beside, as we all have, just a hundred or two, to buy himself out of this squalor?

"It's no worse than Blackfriars Road," Avery said involuntarily; it was meant to comfort him.

"Everyone knows we used to be in Baker Street," Leclerc retorted.

They made their way quickly to the base of the block, past shopwindows filled with old clothes and rusted electric heaters, all the sad muddle of useless things which only the poor will buy. There was a chandler; his candles were yellow and dusty like fragments of a tomb.

"What number?" Leclerc asked.

"You said thirty-four."

They passed between heavy pillars crudely ornamented with mosaics, followed plastic arrows marked with pink numbers; they squeezed between lines of aged, empty cars, until finally they came to a concrete entrance with cartons of milk on the step. There was no door, but a flight of rubberized steps which squeaked as they trod. The air smelled of food and that liquid soap they dispense in railway lavatories. On the heavy stucco wall a hand-painted notice discouraged noise. Somewhere a wireless played. They continued up two flights and stopped before a green door, half-glazed. Mounted on it in letters of white bakelite was the number 34. Leclerc took off his hat and wiped the sweat from his temples. He might have been entering church. It had been raining more than they realized; their coats were quite wet. He pressed the bell. Avery was suddenly very frightened. He glanced at Leclerc and thought, This is your show; you tell her.

The music seemed louder. They strained their ears to catch some other sound, but there was none.

"Why did you call him Malherbe?" Avery asked suddenly.

Leclerc pressed the bell again; and then they heard it, both of them, a whimper midway between the sob of a child and the whine of a cat, a throttled, metallic sigh. While Leclerc stepped back, Avery seized the bronze knocker on the letter box and banged it violently. The echo died away and they heard from inside the flat a light, reluctant tread; a bolt was slid from its housing, a spring lock disengaged. Then they heard again, much louder and more distinctly, the same plaintive monotone. The door opened a few inches and Avery saw a child, a frail, pallid rag of a girl not above ten years old. She wore steel-rimmed spectacles, the kind Anthony wore. In her arms, its pink limbs splayed stupidly about it, its painted eyes staring from between fringes of ragged cotton, was a doll. Its daubed mouth was lolling open, its head hung sideways as if it were broken or dead. It is called a talking doll, but no living thing uttered such a sound.

"Where is your mother?" asked Leclerc. His voice was aggressive, frightened.

The child shook her head. "Gone to work."

"Who looks after you, then?"

She spoke slowly as if she were thinking of something else. "Mum comes back teatimes. I'm not to open the door."

"Where is she? Where does she go?"

"Work."

"Who gives you lunch?" Leclerc insisted.

"What?"

"Who gives you dinner?" Avery said quickly.

"Mrs. Bradley. After school."

Then Avery asked, "Where's your father?" and she smiled and put a finger to her lips.

"He's gone on an airplane," she said. "To get money. But I'm not to say. It's a secret."

Neither of them spoke. "He's bringing me a present," she added.

"Where from?" said Avery.

"From the North Pole, but it's a secret." She still had her hand on the doorknob. "Where Father Christmas comes from."

"Tell your mother some men were here," Avery said. "From your dad's office. We'll come again teatime."

"It's important," said Leclerc.

She seemed to relax when she heard they knew her father.

"He's on an airplane," she repeated.

Avery felt in his pocket and gave her two half crowns, the change from Sarah's ten shillings. She closed the door, leaving them on that damned staircase with the wireless playing dreamy music.

4.

THEY STOOD in the street not looking at one another. Leclerc said, "Why did you ask that question, the question about her father?"

Avery offered no reply; Leclerc did not seem to expect one.

Sometimes Leclerc seemed neither to hear, nor to feel; he drifted away, listening for a sound, like a man who having learned the steps had been deprived of the music. This mood read like a deep sadness, like the bewilderment of a man betrayed.

"I'm afraid I shan't be able to come back here with you this afternoon," Avery said gently. "Perhaps Bruce Woodford would be preferred . . ."

"Bruce is no good." He added: "You'll be at the meeting; at ten forty-five?"

"I may have to leave before the end to get to the Circus and collect my things. Sarah hasn't been well. I'll stay at the office as long as I can. I'm sorry I asked that question, I really am."

"I don't want anyone to know. I must speak to her mother first. There may be some explanation. Taylor's an old hand. He knew the rules."

"I shan't mention it, I promise I shan't. Nor Mayfly."

"I must tell Haldane about Mayfly. He'll object of course. Yes, that's what we'll call it . . . the whole operation. We'll call it Mayfly." The thought consoled him.

They hurried to the office, not to work but for refuge;

for anonymity, a quality they had come to need.

His room was one along from Leclerc's. It had a label
on the door saying ASSISTANT TO THE DIRECTOR. Two
years ago Leclerc had been invited to America, and the
expression dated from his return. Within the department,
staff were referred to by the function they fulfilled. Hence
Avery was known simply as Private Office; though Leclerc
might alter the title every week, he could not alter the ver-
nacular.

At a quarter to eleven Woodford came into his room.
Avery guessed he would: a little chat before the meeting
began, a quiet word about some matter not strictly on the
agenda.

"What's it all about, John?" He lit his pipe, tilted back
his large head and extinguished the match with long,
swinging movements of his hand. He had once been a
schoolmaster; an athletic man.

"You tell me."

"Poor Taylor."

"Precisely."

"I don't want to jump the gun," he said, and settled himself on the edge of the desk, still absorbed in his pipe. "I
don't want to jump the gun, John," he repeated, "but
there's another matter we ought to look at, tragic as Taylor's death is." He stowed the tobacco tin in the pocket of
his green suit and said, "Registry."

"That's Haldane's parish. Research."

"I've got nothing against old Adrian. He's a good scout.
We've been working together for over twenty years." And
therefore you're a good scout too, thought Avery.

Woodford had a way of coming close when he spoke;
riding his heavy shoulder against you like a horse rubbing
itself against a gate. He leaned forward and looked at Avery earnestly: a plain man perplexed, he was saying, a decent man choosing between friendship and duty. His suit
was hairy, too thick to crease, forming rolls like a blanket;
rough-cut buttons of brown bone.

"John, Registry's all to the devil; we both know that. Papers aren't being entered, files aren't brought up on the
right dates." He shook his head in despair. "We've been
missing a policy file on marine freight since mid-October.
Just vanished into thin air."

"Adrian Haldane put out a search notice," Avery said. "We were all involved, not just Adrian. Files do get lost—this is the first since April, Bruce. I don't think that's bad, considering the amount we handle. I thought Registry was one of our best things. The files are immaculate. I understand our Research index is unique. That's all Adrian's doing, isn't it? Still, if you're worried, why not speak to Adrian about it?"

"No, no. It's not *that* important."

Carol came in with the tea. Woodford had his in a pottery jumbo-cup with his initials drawn large, embossed like icing. As Carol put it down, she remarked, "Wilf Taylor's dead."

"I've been here since one," Avery lied, "coping with it. We've been working all night."

"The Director's very upset," she said.

"What was his wife like, Carol?" She was a well-dressed girl, a little taller than Sarah.

"Nobody's met her."

She left the room, Woodford watching her. He took his pipe from his mouth and grinned. Avery knew he was going to say something about sleeping with Carol and suddenly he'd had enough.

"Did your wife make that cup, Bruce?" he asked quickly. "I hear she's quite a potter."

"Made the saucer as well," he said. He began talking about the classes she went to, the amusing way it had caught on in Wimbledon, how his wife was tickled to death.

It was nearly eleven; they could hear the others gathering in the corridor.

"I'd better go next door," Avery said, "and see if he's ready. He's taken quite a beating in the last eight hours."

Woodford picked up his mug and took a sip of tea. "If you get a chance, mention that Registry business to the Boss, John. I don't want to drag it up in front of everyone else. Adrian's getting a bit past it."

"The Director's very tied up at the moment, Bruce."

"Oh, quite."

"He hates to interfere with Haldane. You know that." As they reached the door of his room he turned to Woodford and asked, "Do you remember a man called Malherbe in the Department?"

Woodford stopped dead. "God, yes. A young chap, like you. In the war. Good Lord!" And earnestly, but quite unlike his usual manner: "Don't mention that name to the Boss. He was very cut up about young Malherbe. One of the special fliers. The two of them were quite close in a way."

Leclerc's room by daylight was not so drab as of an impermanent appearance. You would think its occupant had requisitioned it hastily, under conditions of emergency, and had not known how long he would be staying. Maps lay sprawled over the trestle table, not in threes or fours but dozens, some of a scale large enough to show streets and buildings. Teletape, pasted in strips on pink paper, hung in batches on the notice board, fastened with a heavy bulldog clip like galley proofs awaiting correction. A bed had been put in one corner with a bedspread over it. A clean towel hung beside the basin. The desk was new, of gray steel, government issue. The walls were filthy. Here and there the cream paint had peeled, showing dark green beneath. It was a small, square room with Ministry of Works curtains. There had been a row about the curtains, a question of equating Leclerc's rank to the Civil Service scale. It was the one occasion, so far as Avery knew, when Leclerc had made any effort to improve the disorder of the room. The fire was nearly out. Sometimes when it was very windy the fire would not burn at all, and all through the day Avery could hear from next door the soot falling in the chimney.

Avery watched them come in—Woodford first, then Sandford, Dennison and McCulloch. They had all heard about Taylor. It was easy to imagine the news going round the Department, not as headlines, but as a small and gratifying sensation passed from room to room, lending a briskness to the day's activity, as it had to these men; giving them a moment's optimism, like a raise in pay. They would watch Leclerc, watch him as prisoners watch a guard. They knew his routine by instinct, and they waited for him to break it. There would not be a man or woman in the Department but knew they had been called in the middle of the night, and that Leclerc was sleeping in the office.

They settled themselves at the table, putting their cups in front of them noisily like children at a meal, Leclerc at the head, the others on either side, an empty chair at the further end. Haldane came in, and Avery knew as soon as he saw him that it would be Leclerc versus Haldane.

Looking at the empty chair, he said, "I see I'm to take the draftiest place."

Avery rose, but Haldane had sat down. "Don't bother, Avery. I'm a sick man already." He coughed, just as he coughed all year. Not even the summer could help him, apparently; he coughed in all seasons.

The others fidgeted uncomfortably; Woodford helped himself to a biscuit. Haldane glanced at the fire. "Is that the best the Ministry of Works can manage?" he asked.

"It's the rain," Avery said. "The rain disagrees with it. Pine's had a go but he made no difference."

"Ah."

Haldane was a lean man with long, restless fingers; a man locked in himself, slow in his movements, agile in his features, balding, spare, querulous and dry; a man seemingly contemptuous of everything, keeping his own hours and his own counsel; addicted to crossword puzzles and nineteenth-century watercolors.

Carol came in with files and maps, putting them on Leclerc's desk, which in contrast to the remainder of his room was very tidy. They waited awkwardly until she had gone. The door securely closed, Leclerc passed his hand cautiously over his dark hair as if he were not quite familiar with it.

"Taylor's been killed. You've all heard it by now. He was killed last night in Finland traveling under another name." Avery noticed he never mentioned Malherbe. "We don't know the details. He appears to have been run over. I've told Carol to put it about that it was an accident. Is that clear?"

Yes, they said, it was quite clear.

"He went to collect a film from . . . a contact, a Scandinavian contact. You know whom I mean. We don't normally use the routine couriers for operational work, but this was different; something very special indeed. I think

Adrian will back me up there." He made a little upward gesture with his open hands, freeing the wrists from his white cuffs, laying the palms and fingers vertically together; praying for Haldane's support.

"Special?" Haldane repeated slowly. His voice was thin and sharp like the man himself, cultivated, without emphasis and without affectation; an enviable voice. "It was different, yes. Not least because Taylor died. We should never have used him, never," he observed flatly. "We broke a first principle of intelligence. We used a man on the overt side for a clandestine job. Not that we have a clandestine side anymore."

"Shall we let our masters be the judges of that?" Leclerc suggested demurely. "At least you'll agree the Ministry is pressing us daily for results." He turned to those on either side of him, now to the left, now to the right, bringing them in like shareholders. "It is time you all knew the details. We are dealing with something of exceptional security classification, you understand. I propose to limit to Heads of Sections. So far, only Adrian Haldane and one or two of his staff in Research have been initiated. And John Avery as my aide. I wish to emphasize that our sister service knows nothing whatever about it. Now about our own arrangements. The operation has the codeword Mayfly." He was speaking in his clipped, effective voice. "There is one action file, which will be returned to me personally, or to Carol if I am out, at the end of each day; and there is a library copy. That is the system we used in the war for operational files and I think you are all familiar with it. It's the system we shall use henceforth. I shall add Carol's name to the subscription list."

Woodford pointed at Avery with his pipe, shaking his head. Not young John there; John was not familiar with the system. Sandford, sitting beside Avery, explained. The library copy was kept in the cipher room. It was against regulations to take it away. All new serials were to be entered on it as soon as they were made; the subscription list was the list of persons authorized to read it. No pins were allowed; all the papers had to be fast. The others looked on complacently.

Sandford was Administration; he was a fatherly man in gold-rimmed spectacles and came to the office on a motorbike. Leclerc had objected once, on no particular grounds, and now he parked it down the road opposite the Hospital.

"Now, about the operation," Leclerc said. The thin line of his joined hands bisected his bright face. Only Haldane was not watching him; his eyes were turned away toward the window. Outside, the rain was falling gently against the buildings like spring rain in a dark valley.

Abruptly Leclerc rose and went to a map of Europe on the wall. There were small flags pinned to it. Stretching upwards with his arm, riding on his toes to reach the Northern Hemisphere, he said, "We're having a spot of trouble with the Germans." A little laugh went up. "In the area south of Rostock; a place called Kalkstadt, just here." His finger traced the Baltic coastline of Schleswig-Holstein, moved east and stopped an inch or two south of Rostock.

"To put it in a nutshell, we have three indicators which suggest—I cannot say prove—that something big is going on there in the way of military installations."

He swung around to face them. He would remain at the map and say it all from there, to show he had the facts in his memory and didn't need the papers on the table.

"The first indicator came exactly a month ago when we received a report from our representative in Hamburg, Jimmy Gorton."

Woodford smiled. Good God, was old Jimmy still going?

"An East German refugee crossed the border near Lubeck, swam the river; a railwayman from Kalkstadt. He went to our Consulate and offered to sell them information about a new rocket site near Rostock. I need hardly tell you the Consulate threw him out. Since the Foreign Office will not even give us the facilities of its bag service, it is unlikely"—a thin smile—"that they will assist us by buying military information." A nice murmur greeted this joke. "However, by a stroke of luck Gorton got to hear of the man and went to Flensburg to see him."

Woodford would not let this pass. Flensburg? Was not that the place where they had located German submarines in forty-one? Flensburg had been a hell of a show.

Leclerc nodded at Woodford indulgently, as if he too had been amused by the recollection. "The wretched man had been to every allied office in North Germany, but no one would look at him. Jimmy Gorton had a chat with him."

Implicit in Leclerc's way of describing things was an assumption that Gorton was the only intelligent man among a lot of fools. He crossed to his desk, took a cigarette from the silver box, lit it, picked up a file with a heavy red cross on the cover and laid it noiselessly on the table in front of them. "This is Jimmy's report," he said. "It's a first-class bit of work by any standard." The cigarette looked very long between his fingers. "The defector's name," he added inconsequentially, "was Fritsche."

"Defector?" Haldane put in quickly. "The man's a low-grade refugee, a railwayman. We don't usually talk about men like that *defecting*."

Leclerc replied defensively, "The man's not only a railwayman. He's a bit of a mechanic and a bit of a photographer."

McCulloch opened the file and began methodically turning over the serials. Sandford watched him through his gold-rimmed spectacles.

"On the first or second of September—we don't know which because he can't remember—he happened to be doing a double shift in the dumping sheds at Kalkstadt. One of his comrades was sick. He was to work from six till twelve in the morning, and four till ten at night. When he arrived to report for work there were a dozen Vopos, East German people's police, at the station entrance. All passenger traffic was forbidden. They checked his identity papers against a list and told him to keep away from the sheds on the eastern side of the station. They said," Leclerc added deliberately, "that if he approached the eastern sheds he was liable to be shot."

This impressed them. Woodford said it was typical of the Germans.

"It's the Russians we're fighting," Haldane put in.

"He's an odd fish, our man. He seems to have argued with them. He told them he was as reliable as they were, a good German and a Party member. He showed them his union card, photographs of his wife and heaven knows what. It didn't do any good, of course, because they just told him to obey orders and keep away from the sheds. But he must have caught their fancy because when they brewed up some soup at ten o'clock they called him over and offered him a cup. Over the soup he asked them what was going on. They were cagey, but he could see they were excited. Then something happened. Something very important," he continued. "One of the younger ones blurted out that whatever they had in the sheds could blow the Americans out of West Germany in a couple of hours. At this point an officer came along and told them to get back to work."

Haldane coughed a deep, hopeless cough, like an echo in an old vault.

What sort of officer, someone asked, was he—German or Russian?

"German. That is most relevant. There were no Russians in evidence at all."

Haldane interrupted sharply. "The refugee saw none. That's all we know. Let us be accurate." He coughed again. It was very irritating.

"As you wish. He went home and had lunch. He was disgruntled at being ordered around in his own station by a lot of young fellows playing soldiers. He had a couple of glasses of schnapps and sat there brooding about the dumping shed. Adrian, if your cough is troubling you . . ." Haldane shook his head. "He remembered that on the northern side it abutted an old storage hut, and that there was a shutter-type ventilator let into the party wall. He formed the notion of looking through the ventilator to see what was in the shed. As a way of getting his own back on the soldiers."

Woodford laughed.

"Then he decided to go one further and photograph whatever was there."

"He must have been mad," Haldane commented. "I find this part impossible to accept."

"Mad or not, that's what he decided to do. He was cross because they wouldn't trust him. He felt he had a right to know what was in the shed." Leclerc missed a beat, then took refuge in technique. "He had an Exa-two camera, single lens reflex, East German manufacture. It's a cheap housing but takes all the Exakta range lenses; far fewer speeds than the Exakta, of course." He looked inquiringly at the technicians, Dennison and McCulloch. "Am I right, gentlemen?" he asked. "You must correct me." They smiled sheepishly because there was nothing to correct. "He had a good wide-angle lens. The difficulty was the light. His next shift didn't begin till four and by that time dusk would be falling and there would be even less light inside the shed. He had one fast Agfa film which he'd been keeping for a special occasion; it had a DIN speed of twenty-six. He decided to use that." He paused, more for effect than for questions.

"Why didn't he wait till next morning?" Haldane asked.

"In the report," Leclerc continued blandly, "you'll find a very full account by Gorton of how the man got into the hut, stood on an oil drum and took his photographs through the ventilator. I'm not going to repeat all that now. He used the maximum aperture of two-point-eight, speeds ranging from a quarter of a second to two seconds. A fortunate piece of German thoroughness." No one laughed. "The speeds were guesswork, of course. He was bracketing an estimated exposure time of one second. Only the last three frames show anything. Here they are."

Leclerc unlocked the steel drawer of his desk and extracted a set of high-gloss photographs twelve inches by nine. He was smiling a little, like a man looking at his own reflection. They gathered round, all but Haldane and Avery, who had seen them before.

Something was there.

You could see it if you looked quickly; something hidden in the disintegrating shadows; but keep looking and the dark closed in and the shape was gone. Yet something was there—the muffled form of a gun barrel, but pointed and too long for its carriage, the suspicion of a transporter, a vague glint of what might have been a platform.

"They would put protective covers over them, of course," Leclerc commented, studying their faces hopefully, waiting for their optimism.

Avery looked at his watch. It was twenty past eleven. "I shall have to go soon, Director," he said. He still hadn't rung Sarah. "I have to see the accountant about my air ticket."

"Stay another ten minutes," Leclerc pleaded, and Haldane asked, "Where's he going?"

Leclerc replied, throw-away, "To take care of Taylor. He has a date at the Circus first."

"What do you mean, take care of him? Taylor's dead."

There was an uncomfortable silence.

"You know very well that Taylor was traveling under an alias. Somebody has to collect his effects; recover the film. Avery is going out as next of kin. The Ministry has already given its approval; I wasn't aware that I needed yours."

"To claim the body?"

"To get the film," Leclerc repeated hotly.

"That's an operational job; Avery's not trained."

"They were younger than he in the war. He can look after himself."

"Taylor couldn't. What will he do when he's got it; bring it back in his sponge bag?"

"Shall we discuss that afterwards?" Leclerc suggested, and addressed himself once more to the others, smiling patiently as if to say old Adrian must be humored.

"That was all we had to go on till ten days ago. Then came the second indicator. The area around Kalkstadt had been declared a prohibited area." There was an excited murmur of interest. "For a radius of—as far as we can establish—thirty kilometers. Sealed off; closed to all traffic. They brought in frontier guards." He glanced round the table. "I then informed the Minister. I cannot tell even you all the implications. But let me name one." He said the last sentence quickly, at the same time flicking upwards the little horns of graying hair that grew above his ears.

Haldane was forgotten.

"What puzzled us in the beginning"—he nodded at Haldane, a conciliatory gesture at a moment of victory, but Haldane ignored it—"was the absence of Soviet troops. They have units in Rostock, Witmar, Schwerin." His finger darted among the flags. "But none—this is confirmed by other agencies—none in the immediate area of Kalkstadt. If there *are* weapons there, weapons of high destructive capacity, why are there no Soviet troops?"

McCulloch made a suggestion: might there not be technicians, Soviet technicians in civilian dress?

"I regard that as unlikely." A demure smile. "In comparable cases where tactical weapons were being transported we have always identified at least one Soviet unit. On the

other hand, five weeks ago a few Russian troops *were* seen
at Gustweiler, farther south." He was back to the map.
"They billeted for one night at a pub. Some wore artillery
flashes; others had no shoulder-boards at all. They moved
away southward early next morning. One might conclude
they had brought something, left it and gone away again."

Woodford was becoming restless. What did it all add up
to, he wanted to know, what did they make of it over at
the Ministry? Woodford had no patience with riddles.

Leclerc adopted his academic tone. It had a bullying
quality as if facts were facts and could not be disputed.
"Research Section has done a magnificent job. The overall
length of the object in these photographs—they can com-
pute it pretty exactly—is equal to the length of a Soviet
middle-range rocket. On present information"—he lightly
tapped the map with his knuckles so that it swung sideways
on its hook—"the Ministry believes it is *conceivable* we are
dealing with Soviet missiles under East German control.
Research," he added quickly, "is not prepared to go so
far. Now if the Ministry view prevails, if they are right,
that is, we would have on our hands"—this was his moment—"a sort of Cuba situation all over again, only"—he
tried to sound apologetic, to make it a throwaway line—
"more dangerous."

He had them.

"It was at this point," Leclerc explained, "that the
Ministry felt entitled to authorize an overflight. As you
know, for the last four years the Department has been limited to aerial photographs along orthodox civilian or military
air routes. Even these required Foreign Office approval."
He drifted away. "It really was too bad." His eyes seemed
to be searching for something not in the room. The others
watched him anxiously, waiting for him to continue.

"For once the Ministry agreed to waive the ruling, and I
am pleased to say the task of mounting the operation was
given to this Department. We selected the best pilot we
could find on our books: Lansen." Someone looked up in
surprise; agents' names were never used that way. "Lansen
undertook, for a price, to go off course on a charter flight
from Düsseldorf to Finland. Taylor was dispatched to collect the film; he died at the landing field. A road accident,
apparently."

Outside they could hear the sound of cars moving through the rain like the rustling of paper in the wind. The fire had gone out; only the smoke remained, hanging like a shroud over the table.

Sandford had raised his hand. What kind of missile was this supposed to be?

"A Sandal, Medium Range. I am told by Research that it was first shown in Red Square in November sixty-two. It has achieved a certain notoriety since then. It was the Sandal which the Russians installed in Cuba. The Sandal is also"—a glance at Woodford—"the linear descendant of the wartime German V-2."

He fetched other photographs from the desk and laid them on the table.

"Here is a Research Section photograph of the Sandal missile. They tell me it is distinguished by what is called a flared skirt"—he pointed to the formation at the base—"and by small fins. It is about forty feet long from base to cone. If you look carefully you will see tucks near the clamp—just here—which hold the protective cloth cover in position. There is, ironically, no extant picture of the Sandal in protective covers. Possibly the Americans have one, but I don't feel able to approach them at this stage."

Woodford reacted quickly. "Of course not," he said.

"The Minister was anxious that we shouldn't alarm them prematurely. One only has to *suggest* rockets to the Americans to get the most drastic reaction. Before we know where they are they'll be flying U-2s over Rostock." Encouraged by their laughter, Leclerc continued. "The Minister made another point which I think I might pass on to you. The country which comes under maximum threat from these rockets—they have a range of around eight hundred miles—might well be our own. It is certainly not the United States. Politically, this would be a bad moment to go hiding our faces in the Americans' skirts. After all, as the Minister put it, we still *have* one or two teeth of our own."

Haldane said sarcastically, "That is a charming notion," and Avery turned on him with all the anger he had fought away.

"I think you might do better than that," he said. He nearly added: Have a little mercy.

Haldane's cold gaze held Avery for a moment, then re-leased him, his case not forgiven but suspended.

Someone asked what they would do next: suppose Avery did not find Taylor's film? Suppose it just wasn't there? Could they mount another overflight?

"No," Leclerc replied. "Another overflight is out of the question. Far too dangerous. We shall have to try something else." He seemed disinclined to go further, but Haldane said, "What, for instance?"

"We may have to put a man in. It seems to be the only way."

"This Department?" Haldane asked incredulously. "Put a man in? The Ministry would never tolerate such a thing. You mean, surely, you'll ask the Circus to do it?"

"I have already told you the position. Heaven knows, Adrian, you're not going to tell me we can't do it?" He looked appealing round the table. "Every one of us here except young Avery has been in the business twenty years or more. You yourself have forgotten more about agents than half those people in the Circus ever knew."

"Hear, hear!" Woodford cried.

"Look at your own section, Adrian; look at Research. There must have been half-a-dozen occasions in the last five years when the Circus actually came to you, asked you for advice, used your facilities and skills. The time may come when they do the same with agents! The Ministry granted us an overflight. Why not an agent too?"

"You mentioned a third indicator. I don't follow you. What was that?"

"Taylor's death," said Leclerc.

Avery got up, nodded goodbye and tiptoed to the door. Haldane watched him go.

5.

THERE WAS A NOTE on his desk from Carol: *Your wife rang.*

He walked into her office and found her sitting at her typewriter but not typing. "You wouldn't talk about poor Wilf Taylor like that," she said, "if you'd known him better."

"Like what? I haven't talked about him at all."

He thought he should comfort her, because sometimes they touched one another; he thought she might expect that now.

He bent forward, advancing until the sharp ends of her hair touched his cheek. Inclining his head inward so that their temples met, he felt her skin travel slightly across the flat bone of her skull. For a moment they remained thus, Carol sitting upright, looking straight ahead of her, her hands either side of the typewriter, Avery awkwardly stooping. He thought of putting his hand beneath her arm and touching her breast, but did not; both gently recoiling, they separated and were alone again. Avery stood up.

"Your wife telephoned," she said. "I told her you were at the meeting. She wants to talk to you urgently."

"Thanks. I'm on my way."

"John, what *is* going on? What's all this about the Circus? What's Leclerc up to?"

"I thought you knew. He said he'd put you on the list."

"I don't mean that. Why's he lying to them again? He's dictated a memorandum to Control about some training scheme and you going abroad. Pine took it around by hand. He's gone mad about her pension; Mrs. Taylor's; looking up precedents and heaven knows what. Even the application is Top Secret. He's building one of his card houses, John, I know he is. Who's Leiser, for instance?"

"You're not supposed to know. He's an agent; a Pole."

"Does he work for the Circus?" She changed her tack.

"Well, why are *you* going? That's another thing I don't understand. For that matter, why did Taylor have to go? If the Circus has couriers in Finland, why couldn't we have used them in the first place? Why send poor Taylor? Even now the F.O. could iron it out, I'm sure they could. He just won't give them a chance: he *wants* to send you."

"You don't understand," Avery said shortly.

"Another thing," she demanded as he was going, "why does Adrian Haldane hate you so?"

He visited the accountant, then took a taxi to the Circus. Leclerc had said he could claim for it. He was cross that Sarah had tried to reach him at such a moment. He had told her never to ring him at the Department. Leclerc said it was insecure.

"What did you read at Oxford? It was Oxford, wasn't it?" Smiley asked, and gave him a cigarette, rather a muddled one from a packet of ten.

"Languages." Avery patted his pockets for a match. "German and Italian." When Smiley said nothing he added, "German principally."

Smiley was a small, distracted man with plump fingers and a shadowy, blinking way with him which suggested discomfort. Whatever Avery had expected, it was not this.

"Well, well." Smiley nodded to himself, a very private comment. "It's a question of a courier, I believe, in Helsinki. You want to give him a film. A training scheme."

"Yes."

"It's a most unusual request. You're sure . . . do you know the *size* of the film?"

"No."

A long pause.

"You should try to find out that kind of thing," Smiley said kindly. "I mean, the courier may want to conceal it, you see."

"I'm sorry."

"Oh, it doesn't matter."

Avery was reminded of Oxford, and reading essays to his tutor.

"Perhaps," said Smiley thoughtfully, "I might say one thing. I'm sure Leclerc has already had it from Control. We want to give you all the help we can—*all* the help. There used to be a time," he mused, with that curious air of indirection which seemed to characterize all his utterances, "when our departments *competed*. I always found that very painful. But I wondered whether you could tell me a *little*, just a little. . . . Control was so anxious to help. We should hate to do the wrong thing out of ignorance."

"It's a training exercise. Full dress. I don't know much about it myself."

"We want to help," Smiley repeated simply. "What is your target country, your *putative* target?"

"I don't know. I'm only playing a small part. It's training."

"But if it's training, why so much secrecy?"

"Well, Germany," Avery said.

"Thank you."

Smiley seemed embarrassed. He looked at his hands folded lightly on the desk before him. He asked Avery whether it was still raining. Avery said he was afraid so.

"I'm sorry to hear about Taylor," he said. Avery said yes he was a good man.

"Do you know what time you'll have your film? Tonight? Tomorrow? Leclerc rather thought tonight, I gather."

"I don't know. It depends how it goes. I just can't tell at the moment."

"No." There followed a long, unexplained silence. He's like an old man, thought Avery, he forgets he's not alone. "No, there are so many imponderables. Have you done this kind of thing before?"

"Once or twice." Again Smiley said nothing and did not seem to notice the gap.

"How *is* everyone in Blackfriars Road? Do you know Haldane at all?" Smiley asked. He didn't care about the reply.

"He's Research now."

"Of course. A good brain. Your Research people enjoy quite a reputation, you know. We have consulted them ourselves more than once. Haldane and I were contemporaries at Oxford. Then in the war we worked together for a while. A Greats man. We'd have taken him here after the war; I think the medical people were worried about his chest."

"I hadn't heard."

"Hadn't you?" The eyebrows rose comically. "There's a hotel in Helsinki called the Prince of Denmark. Opposite the main station. Do you know it by any chance?"

"No. I've never been to Helsinki."

"Haven't you now?" Smiley peered at him anxiously. "It's a very *strange* story. This Taylor: was he training too?"

"I don't know. But I'll find the hotel," Avery said with a touch of impatience.

"They sell magazines and postcards just inside the door. There's only the one entrance." He might have been talking about the house next door. "And flowers. I think the best arrangement would be for you to go there once you have the film. Ask the people at the flower stall to send a dozen red roses to Mrs. Avery at the Imperial Hotel at Torquay. Or half a dozen would be enough, we don't want to waste money, do we? Flowers are so expensive there. Are you traveling under your own name?"

"Yes."

"Any particular reason? I don't mean to be curious," he added hastily, "but one has such a short life anyway . . . I mean before one's blown."

"I gather it takes a bit of time to get a fake passport. The Foreign Office . . ." He shouldn't have answered. He should have told him to mind his own business.

"I'm sorry," said Smiley, and frowned as if he had made an error of tact. "You can always come to us, you know. For passports, I mean." It was meant as a kindness. "Just send the flowers. As you leave the hotel, check your watch by the hall clock. Half an hour later return to the main entrance. A taxi driver will recognize you and open the door of his car. Get in, drive around, give him the film. Oh, and pay him please. Just the ordinary fare. It's so easy to forget the *little* things. What *kind* of training precisely?"

"What if I don't get the film?"

"In that case do nothing. Don't go near the hotel. Don't go to Helsinki. Forget about it." It occurred to Avery that his instructions had been remarkably clear.

"When you were reading German, did you touch on the seventeenth century by any chance?" Smiley inquired hopefully as Avery rose to go. "Gryphius, Lohenstein; those people?"

"It was a special subject. I'm afraid I didn't."

"*Special*," muttered Smiley. "What a *silly* word. I suppose they mean extrinsic; it's a very impertinent notion."

As they reached the door he said, "Have you a briefcase or anything?"

"Yes."

"When you have that film, put it in your pocket," he suggested, "and carry the briefcase in your hand. If you *are* followed, they tend to watch the briefcase. It's natural, really. If you just drop the briefcase somewhere, they may go looking for that instead. I don't think the Finns are very *sophisticated* people. It's only a training hint, of course. But don't *worry*. It's such a mistake, I always feel, to put one's trust in *technique*." He saw Avery to the door, then made his way ponderously along the corridor to Control's room.

Avery walked upstairs to the flat, guessing how Sarah would react. He wished he had telephoned after all because he hated to find her in the kitchen, and Anthony's toys all over the drawing room carpet. It never worked, turning up without warning. She took fright as if she expected him to have done something dreadful.

He did not carry a key; Sarah was always in. She had no friends of her own as far as he knew; she never went to coffee parties or took herself shopping. She seemed to have no talent for independent pleasure.

He pressed the bell, heard Anthony calling Mummy, Mummy, and waited to hear her step. The kitchen was at the end of the passage, but this time she came from the bedroom, softly as though she were barefooted.

She opened the door without looking at him. She was wearing a cotton nightdress and a cardigan.

"God, you took your time," she said, turned and walked uncertainly back to the bedroom. "Something wrong?" she asked over her shoulder. "Someone else been murdered?"

"What's the matter, Sarah? Aren't you well?"

Anthony was running about shouting because his father had come home. Sarah climbed back into bed. "I rang the doctor. *I* don't know what it is," she said, as if illness were not her subject.

"Have you a temperature?"

She had put a bowl of cold water and the bathroom flannel beside her. He wrung out the flannel and laid it on her head. "You'll have to cope," she said. "I'm afraid it's not as exciting as spies. Aren't you going to ask me what's wrong?"

"When's the doctor arriving?"

"He has surgery till twelve. He'll turn up after that, I suppose."

He went to the kitchen, Anthony following. The breakfast things were still on the table. He telephoned her mother in Reigate and asked her to come straightaway.

It was just before one when the doctor arrived. A fever, he said; some germ that was going the rounds.

He thought she would weep when he told her he was going abroad; she took it in, reflected for a while and then suggested he go and pack.

"Is it important?" she said suddenly.

"Of course. Terribly."

"Who for?"

"You, me. All of us, I suppose."

"And for Leclerc?"

"I told you. For all of us."

He promised Anthony he would bring him something.

"Where are you going?" Anthony asked.

"In an airplane."

"Where?"

He was going to tell him it was a great secret when he remembered Taylor's little girl.

He kissed her goodbye, took his suitcase to the hall and put it on the mat. There were two locks on the door for Sarah's sake and they had to be turned simultaneously. He heard her say:

"Is it dangerous too?"

"I don't know. I only know it's very big."

"You're really sure of that, are you?"

He called almost in despair, "Look, how far am I supposed to think? It isn't a question of politics, don't you see? It's a question of fact. Can't you believe? Can't you tell me for once in my life that I'm doing something good?" He went into the bedroom, reasoning with her. She held a paperback in front of her and was pretending to read. "We all have to, you know, we all have to draw a line round our lives. It's no good asking me the whole time, 'Are you sure?' It's like asking whether we should have children, whether we should have married. There's just no point."

"Poor John," she observed, putting down the book and analyzing him. "Loyalty without faith. It's very hard for you." She said this with total dispassion as if she had identified a social evil. The kiss was like a betrayal of her standards.

Haldane watched the last of them leave the room; he had arrived late, he would leave late, never with the crowd.

Leclerc said, "Why do you do that to me?" He spoke like an actor tired from the play. The maps and photographs were strewn on the table with the empty cups and ashtrays.

Haldane didn't answer.

"What are you trying to prove, Adrian?"

"What was that you said about putting a man in?"

Leclerc went to the basin and poured himself a glass of water from the tap. "You don't care for Avery, do you?" he asked.

"He's young. I'm tired of that cult."

"I get a sore throat, talking all the time. Have some yourself. Do your cough good."

"How old is Gorton?" Haldane accepted the glass, drank and handed it back.

"Fifty."

"He's more. He's our age. He was our age in the war."

"One forgets. Yes, he must be fifty-five or-six."

"Established?" Haldane persisted.

Leclerc shook his head. "He's not qualified. Broken service. He went to the Control Commission after the war. When that packed up he wanted to stay in Germany. German wife, I think. He came to us and we gave him a contract. We could never afford to keep him there if he were established." He took a sip of water, delicately, like a girl. "Ten years ago we'd thirty men in the field. Now we've nine. We haven't even got our own couriers, not clandestine ones. They all knew it this morning; why didn't they say so?"

"How often does he put in a refugee report?"

Leclerc shrugged. "I don't see all his stuff," he said. "Your people should know. The market's dwindling, I suppose, now they've closed the Berlin border."

"They only put the better reports up to me. This must be the first I've seen from Hamburg for a year. I always imagined he had some other function."

Leclerc shook his head. Haldane asked, "When does his contract come up for renewal?"

"I don't know. I just don't know."

"I suppose he must be fairly worried. Does he get a gratuity on retirement?"

"It's just a three-year contract. There's no gratuity. No frills. He has the chance of going on after sixty, of course, if we want him. That's the advantage of being a temporary."

"When was his contract last renewed?"

"You'd better ask Carol. It must be two years ago. Maybe longer."

Haldane said again, "You talked about putting a man in."

"I'm seeing the Minister again this afternoon."

"You've sent Avery already. You shouldn't have done that, you know."

"Somebody had to go. Did you want me to ask the Circus?"

"Avery was very impertinent," Haldane observed.

The rain was running in the gutters, tracing gray tracks on the dingy panes. Leclerc seemed to want Haldane to speak, but Haldane had nothing to say. "I don't know yet what the Minister thinks about Taylor's death. He'll ask me this afternoon and I shall give him my opinion. We're all in the dark, of course." His voice recovered its strength. "But he may instruct me—it's in the cards, Adrian—he may *instruct* me to get a man in."

"Well?"

"Suppose I asked you to form an operations section, make the research, prepare the papers and equipment; suppose I asked you to find, train and field the agent. Would you do it?"

"Without telling the Circus?"

"Not in detail. We may need their facilities from time to time. That doesn't mean we need tell them the whole story. There's the question of security: *need to know.*"

"Then without the Circus?"

"Why not?"

Haldane shook his head. "Because it isn't our work. We're just not equipped. Give it to the Circus and help them out with the military stuff. Give it to an old hand, someone like Smiley or Leamas—"

"Leamas is dead."

"All right then—Smiley."

"Smiley is blown."

Haldane colored. "Then Guillam or one of the others. One of the pros. They've got a big enough stable these days. Go and see Control, let him have the case."

"No," Leclerc said firmly, putting his glass on the table. "No, Adrian. You've been in the Department as long as I have, you know our brief. *Take all necessary steps*—that's what it says—*all necessary steps for the procurement, analysis and verification of military intelligence in those areas where the requirement cannot be met from conventional military resources.*" He beat out the words with his little fist as he spoke. "How else do you think I got authority for the overflight?"

"All right," Haldane conceded. "We have our brief. But things have changed. It's a different game now. In those days we were top of the tree—rubber boats on a moonless night; a captured enemy plane; wireless and all that. You and I know; we did it together. But it's changed. It's a different war; a different kind of fighting. They know that at the Ministry perfectly well." He added, "And don't place too much trust in the Circus; you'll get no charity from those people."

They looked at one another in surprise, a moment of recognition. Leclerc said, his voice scarcely above a whisper: "It began with the networks, didn't it? Do you remember how the Circus swallowed them up one by one? The

Ministry would say: 'We're in danger of duplication on the Polish desks, Leclerc. I've decided Control should look after Poland.' When was that? July forty-eight. Year after year it's gone on. Why do you think they patronize your Research Section? Not just for your beautiful files; they've got us where they want us, don't you see? Satellites! Non-operational! It's a way of putting us to sleep! You know what they call us in Whitehall these days? The Grace and Favor boys."

There was a long silence.

Haldane said, "I'm a collator, not an operational man."

"You *used* to be operational, Adrian."

"So did we all."

"You know the target. You know the whole background. There's no one else. Take whom you want—Avery, Woodford, whomever you want."

"We're not used to people anymore. Handling them, I mean." Haldane had become unusually diffident. "I'm a Research man. I work with files."

"We've had nothing else to give you until now. How long is it? Twenty years."

"Do you know what it means, a rocket site?" Haldane demanded. "Do you know how much mess it makes? They need launch pads, blast shields, cable troughs, control buildings; they need bunkers for storing the warheads, trailers for fuel and oxidizers. All those things come first. Rockets don't creep about in the night, they move like a traveling fair; we'd have other indicators before now; or the Circus would. As for Taylor's death—"

"For heaven's sake, Adrian, do you think Intelligence consists of unassailable philosophical truths? Does every priest have to *prove* that Christ was born on Christmas Day?"

His little face was thrust forward as he tried to draw from Haldane something he seemed to know was there. "You can't do it all by sums, Adrian. We're not academics, we're Civil Servants. We have to deal with things as they are. We have to deal with people, with events!"

"Very well, events then: if he swam the river, how did he preserve the film? How did he *really* take the pictures? Why isn't there any trace of camera shake? He'd been drinking, he was balancing on tiptoe; they're long enough exposures, you know, time exposures," he said. Haldane seemed afraid, not of Leclerc, not of the operation, but of himself. "Why did he give Gorton for nothing what he'd offered elsewhere for money? Why did he risk his life at all, taking those photographs? I sent Gorton a list of supplementaries. He's still trying to find the man, he says."

His eyes drifted to the model airplane and the files on Leclerc's desk. "You're thinking of Peenemünde, aren't you?" he continued. "You want it to be like Peenemünde."

"You haven't told me what you'll do if I get those instructions."

"You never will. You never, never will." He spoke with great finality, almost triumph. "We're dead, don't you see? You said it yourself. They want us to go to sleep, not go to war." He stood up. "So it doesn't matter. It's all academic after all. Can you *really* imagine Control would help us?"

"They've agreed to help us with a courier."

"Yes. I find that most odd."

Haldane stopped before a photograph by the door. "That's Malherbe, isn't it? The boy who died. Why did you choose that name?"

"I don't know. It just came into my head. One's memory plays odd tricks."

"You shouldn't have sent Avery. We've no business to use him for a job like that."

Leclerc said, "I went through the cards last night. We've got a man who'd do. Trained wireless operator, German speaker, unmarried." Haldane stood quite still.

"Age?" he asked at last.

"Forty. A bit over."

"He must have been very young."

"He put up a good show. They caught him in Holland and he got away."

"How did he get caught?"

The slightest pause. "It isn't recorded."

"Intelligent?"

"He seems quite well qualified."

The same long silence.

"So am I. Let's see what Avery brings back."

"Let's see what the Ministry says."

Leclerc waited till the sound of coughing had faded

down the corridor before he put on his coat. He would go for a walk, take some fresh air and have lunch at his club; the best they had. He wondered what it would be; the place had gone off badly in the last few years. After lunch he would go round to Taylor's widow. Then to the Ministry.

Woodford, lunching with his wife at Gorringe's, said, "Young Avery's on his first run. Clarkie sent him. He should make a good job of it."

"Perhaps he'll get himself killed, too," she said nastily. She was off the drink, doctor's orders. "Then you can have a real ball. Christ, that would be a party and a half! Come to the Blackfriars' Ball!" Her lower lip was quivering. "Why are the young ones so bloody marvelous? We were young, weren't we . . . ? Christ, we still are. What's wrong with us? We can't wait to get old, can we? We can't . . ."

"All right, Babs," he said. He was afraid she might cry.

6.

Takeoff

AVERY SAT in the airplane remembering the day when Haldane failed to appear. It was, by coincidence, the first of the month, July it must have been, and Haldane did not come to the office. Avery knew nothing of it until Woodford rang him on the internal telephone to tell him. Haldane was probably ill, Avery had said; some personal matter had cropped up. But Woodford was adamant. He had been to Leclerc's room, he said, and had looked at the leave roster: Haldane was not due for leave till August.

"Telephone his flat, John, telephone his flat," he had urged. "Speak to his wife. Find out what's become of him." Avery was so astonished that he did not know what to say: those two had worked together for twenty years, and even he knew Haldane was a bachelor.

"Find out where he is," Woodford had persisted. "Go on, I order you: ring his flat."

So he did. He might have told Woodford to do it himself, but he hadn't the heart. Haldane's sister answered. Haldane was in bed, his chest was playing him up; he had refused to tell her the Department's telephone number. As Avery's eye caught the calendar, he realized why Woodford had been so agitated: it was the beginning of a quarter. Haldane might have got a new job and left the Department without telling Woodford. A day or two later, when Haldane returned, Woodford was uncommonly warm toward him, bravely ignoring his sarcasm; he was grateful to him for coming back. For some time after that, Avery had

been frightened. His faith shaken, he examined more closely its object.

He noticed that they ascribed—it was a plot in which all
but Haldane compounded—legendary qualities to one another. Leclerc, for instance, would seldom introduce Avery
to a member of his parent Ministry without some catchword. "Avery is the brightest of our new stars"—or, to
more senior men, "John is my memory. You must ask
John." For the same reason they lightly forgave one another their trespasses, because they dared not think, for their
own sakes, that the Department had room for fools. He
recognized that it provided shelter from the complexities of
modern life, a place where frontiers still existed. For its
servants, the Department had a religious quality. Like
monks, they endowed it with a mystical identity far away
from the hesitant, sinful band which made up its ranks.
While they might be cynical of the qualities of one another, contemptuous of their own hierarchical preoccupations,
their faith in the Department burned in some separate
chapel and they called it patriotism.

For all that, as he glanced at the darkening sea beneath
him, at the cold sunlight slanting on the waves, he felt his
heart thrilling with love. Woodford with his pipe and his
plain way became part of that secret elite to which Avery
now belonged; Haldane, Haldane above all, with his cross-
words and his eccentricities, fitted into place as the uncom-
promising intellectual, irritable and aloof. He was sorry he
had been rude to Haldane. He saw Dennison and Mc-
Culloch as the matchless technicians, quiet men, not articulate at meetings, but tireless and in the end, right. He
thanked Leclerc, thanked him warmly, for the privilege of
knowing these men, for the excitement of this mission; for
the opportunity to advance from the uncertainty of the
past toward experience and maturity, to become a man,
shoulder to shoulder with the others, tempered in the fire
of war; he thanked him for the precision of command,
which made order out of the anarchy of his heart. He
imagined that when Anthony grew up, he too might be led
into those dowdy corridors and be presented to old Pine,
who with tears in his eyes would stand up in his box and
warmly grasp the child's tender hand.

It was a scene in which Sarah played no part.

Avery lightly touched a corner of the long envelope in his inside pocket. It contained his money: two hundred pounds in a blue envelope with the Government crest. He had heard of people in the war sewing such things into the lining of their clothes, and he rather wished they had done that for him. It was a childish conceit, he knew; he even smiled to discover himself given to such fancies.

He remembered Smiley that morning; in retrospect he was just a little frightened of Smiley. And he remembered the child at the door. A man must steel himself against sentiment.

"Your husband did a very good job," Leclerc was saying. "I cannot tell you the details. I am sure that he died very gallantly."

Her mouth was stained and ugly. Leclerc had never seen anyone cry so much; it was like a wound that would not close.

"What do you mean, gallantly?" She blinked. "We're not fighting a war. That's finished, all that fancy talk. He's dead," she said stupidly, and buried her face in her crooked arm, slouching across the dining room table like a puppet abandoned. The child was staring from a corner.

"I trust," Leclerc said, "that I have your permission to apply for a pension. You must leave all that to us. The sooner we take care of it the better. A pension," he declared, as if it were the maxim of his house, "can make a lot of difference."

The Consul was waiting beside the Immigration Officer; he came forward without a smile as if he were doing his duty. "Are you Avery?" he asked. Avery had the impression of a tall man in a trilby and a dark overcoat, red-faced and severe. They shook hands.

"You're the British Consul. Mr. Sutherland."

"H. M. Consul, actually," he replied a little tartly. "There's a difference, you know." He spoke with a Scottish accent. "How did you know my name?"

They walked together toward the main entrance. It was all very simple. Avery noticed the girl at the desk; fair and rather pretty.

"It's kind of you to come all this way," Avery said.

"It's only three miles from the town." They got into the car.

"He was killed just up the road," said Sutherland. "Do you want to see the spot?"

"I might as well. To tell my mother." He was wearing a black tie.

"Your name *is* Avery, isn't it?"

"Of course it is; you saw my passport at the desk." Sutherland didn't like that, and Avery rather wished he hadn't said it. He started the engine. They were about to pull into the center of the road when a Citroën swung out and overtook them.

"Damn fool," Sutherland snapped. "Roads are like ice. One of these pilots, I suppose. No idea of speed." They could see a peaked cap silhouetted against the windshield as the car hurried down the long road across the dunes, throwing up a small cloud of snow behind it.

"Where do you come from?" he asked.

"London."

Sutherland pointed straight ahead: "That's where your brother died. Up there on the brow. The police reckon the driver must have been tight. They're very hot on drunken driving here, you know." It sounded like a warning. Avery stared at the flat reaches of snowbound country on either side and thought of lonely, English Taylor struggling along the road, his weak eyes streaming from the cold.

"We'll go to the police afterward," said Sutherland. "They're expecting us. They'll tell you all the details. Have you booked yourself a room here?"

"No."

As they reached the top of the rise Sutherland said with grudging deference, "It was just here if you want to get out."

"It's all right."

Sutherland accelerated a little as if he wanted to get away from the place.

"Your brother was walking to the hotel. The Regina, just here. There was no taxi." They descended the slope on the other side; Avery caught sight of the long lights of a hotel across the valley.

"No distance at all, really," Sutherland commented. "He'd have done it in fifteen minutes. Less. Where does your mother live?"

The question took Avery by surprise.

"Woodbridge, in Suffolk." There was a by-election going on there; it was the first town that came into his head, though he had no interest in politics.

"Why didn't he put her down?"

"I'm sorry, I don't understand."

"As next of kin. Why didn't Malherbe put his mother down instead of you?"

Perhaps it was not meant as a serious question; perhaps he just wanted to keep Avery talking because he was upset; nevertheless, it was unnerving. He was still strung up from the journey, he wanted to be taken for granted, not subjected to this interrogation. He realized, too, that he had not sufficiently worked out the supposed relationship between Taylor and himself. What had Leclerc written in the teleprint; half brother or stepbrother? Hastily he tried to visualize a train of family events, death, remarriage or estrangement, which would lead him to the answer to Sutherland's question.

"There's the hotel," the Consul said suddenly, and then, "It's nothing to do with me, of course. He can put down whoever he wants." Resentment had become a habit of speech with Sutherland, a philosophy. He spoke as if everything he said were the contradiction of a popular view.

"She's old," Avery replied at last. "It's a question of protecting her from shock. I expect that's what he had in mind when he filled in his passport application. She's been ill; a bad heart. She's had an operation." It sounded very childish.

"Ah."

They had reached the outskirts of the town.

"There has to be a postmortem," Sutherland said. "It's the law here, I'm afraid, in the case of violent death."

Leclerc was going to be angry about that. Sutherland continued, "For us, it makes the formalities more complicated. The Criminal Police take over the body until the postmortem is complete. I asked them to be quick, but one can't insist."

"Thanks. I thought I'd have the body flown back." As

they turned off the main road into the market square, Avery asked casually, as if he had no personal interest in the outcome, "What about his effects? I'd better take them with me, hadn't I?"

"I doubt whether the police will hand them over until they've the go-ahead from the public prosecutor. The post-mortem report goes to him; he gives clearance. Did your brother leave a will?"

"I've no idea."

"You'd not happen to know whether you're an executor?"

"No."

Sutherland gave a dry, patient laugh. "I can't help feeling you're a little premature. Next of kin is not quite the same as executor," he said. "It gives you no legal rights, I'm afraid, apart from the disposal of the body." He paused, looking back over his seat while he reversed the car into a parking space. "Even if the police hand your brother's effects over to me, I'm not allowed to release them until I've had instructions from the Office, and *they,*" he continued quickly, for Avery was about to interrupt him, "won't issue such instructions to *me* until a grant of probate has been made or a Letter of Administration issued. But I can give you a death certificate," he added consolingly, opening his door, "if the insurance companies require it." He looked at Avery sideways, as if wondering whether he stood to inherit anything. "It'll cost you five shillings for the Consular registration and five shillings per certified copy. What was that you said?"

"Nothing." Together they climbed the steps to the police station.

"We'll be seeing Inspector Peersen," Sutherland explained. "He's quite well disposed. You'll kindly let me handle him."

"Of course."

"He's been a lot of help with my DBS problems."

"Your what?"

"Distressed British Subjects. We get one a day in summer. They're a disgrace. Did your brother drink a lot, incidentally? There's some suggestion he was—"

"It's possible," Avery said. "I hardly knew him in the last few years." They entered the building.

Leclerc himself was walking carefully up the broad steps of the Ministry. It lay between Whitehall Gardens and the river; the doorway was large and new, surrounded with that kind of fascist statuary which is admired by local authorities. Partly modernized, the building was guarded by sergeants in red sashes and contained two escalators; the one which descended was full, for it was half past five.

"Under Secretary," Leclerc began diffidently, "I shall have to ask the Minister for another overflight."

"You'll be wasting your time," he replied with satisfaction. "He was most apprehensive about the last one. He's made a policy decision; there'll be no more."

"Even with a target like this?"

"Particularly with a target like this."

The Under Secretary lightly touched the corners of his in-tray as a bank manager might touch a statement. "You'll have to think of something else," he said. "Some other way. Is there no *painless* method?"

"None. I suppose we could try to stimulate a defection from the area. That's a lengthy business. Leaflets, propaganda broadcasts, financial inducements. It worked well in the war. We would have to approach a lot of people."

"It sounds a most improbable notion."

"Yes. Things are different now."

"What other ways are there then?" he insisted.

Leclerc smiled again, as if he would like to help a friend but could not work miracles. "An agent. A short-term operation. In and out: a week altogether perhaps."

The Under Secretary said, "But who could you find for a job like that? These days?"

"Who indeed? It's a very long shot."

The Under Secretary's room was large but dark, with rows of bound books. Modernization had encroached as far as his private office, which was done in the contemporary style, but there the process had stopped. They could wait till he retired to do his room. A gas fire burned in the marble fireplace. On the wall hung an oil painting of a battle at sea. They could hear the sound of barges in the fog. It was an oddly maritime atmosphere.

"Kalkstadt's pretty close to the border," Leclerc suggested. "We wouldn't have to use a scheduled airline. We could do a training flight, lose our way. It's been done before."

"Precisely," said the Under Secretary; then: "This man of yours who died."

"Taylor?"

"I'm not concerned with names. He was murdered, was he?"

"There's no proof," Leclerc said.

"But you assume it?"

Leclerc smiled patiently. "I think we both know, Under Secretary, that it is very dangerous to make broad assumptions when decisions of policy are involved. I'm still asking for another overflight."

The Under Secretary colored.

"I told you it's out of the question. No! Does that make it clear? We were talking of alternatives."

"There's one alternative, I suppose, which would scarcely touch on my Department. It's more a matter for yourselves and the Foreign Office."

"Oh?"

"Drop a hint to the London newspapers. Stimulate publicity. Print the photographs."

"And?"

"Watch them. Watch the East German and Soviet diplomacy, watch their communications. Throw a stone into the nest and see what comes out."

"I can tell you exactly what would come out. A protest from the Americans that would ring through these corridors for another twenty years."

"Of course. I was forgetting that."

"Then you're very lucky. You suggested putting an agent in."

"Only tentatively. We've no one in mind."

"Look," said the Under Secretary, with the finality of a man much tried. "The Minister's position is very simple. You have produced a report. If it is true, it alters our entire defense position. In fact it alters everything. I detest sensation, so does the Minister. Having put up the hare, the least you can do is have a shot at it."

Leclerc said, "If I found a man there's the problem of resources. Money, training and equipment. Extra staff perhaps. Transport. Whereas an overflight . . ."

"Why do you raise so many difficulties? I understood you people existed for this kind of thing."

"We have the expertise, Under Secretary. But I cut down, you know. I have cut down a lot. Some of our functions have lapsed: one must be honest. I have never tried to put the clock back. This is, after all"—a delicate smile—"a slightly *anachronistic* situation."

The Under Secretary glanced out of the window at the lights along the river.

"It seems pretty contemporary to me. Rockets and that kind of thing. I don't think the Minister considers it anachronistic."

"I'm not referring to the target but the method of attack: it would have to be a crash operation at the border. That has scarcely been done since the war. Although it is a form of clandestine warfare with which my Department is traditionally at home. Or used to be."

"What are you getting at?"

"I'm only thinking aloud, Under Secretary. I wonder whether the Circus might not be better equipped to deal with this. Perhaps you should approach Control. I can promise him the support of my armaments people."

"You mean you don't think you can handle it?"

"Not with my existing organization. Control can. As long, that is, as the Minister doesn't mind bringing in another Department. Two, really. I didn't realize you were so worried about publicity."

"Two?"

"Control will feel bound to inform the Foreign Office. It's his duty. Just as I inform you. And from then on, we must accept that it will be their headache."

"If *those* people know," the Under Secretary said with contempt, "it'll be round every damned club by tomorrow."

"There is that danger," Leclerc conceded. "More particularly, I wonder whether the Circus has the *military* skills. A rocket site is a complicated affair: launch pads, blast shields, cable troughs; all these things require proper processing and evaluation. Control and I could combine forces, I suppose—"

"That's out of the question. You people make poor bedfellows. Even if you succeeded in cooperating, it would be against policy: no monolith."

"Ah yes. Of course."

"Assume you do it yourself, then; assume you find a man. What would that involve?"

"A supplementary estimate. Immediate resources. Extra staff. A training establishment. Ministerial protection; special passes and authority." The knife again. "And *some* help from Control . . . we could obtain that under a pretext."

A foghorn echoed mournfully across the water.

"If it's the only way . . ."

"Perhaps you'd put it to the Minister," Leclerc suggested.

Silence. Leclerc continued, "In practical terms we need the best part of thirty thousand pounds."

"Accountable?"

"Partially. I understood you wanted to be spared details."

"Except where the Treasury's concerned. I suggest that you make a memo about costs."

"Very well. Just an outline."

The silence returned.

"That is hardly a large sum when set against the risk," the Under Secretary said, consoling himself.

"The potential risk. We want to clarify. I don't pretend to be convinced. Merely suspicious, heavily suspicious." He couldn't resist adding, "The Circus would ask twice as much. They're very free with money."

"Thirty thousand pounds, then, and our protection?"

"And a man. But I must find him for myself." A small laugh. The Under Secretary said abruptly, "There are certain details the Minister will not want to know. You realize that?"

"Of course. I imagine you will do most of the talking."

"I imagine the Minister will. You've succeeded in worrying him a good deal."

This time Leclerc remarked with impish piety, "We should never do that to our master; our common master."

The Under Secretary did not seem to feel they had one. They stood up.

"Incidentally," Leclerc said, "Mrs. Taylor's pension. I'm making an application to the Treasury. They feel the Minister should sign it."

"Why, for God's sake?"

"It's a question of whether he was killed in action."

The Under Secretary froze. "That is most presumptuous. You're asking for Ministerial confirmation that Taylor was murdered."

"I'm asking for a widow's pension," Leclerc protested gravely. "He was one of my best men."

"Of course. They always are."

The Minister did not look up as they came in.

But the Police Inspector rose from his chair, a short, plump man with a shaven neck. He wore plain clothes. Avery supposed him to be a detective. He shook their hands with an air of professional bereavement, sat them in modern chairs with teak arms and offered cigars out of a tin. They declined, so he lit one himself and used it thereafter both as a prolongation of his short fingers when making gestures of emphasis, and as a drawing instrument to describe in the smoke-filled air objects of which he was speaking. He deferred frequently to Avery's grief by thrusting his chin downward into his collar and casting from the shadow of his lowered eyebrows confiding looks of sympathy. First he related the circumstances of the accident, praised in tiresome detail the efforts of the police to track down the car, referred frequently to the personal concern of the President of Police, whose anglophilia was a byword, and stated his own conviction that the guilty man would be found out and punished with the full severity of Finnish law. He dwelt for some time on his own admiration of the British, his affection for the Queen and Sir Winston Churchill, the charms of Finnish neutrality, and finally he came to the body.

The postmortem, he was proud to say, was complete, and Mr. Public Prosecutor (his own words) had declared that the circumstances of Mr. Malherbe's death gave no grounds for suspicion despite the presence of a considerable amount of alcohol in the blood. The barman at the airport accounted for five glasses of Steinhäger. He turned to Sutherland.

"Does he want to see his brother?" he inquired, thinking it apparently a delicacy to refer the question to a third party.

Sutherland was embarrassed. "That's up to Mr. Avery," he said, as if the matter were outside his competence. They both looked at Avery.

"I don't think so," Avery said.

"There is one difficulty. About the identification," Peersen said.

"Identification?" Avery repeated. "Of my brother?"

"You saw his passport," Sutherland put in, "before you sent it up to me. What's the difficulty?"

The policeman nodded. "Yes, yes." Opening a drawer, he took out a handful of letters, a wallet and some photographs.

"His name was Malherbe," he said. He spoke fluent English with a heavy American accent which somehow suited the cigar. "His passport was Malherbe. It was a *good* passport, wasn't it?" Peersen glanced at Sutherland. For a second, Avery thought he detected in Sutherland's clouded face a certain honest hesitation.

"Of course."

Peersen began to sort through the letters, putting some in a file before him and returning others to the drawer. Every now and then, as he added to the pile, he muttered: "Ah, so," or "Yes, yes." Avery could feel the sweat running down his body; it drenched his clasped hands.

"And your brother's name was Malherbe?" he asked again, when he had finished his sorting.

Avery nodded. "Of course."

Peersen smiled. "Not of course," he said, pointing his cigar and nodding in a friendly way as if he were making a debating point. "All his possessions, his letters, his clothes, driving license, all belong to Mr. Taylor. You know anything of Taylor?"

A dreadful block was forming in Avery's mind. The envelope, what should he do with the envelope? Go to the lavatory, destroy it now before it was too late? He doubted whether it would work: the envelope was stiff and shiny. Even if he tore it, the pieces would float. He was aware of Peersen and Sutherland looking at him, waiting for him to speak, and all he could think of was the envelope weighing so heavily in his inside pocket.

He managed to say, "No, I don't. My brother and I . . ." Stepbrother or half brother? "My brother and I did not have much to do with one another. He was older. We didn't really grow up together. He had a lot of different jobs, he could never quite settle down to anything. Perhaps this Taylor was a friend of his . . . who . . ." Avery shrugged, bravely trying to imply that Malherbe had been something of a mystery to him also.

"How old are you?" Peersen asked. His respect for the bereaved seemed to be dwindling.

"Thirty-two."

"And Malherbe?" he threw out conversationally. "He was how many years older, please?"

Sutherland and Peersen had seen his passport and knew his age. One remembers the age of people who die. Only Avery, his brother, had no idea how old the dead man was.

"Twelve," he hazarded. "My brother was forty-four." Why did he have to say so much?

Peersen raised his eyebrows. "Only forty-four? Then the passport is wrong as well."

Peersen turned to Sutherland, poked his cigar toward the door at the far end of the room and said happily, as if he had ended an old argument between friends, "Now you are seeing why I have a problem about identification."

Sutherland was looking very angry.

"It would be nice if Mr. Avery looked at the body," Peersen suggested. "Then we can be sure."

Sutherland said, "Inspector Peersen. The identity of Mr. Malherbe has been established from his passport. The Foreign Office in London has ascertained that Mr. Avery's name was quoted by Mr. Malherbe as his next of kin. You tell me there is nothing suspicious about the circumstances of his death. The customary procedure is now for you to release his effects to me for custody pending the completion of formalities in the United Kingdom. Mr. Avery may presumably take charge of his brother's body."

Peersen seemed to deliberate. He extracted the remainder of Taylor's papers from the steel drawer of his desk, added them to the pile already in front of him. He telephoned somebody and spoke in Finnish. After some minutes an orderly brought in an old leather suitcase with an inventory which Sutherland signed. Throughout all this, neither Avery nor Sutherland exchanged a word with the Inspector.

Peersen accompanied them all the way to the front door. Sutherland insisted on carrying the suitcase and papers himself. They went to the car. Avery waited for Sutherland to speak, but he said nothing. They drove for about ten minutes. The town was poorly lit. Avery noticed there was chemical on the road, in two lanes. The crown and gutters were still covered with snow. He was reminded of riding in the Mall, a thing he had never done. The streetlamps were neon, shedding a sickly light which seemed to shrink before the gathering darkness. Now and then Avery was aware of steep timbered roofs, the clanging of a tram or the tall white hat of a policeman.

Occasionally he stole a glance through the rear window.

7.

WOODFORD STOOD in the corridor smoking his pipe, grinning at the staff as they left. It was his hour of magic. The mornings were different. Tradition demanded that the junior staff arrive at half past nine; officer grades at ten or quarter past. Theoretically, senior members of the Department stayed late in the evening, clearing their papers. A gentleman, Leclerc would say, never watched the clock. The custom dated from the war, when officers spent the early hours of the morning debriefing reconnaissance pilots back from a run, or the late hours of the night dispatching an agent. The junior staff had worked shift in those days, but not the officers, who came and went as their work allowed. Now tradition fulfilled a different purpose. Now there were days, often weeks, when Woodford and his colleagues scarcely knew how to fill the time until five-thirty; all but Haldane, who supported on his stooping shoulders the Department's reputation for research. The rest would draft projects which were never submitted, bicker gently among themselves about leave, duty rosters and the quality of their official furniture; give excessive attention to the problems of their section staff.

Berry, the cipher clerk, came into the corridor, stooped and put on his bicycle clips.

"How's the missus, Berry?" Woodford asked. A man must keep his finger on the pulse.

"Doing very nicely, thank you, sir." He stood up, ran a comb through his hair. "Shocking about Wilf Taylor, sir."

"Shocking. He was a good scout."

"Mr. Haldane's locking up Registry, sir. He's working late."

"Is he? Well, we all have our hands full just now."

Berry lowered his voice. "And the boss is sleeping in, sir. Quite a crisis, really. I hear he's gone to see the Minister. They sent a car for him."

"Good night, Berry." They hear too much, Woodford reflected with satisfaction, and began sauntering along the passage.

The illumination in Haldane's room came from an adjustable reading lamp. It threw a brief, intense beam on to the file in front of him, touching the contours of his face and hands.

"Working late?" Woodford inquired.

Haldane pushed one file into his out-tray and picked up another.

"Wonder how young Avery's faring; he'll do well, that boy. I hear the Boss isn't back yet. Must be a long session." As he spoke, Woodford settled himself in the leather armchair. It was Haldane's own, he had brought it from his flat and sat in it to do his crossword puzzle after luncheon.

"Why should he do well? There is no particular precedent," Haldane said, without looking up.

"How did Clarkie get on with Taylor's wife?" Woodford now asked. "How'd she take it?"

Haldane sighed and put his file aside.

"He broke it to her. That's all I know," he said.

"You didn't hear how she took it? He didn't tell you?"

Woodford always spoke a little louder than necessary, for he was used to competing with his wife.

"I've really no idea. He went alone, I understand. Leclerc prefers to keep these things to himself."

"I thought perhaps with you . . ."

Haldane shook his head. "Only Avery," he muttered.

"It's a big thing, this, isn't it, Adrian . . . could be?"

"It could be. We shall see," Haldane said gently. He was not always unkind toward Woodford.

"Anything new on the Taylor front?" Woodford inquired.

"The Air Attaché at Helsinki has located Lansen. He confirms that he handed Taylor the film. Apparently the

Russians intercepted him over Kalkstadt; two MIGs. They buzzed him, then let him go."

"God," said Woodford stupidly. "That clinches it."

"It does nothing of the kind; it's consistent with what we know. If they declare the area closed why shouldn't they patrol it? They probably closed it for maneuvers, ground-air exercises. Why didn't they force Lansen down? The whole thing is entirely inconclusive."

Leclerc was standing in the doorway. He had put on a clean collar for the Minister and a black tie for Taylor.

"I came by car," he said. "They've given us one from the Ministry pool on indefinite loan. The Minister was quite distressed to hear we hadn't one. It's a Humber, chauffeur-driven like Control's. They tell me the chauffeur is a secure sort of person." He looked at Haldane. "I've decided to form Special Section, Adrian. I want you to take it over. I'm giving research to Sandford for the time being. The change will do him good." His face broke into a smile as if he could contain himself no longer. He was very excited. "We're putting a man in. The Minister's given his consent. We go to work at once. I want to see Heads of Sections first thing tomorrow. Adrian, I'll give you Woodford and Avery. Bruce, you keep in touch with the boys; get on to the old training people. The Minister will support three-month contracts for temporary staff. No peripheral liabilities, of course. The usual program: wireless, weapon training, ciphers, observation, unarmed combat and cover. Adrian, we'll need a house. Perhaps Avery could go into that when he comes back. I'll approach Control about documentation; the forgers all went over to him. We'll want frontier records for the Lübeck area, refugee reports, details of minefields and obstructions." He glanced at his watch. "Adrian, shall we have a word?"

"Tell me one thing," Haldane said. "How much does the Circus know about this?"

"Whatever we choose to tell them. Why?"

"They know Taylor is dead. It's all over Whitehall."

"Possibly."

"They know Avery's picking up a film in Finland. They may very well have noticed the Air Safety Center report on Lansen's plane. They have a way of noticing things. . . ."

"Well?"

"So it isn't only a question of what we tell them, is it?"

"You'll come to tomorrow's meeting?" Leclerc asked a little pathetically.

"I think I have the meat of my instructions. If you have no objection I would like to make one or two inquiries. This evening and tomorrow perhaps."

Leclerc, bewildered, said, "Excellent. Can we help you?"

"Perhaps I might have the use of your car for an hour?"

"Of course. I want us all to use it—to our common benefit. Adrian—this is for you."

He handed him a green card in a cellophane folder.

"The Minister signed it, personally." He implied that, like a Papal blessing, there were degrees of authenticity in a Ministerial signature. "Then you'll do it, Adrian? You'll take the job?"

Haldane might not have heard. He had reopened the file and was looking curiously at the photograph of a Polish boy who had fought the Germans twenty years ago. It was a young, strict face; humorless. It seemed to be concerned not with living but with survival.

"Why, Adrian," Leclerc cried with sudden relief. "You've taken the second vow!"

Reluctantly Haldane smiled, as if the phrase had called to mind something that he had thought forgotten. "He seems to have a talent for survival," he observed, finally indicating the file. "Not an easy man to kill."

"As next of kin," Sutherland began, "you have the right to state your wishes concerning the disposal of your brother's body."

"Yes."

Sutherland's house was a small building with a picture window full of potted plants. Only these distinguished it, either externally or internally, from its model in the dormitory areas of Aberdeen. As they walked down the drive, Avery caught sight of a middle-aged woman in the window. She wore an apron and was dusting something.

"I have an office at the back," said Sutherland, as if to emphasize that the place was not wholly given over to luxury. "I suggest we tie up the rest of the details now. I shan't keep you long." He was telling Avery he needn't expect to stay to supper. "How do you propose to get him back to England?"

They sat down on either side of the desk. Behind Sutherland's head hung a watercolor of mauve hills reflected in a Scottish loch.

"I should like it flown home."

"You know that is an expensive business?"

"I should like him flown all the same."

"For burial?"

"Of course."

"It isn't of course at all," Sutherland countered with distaste. "If your 'brother' "—he said it in inverted commas now, but he would play the game to the end—"were to be cremated, the flight regulations would be totally different."

"I see. I'm sorry."

"There is a firm of undertakers in the town, Barford and Company. One of the partners is English, married to a Swedish girl. There is a substantial Swedish minority here. We do our best to support the British community. In the circumstances, I would prefer you to return to London as soon as you can. I suggest you empower me to use Barford."

"All right."

"As soon as he has taken over the body, I will provide him with your brother's passport. He will have to obtain a medical certificate regarding the cause of death. I'll put him in touch with Peersen."

"Yes."

"He will also require a death certificate issued by a local registrar. It is cheaper if one attends to that side of things oneself. If money matters to your people."

Avery said nothing.

"When he has found out a suitable flight he will look after the freight warrant and bill of lading. I understand these things are usually moved at night. The freight rate is cheaper and—"

"That's all right."

"I'm glad. Barford will make sure the coffin is airtight. It may be of metal or wood. He will also append his own certificate that the coffin contains nothing but the body—and the same body as that to which the passport and the death certificate refer. I mention this for when you take delivery

in London. Barford will do all this very quickly. I shall see
to that. He has some pull with the charter companies here.
The sooner he—"

"I understand."

"I'm not sure you do." Sutherland raised his eyebrows as
if Avery had been impertinent. "Peersen has been very
reasonable. I don't wish to test his patience. Barford will
have a correspondent firm in London—it *is* London, isn't
it?"

"London, yes."

"I imagine he will expect some payment in advance. I
suggest you leave the money with me against a receipt. As
regards your brother's effects, I take it that whoever sent
you wished you to recover these letters?" He pushed them
across the table.

Avery muttered, "There was a film, an undeveloped
film." He put the letters in his pocket.

Deliberately Sutherland extracted a copy of the inventory which he had signed at the police station, spread it out
before him and ran his finger down the left-hand column
suspiciously, as if he were checking someone else's figures.

"There is no film entered here. Was there a camera
too?"

"No."

"Ah."

He saw Avery to the door. "You'd better tell whoever
sent you that Malherbe's passport was not valid. The Foreign Office sent out a circular about a group of numbers,
twenty-odd. Your brother's was one of them. There must
have been a slip-up. I was about to report it when a Foreign Office teleprint arrived empowering you to take over
Malherbe's effects." He gave a short laugh. He was very
angry. "That was nonsense, of course. The Office would
never have sent that on their own. They've no authority, not
unless you'd Letters of Administration, and you couldn't
have got *those* in the middle of the night. Have you
somewhere to stay? The Regina's quite good, near the airport. Out of town, too. I assume you can find your own
way. I gather you people get excellent subsistence."

Avery made his way quickly down the drive, carrying in
his memory the indelible image of Sutherland's thin, bitter
face set angrily against the Scottish hills. The wooden

houses beside the road shone half white in the darkness
like shadows around an operating table.

Somewhere not far from Charing Cross, in the basement
of one of those surprising eighteenth-century houses
between Villiers Street and the river, is a club with no
name on the door. You reach it by descending a curving
stone staircase. The railing, like the woodwork of the
house in Blackfriars Road, is painted dark green and needs
replacing.

Its members are an odd selection. Some of a military
kind, some in the teaching profession, others clerical; others again from that no-man's-land of London society which
lies between the bookmaker and the gentleman, presenting
to those around them, and perhaps even to themselves, an
image of vacuous courage; conversing in codes and phrases
which a man with a sense of language can only listen to at
a distance. It is a place of old faces and young bodies; of
young faces and old bodies; where the tensions of war have
become the tensions of peace, and voices are raised to
drown the silence, and glasses to drown the loneliness; it is
the place where the searchers meet, finding no one but
each other and the comfort of a shared pain; where the
tired watchful eyes have no horizon to observe. It is their
battlefield still; if there is love, they find it here in one another, shyly like adolescents, thinking all the time of other
people.

From the war, none but the dons were missing.

It is a small place run by a thin, dry man called Major
Dell; he has a moustache, and a tie with blue angels on a
black background. He stands the first drink, and they buy
him the others. It is called the Alias Club, and Woodford
was a member.

It is open in the evenings. They come at about six, de-
taching themselves with pleasure from the moving crowd,
furtive but determined, like men from out of town visiting
a disreputable theatre. You notice first the things that are
not there: no silver cups behind the bar, no visitors' book
nor list of membership; no insignia, crest or title. Only on
the whitewashed brick walls a few photographs hang,
framed in decorative adhesive tape, like the photographs in
Leclerc's room. The faces are indistinct, some enlarged, ap-

parently from a passport, taken from the front with both ears showing according to the regulation; some are women, a few of them attractive, with high square shoulders and long hair after the fashion of the war years. The men are wearing a variety of uniforms; Free French and Poles mingle with their British comrades. Some are fliers. Of the English faces one or two, grown old, still haunt the club.

When Woodford came in everyone looked around and Major Dell, much pleased, ordered his pint of beer. A florid, middle-aged man was talking about a sortie he once made over Belgium, but he stopped when he lost the attention of his audience.

"Hello, Woodie," somebody said in surprise. "How's the lady?"

"Fit." Woodford smiled genially. "Fit." He drank some beer. Cigarettes were passed around. Major Dell said, "Woodie's jolly shifty tonight."

"I'm looking for someone. It's all a bit top secret."

"We know the form," the florid man replied. Woodford glanced around the bar and asked quietly, a note of mystery in his voice, "What did Dad do in the war?"

A bewildered silence. They had been drinking for some time.

"Kept Mum, of course," said Major Dell uncertainly and they all laughed.

Woodford laughed with them, savoring the conspiracy, reliving the half-forgotten ritual of secret mess nights somewhere in England.

"And where did he keep her?" he demanded, still in the same confiding tone. This time two or three voices called in unison, "Under his blooming hat!"

They were louder, happier.

"There was a man called Johnson," Woodford continued quickly, "Jack Johnson. I'm trying to find out what became of him. He was a trainer in wireless transmission; one of the best. He was at Bovingdon first with Haldane until they moved him up to Oxford."

"Jack Johnson!" the florid man cried excitedly. "The WT man? I bought a car radio from Jack two weeks ago! Johnson's Fair Deal in the Clapham Broadway, that's the fellow. Drops in here from time to time. Amateur wireless enthusiast. Little bloke, speaks out of the side of his face?"

"That's him," someone else said. "He knocks off twenty percent for the old gang."

"He didn't for me," the florid man said.

"That's Jack; he lives at Clapham."

The others took it up: that was the fellow and he ran this shop, at Clapham; king of ham radio, been a ham before the war even when he was a kid; yes, on the Broadway, hung out there for years; must be worth a ransom. Liked to come into the club around Christmas time. Woodford, flushed with pleasure, ordered drinks.

In the bustle that followed, Major Dell took Woodford gently by the arm and guided him to the other end of the bar.

"Woodie, is it true about old Wilf Taylor? Has he really bought it?"

Woodford nodded, his face grave. "He was on a job. We think someone's been a little bit naughty."

Major Dell was all solicitude. "I haven't told the boys. It would only worry them. Who's caring for the Missus?"

"The Boss is taking that up now. It looks pretty hopeful."

"Good," said the Major. "Good." He nodded, patting Woodford's arm in a gesture of consolation. "We'll keep it from the boys, shall we?"

"Of course."

"He had one or two bills. Nothing very big. He liked to drop in Friday nights." The Major's accent slipped from time to time like a made-up tie.

"Send them along. We'll take care of those."

"There was a kid, wasn't there? A little girl?" They were moving back to the bar. "How old was she?"

"Eightish. Maybe more."

"He talked about her a lot," said the Major.

Somebody called, "Hey, Bruce, when are you chaps going to take another crack at the Jerries? They're all over the bloody place. Took the wife to Italy in the summer—full of arrogant Germans."

Woodford smiled. "Sooner than you think. Now let's try this one." The conversation died. Woodford was real. He still did the job.

"There was an unarmed combat man, a staff sergeant; a Welshman. He was short too."

"Sounds like Sandy Lowe," the florid man suggested.

"Sandy, that's him!" They all turned to the florid man in admiration. "He was a Taffy. Randy Sandy we called him."

"Of course," said Woodford contentedly. "Now didn't he go off to some public school as a boxing instructor?" He was looking at them narrowly, holding a good deal back, playing it long because it was so secret.

"That's him, that's Sandy!"

Woodford wrote it down, taking care because he had learned from experience that he tended to forget things which he entrusted to memory.

As he was going, the Major asked, "How's Clarkie?"

"Busy," Woodford said. "Working himself to death, as always."

"The boys talk about him a lot, you know. I wish he'd come here now and then, give them a hell of a boost, you know. Perk them up."

"Tell me," said Woodford. They were by the door. "Do you remember a fellow called Leiser? Fred Leiser, a Pole? Used to be with our lot. He was in the Holland show."

"Still alive?"

"Yes."

"Sorry," said the Major vaguely. "The foreigners have stopped coming; I don't know why. I don't discuss it with the boys."

Closing the door behind him, Woodford stepped into the London night. He looked about him, loving all he saw— the Mother city in his rugged care. He walked slowly, an old athlete on an old track.

8.

Avery, on the other hand, walked fast. He was afraid. There is no terror so consistent, so elusive to describe, as that which haunts a spy in a strange country. The glance of a taxi driver, the density of people in the street, the variety of official uniforms—was he a policeman or a postman?—the obscurity of custom and language, and the very noises which comprised the world into which Avery had moved contributed to the state of constant anxiety, which, like a nervous pain, became virulent now that he was alone. In the shortest time his spirit ranged between panic and cringing love, responding with unnatural gratitude to a kind glance or word. It was part of an effeminate dependence upon those whom he deceived. Avery needed desperately to win from the uncaring faces around him the absolution of a trusting smile. It was no help that he told himself: you do them no harm, you are their protector. He moved among them like a hunted man in search of rest and food.

He took a cab to the hotel and asked for a room with a bath. They gave him the register to sign. He had actually put his pen to the page when he saw, not ten lines above, done in a laborious hand, the name Malherbe, broken in the middle as if the writer could not spell it. His eye followed the entry along the line: ADDRESS, London; PROFESSION, Major (retired); DESTINATION, London. His last vanity, Avery thought, a false profession, a false rank, but little English Taylor had stolen a moment's glory. Why not Colonel? Or Admiral? Why not give himself a peerage and an address in Park Lane? Even when he dreamed, Taylor had known his limits.

The concierge said, "The valet will take your luggage."

"I'm sorry," said Avery, a meaningless apology, and signed his name while the man watched him curiously.

He gave the valet a coin and it occurred to him as he did so that he had given him eight and six. He closed the bedroom door. For a while he sat on his bed. It was a carefully planned room but bleak and without sympathy. On the door was a notice in several languages warning against the perils of theft, and by the bed another which explained the financial disadvantages of failing to breakfast in the hotel. There was a magazine about travel on the writing desk, and a Bible bound in black. There was a small bathroom, very clean, and a built-in wardrobe with one coat hanger. He had forgotten to bring a book. He had not anticipated having to endure leisure.

He was cold and hungry. He thought he would have a bath. He ran it and undressed. He was about to get into the water when he remembered Taylor's letters in his pocket. He put on a dressing gown, sat on the bed and looked through them. One from his bank about an overdraft, one from his mother, one from a friend which began Dear Old Wilf, the rest from a woman. He was suddenly frightened of the letters: they were evidence. They could compromise him. He determined to burn them all. There was a second basin in the bedroom. He put all the papers into it and held a match to them. He had read somewhere that was the thing to do. There was a membership card for the Alias Club made out in Taylor's name so he burned that too, then broke up the ash with his fingers and turned on the water; it rose swiftly. The plug was a built-in metal affair operated by a lever between the taps. The sodden ash was packed beneath it. The basin was blocked.

He looked for some instrument to probe under the lip of the plug. He tried his fountain pen but it was too fat, so he fetched the nail file. After repeated attempts he persuaded the ash into the outlet. The water ran away, revealing a heavy brown stain on the enamel. He rubbed it, first with his hand then with the scrubbing brush, but it wouldn't go. Enamel didn't stain like that, there must have been some quality in the paper, tar or something. He went into the bathroom, looking vainly for a detergent.

As he reentered his bedroom he became aware that it
was filled with the smell of charred paper. He went quickly
to the window and opened it. A blast of freezing wind
swept over his naked limbs. He was gathering the dressing
gown more closely about him when there was a knock on
the door. Paralyzed with fear he stared at the door handle,
heard another knock, called, watched the handle turn. It
was the man from Reception.

"Mr. Avery?"

"Yes?"

"I'm sorry. We need your passport. For the police."

"Police?"

"It's the customary procedure."

Avery had backed against the basin. The curtains were
flapping wildly beside the open window.

"May I close the window?" the man asked.

"I wasn't well. I wanted some fresh air."

He found his passport and handed it over. As he did so,
he saw the man's gaze fixed upon the basin, on the brown
mark and the small flakes which still clung to the sides.

He wished as never before that he was back in England.

The row of villas which lines Western Avenue is like a
row of pink graves in a field of gray; an architectural
image of middle age. Their uniformity is the discipline of
growing old, of dying without violence and living without
success. They are houses which have got the better of their
occupants; whom they change at will, and do not change
themselves. Furniture vans glide respectfully among them
like hearses, discreetly removing the dead and introducing
the living. Now and then some tenant will raise his hand,
expending pots of paint on the woodwork or labor on the
garden, but his efforts no more alter the house than flowers
a hospital ward, and the grass will grow its own way, like
grass on a grave.

Haldane dismissed the car and turned off the road toward South Park Gardens, a crescent five minutes from the
Avenue. A school, a post office, four shops and a bank. He
stooped a little as he walked; a black briefcase hung from
his thin hand. He made his way quietly along the pavement; the tower of a modern church rose above the houses;
a clock struck seven. A grocer's on the corner, new façade,

self-service. He looked at the name: Smethwick. Inside, a youngish man in overalls was completing a pyramid of cereal foods. Haldane rapped on the glass. The man shook his head and added a packet to the pyramid. He knocked again, sharply. The grocer came to the door.

"I'm not allowed to sell you anything," he shouted, "so it's no good knocking, is it?" He noticed the briefcase and asked, "Are you a rep then?"

Haldane put his hand in his inside pocket and held something to the window—a card in a cellophane wrapper like a season ticket. The grocer stared at it. Slowly he turned the key.

"I want a word with you in private," Haldane said, stepping inside.

"I've never seen one of those," the grocer observed uneasily. "I suppose it's all right."

"It's quite all right. A security inquiry. Someone called Leiser, a Pole. I understand he worked here long ago."

"I'll have to call my dad," the grocer said. "I was only a kid then."

"I see," said Haldane, as if he disliked the youth.

It was nearly midnight when Avery rang Leclerc. He answered straightaway. Avery could imagine him sitting up in the steel bed, the Air Force blankets thrown back, his small alert face anxious for the news.

"It's John," he said cautiously.

"Yes, yes, I know who you are." He sounded cross that Avery had mentioned his name.

"The deal's off, I'm afraid. They're not interested . . . negative. You'd better tell the man I saw; the little, fat man . . . tell him we shan't need the services of his friend here."

"I see. Never mind." He sounded utterly uninterested.

Avery didn't know what to say; he just didn't know. He needed desperately to go on talking to Leclerc. He wanted to tell him about Sutherland's contempt and the passport that wasn't right. "The people here, the people I'm negotiating with, are rather worried about the whole deal."

He waited.

He wanted to call him by his name but he had no name for him. They did not use "Mister" in the Department; the elder men addressed one another by their surnames and called the juniors by their Christian names. There was no established style of addressing one's superior. So he said, "Are you still there?" and Leclerc replied, "Of course. Who's worried? What's gone wrong?" Avery thought: I could have called him "Director," but that would have been insecure.

"The representative here, the man who looks after our interests . . . he's found out about the deal," he said. "He seems to have guessed."

"You stressed it was highly confidential?"

"Yes, of course." How could he ever explain about Sutherland?

"Good. We don't want any trouble with the Foreign Office just now." In an altered tone Leclerc continued, "Things are going very well over here, John, very well. When do you get back?"

"I've got to cope with the . . . with bringing our friend home. There are a lot of formalities. It's not as easy as you'd think."

"Never mind. When will you be finished?"

"Tomorrow."

"I'll send a car to meet you at Heathrow. A lot's happened in the last few hours; a lot of improvements. We need you badly." Leclerc added, throwing him a coin, "And well done, John, well done indeed."

"All right."

He expected to sleep heavily that night, but after what might have been an hour he woke, alert and watchful. He looked at his watch; it was ten past one. Getting out of bed he went to the window and looked on to the snow-covered landscape, marked by the darker lines of the road which led to the airport; he thought he could discern the little rise where Taylor had died.

He was desolate and afraid. His mind was obsessed by confused visions: Taylor's dreadful face, the face he so nearly saw, drained of blood, wide-eyed as if communicating a crucial discovery; Leclerc's voice, filled with vulnerable optimism: the fat policeman, staring at him in envy, as if he were something he could not afford to buy. He realized he was a person who did not take easily to solitude. Solitude saddened him, made him sentimental. He found

himself thinking, for the first time since he had left the flat
that morning, of Sarah and Anthony. Tears came suddenly
to his tired eyes when he recalled his boy, the steel-rimmed
spectacles like tiny irons; he wanted to hear his voice, he
wanted Sarah, and the familiarity of his home. Perhaps he
could telephone the flat, speak to her mother, ask after her.
But what if she were ill? He had suffered enough pain that
day, he had given enough of his energy, fear and invention.
He had lived a nightmare: he could not be expected to ring
her now. He went back to bed.

Try as he might, he could not sleep. His eyelids were hot
and heavy, his body deeply tired, but still he could not
sleep. A wind rose, rattling the double windows; now he
was too hot, now too cold. Once he dozed, only to be wakened violently from his uneasy rest by the sound of crying,
it might have been in the next room, it might have been
Anthony, or it might have been—since he did not hear it
properly, but only half knew in waking what kind of a
sound it had been—the metallic sobbing of a child's doll.

And once, it was shortly before dawn, he heard a footfall outside his room, a single tread in the corridor, not
imagined but real, and he lay in chill terror waiting for the
handle of his door to turn or the peremptory knocking of
Inspector Peersen's men. As he strained his ears he swore
he detected the faintest rustle of clothing, the subdued in-
take of human breath, like a tiny sigh; then silence.
Though he listened for minutes on end, he heard nothing
more.

Putting on the light, he went to the chair, felt in his
jacket for his fountain pen. It was by the basin. From his
briefcase he took a leather holdall which Sarah had given
him.

Settling himself at the flimsy table in front of the window, he began writing a love letter to a girl, it might have
been to Carol, he did not know. When at last morning
came he destroyed it, tearing it into small pieces and flush-
ing them down the lavatory. As he did so he caught sight
of something white on the floor. It was a photograph of
Taylor's child carrying a doll; she was wearing glasses, the
kind Anthony wore. It must have been among his papers.
He thought of destroying it but somehow he couldn't. He
slipped it into his pocket.

9.

Homecoming

LECLERC was waiting at Heathrow as Avery knew
he would be, standing on tiptoe, peering anxiously between
the heads of the waiting crowd. He had squared the cus-
toms somehow, he must have got the Ministry to do it, and
when he saw Avery he came forward into the hall and
guided him in a managing way as if he were used to being
spared formalities. This is the life we lead, Avery thought;
the same airport with different names; the same hurried,
guilty meetings; we live outside the walls of the town,
blackfriars from a dark house in Lambeth. He was desperately tired. He wanted Sarah. He wanted to say I'm sorry,
make it up with her, get a new job, try again; play with
Anthony more. He felt ashamed.

"I'll just make a telephone call. Sarah wasn't too well
when I left."

"Do it from the Office," Leclerc said. "Do you mind? I
have a meeting with Haldane in an hour." Thinking he detected a false note in Leclerc's voice, Avery looked at him
suspiciously, but the other's eyes were turned away toward
the black Humber standing in the privilege car park. Leclerc let the driver open the door for him; a silly muddle
took place until Avery sat on his left as protocol apparently demanded. The driver seemed tired of waiting. There
was no partition between him and themselves.

"This is a change," Avery said, indicating the car.

Leclerc nodded in a familiar way as if the acquisition

were no longer new. "How are things?" he asked, his mind elsewhere.

"All right. There's nothing the matter, is there? With Sarah, I mean."

"Why should there be?"

"Blackfriars Road?" the driver inquired without turning his head, as a sense of respect might have indicated.

"Headquarters, yes please."

"There was a hell of a mess in Finland," Avery observed brutally. "Our friend's papers . . . Malherbe's . . . weren't in order. The Foreign Office had cancelled his passport."

"Malherbe? Ah yes. You mean Taylor. We know all about that. It's all right now. Just the usual jealousy. Control is rather upset about it, as a matter of fact. He sent round to apologize. We've a lot of people on our side now, John, you've no idea. You're going to be very useful, John; you're the only one who's seen it on the ground." Seen what? Avery wondered. They were together again. The same intensity, the same physical unease, the same absences. As Leclerc turned to him Avery thought for one sickening moment he was going to put a hand on his knee. "You're tired, John, I can tell. I know how it feels. Never mind—you're back with us now. Listen, I've good news for you. The Ministry's waked up to us in a big way. We're to form a special operational unit to mount the next phase."

"Next phase?"

"Of course. The man I mentioned to you. We can't leave things as they are. We're clarifiers, John, not simply collators. I've revived Special Section; do you know what that is?"

"Haldane ran it during the war; training—"

Leclerc interrupted quickly for the driver's sake: "— training the traveling salesmen. And he's going to run it again now. I've decided you're to work with him. You're the two best brains I've got." A sideways glance.

Leclerc had altered. There was a new quality to his bearing, something more than optimism or hope. When Avery had seen him last he had seemed to be living against adversity; now he had a freshness about him, a purpose, which was either new or very old.

"And Haldane accepted?"

"I told you. He's working night and day. You forget, Adrian's a professional. A real technician. Old heads are the best for a job like this. With one or two young heads among them."

Avery said, "I want to talk to you about the whole operation . . . about Finland. I'll come to your office after I've rung Sarah."

"Come straightaway, then I can put you in the picture."

"I'll phone Sarah first."

Again Avery had the unreasonable feeling that Leclerc was trying to keep him from communicating with Sarah.

"She *is* all right, isn't she?"

"So far as I know. Why do you ask?" Leclerc went on, charming him: "Glad to be back, John?"

"Yes, of course."

He sank back into the cushions of the car. Leclerc, noticing his hostility, abandoned him for a time; Avery turned his attention to the road and the pink, healthy villas drifting past in the light rain.

Leclerc was talking again, his committee voice. "I want you to start straightaway. Tomorrow if you can. We've got your room ready. There's a lot to be done. This man: Haldane has him in play. We should hear something when we get home. From now on you're Adrian's creature. I trust that pleases you. Our masters have agreed to provide you with a special Ministry pass. The same kind of thing that they have in the Circus."

Avery was familiar with Leclerc's habit of speech; there were times when he resorted entirely to oblique allusion, offering a raw material which the consumer, not the purveyor, must refine.

"I want to talk to you about the whole thing. When I've rung Sarah."

"That's right," Leclerc replied nicely, "come and talk to me about it. Why not come now?" He looked at Avery, offering his whole face; a thing without depth, a moon with one side. "You've done well," he said generously. "I hope you'll keep it up." They entered London. "We're getting some help from the Circus," he added. "They seem to be quite willing. They don't know the whole picture of course. The Minister was very firm on that point."

They passed down Lambeth Road, where the God of Battles presides; the Imperial War Museum at one end, schools the other, hospitals in-between; a cemetery wired off like a tennis court. You cannot tell who lives there. The houses are too many for the people, the schools too large for the children. The hospitals may be full, but the blinds are drawn. Dust hangs everywhere, like the dust of war. It hangs over the hollow façades, chokes the grass in the graveyards: it has driven away the people, save those who loiter in the dark places like the ghosts of soldiers, or wait sleepless behind their yellow-lighted windows. It is a road which people seem to have left often. The few who returned brought something of the living world, according to their voyages. One a piece of field, another a broken Regency terrace, a warehouse or dumping yard; or a pub called the Flowers of the Forest.

It is a road filled with faithful institutions. Over one presides our Lady of Consolation, over another, Archbishop Amigo. Whatever is not hospital, school, pub or seminary is dead, and the dust has got its body. There is a toyshop with a padlocked door. Avery looked into it every day on the way to the office; the toys were rusting on the shelves. The window looked dirtier than ever; the lower part was striped with children's fingermarks. There is a place that mends your teeth while you wait. He glimpsed them now from the car, counting them off as they drove past, wondering whether he would ever see them again as a member of the Department. There are warehouses with barbed wire across their gates, and factories which produce nothing. In one of them a bell rang but no one heard. There is a broken wall with posters on it. You are Somebody today in the Regular Army. They rounded Saint George's Circus and entered Blackfriars Road for the home run.

As they approached the building, Avery sensed that things had changed. For a moment he imagined that the very grass on the wretched bit of lawn had thickened and revived during his brief absence; that the concrete steps leading to the front door, which even in midsummer managed to appear moist and dirty, were now clean and inviting. Somehow he knew, before he entered the building at all, that a new spirit had infected the Department.

It had reached the most humble members of the staff. Pine, impressed no doubt by the black staff car and the sudden passage of busy people, looked spruce and alert. For once he said nothing about cricket scores. The staircase was daubed with wax polish.

In the corridor they met Woodford. He was in a hurry. He was carrying a couple of files with red caution notices on the cover.

"Hullo, John! You've landed safely, then? Good party?" He really did seem pleased to see him. "Sarah all right now?"

"He's done well," said Leclerc quickly. "He had a very difficult run."

"Ah yes; poor Taylor. We shall need you in the new section. Your wife will have to spare you for a week or two."

"What was that about Sarah?" Avery asked. Suddenly he was frightened. He hastened down the corridor. Leclerc was calling but he took no notice. He entered his room and stopped dead. There was a second telephone on his desk, and a steel bed like Leclerc's along the side wall. Beside the new telephone was a piece of military board with a list of emergency telephone numbers pinned to it. The numbers for use during the night were printed in red. On the back of the door hung a two-color poster depicting in profile the head of a man. Across his skull was written KEEP IT HERE, and across his mouth, DON'T LET IT OUT HERE. It took him a moment or two to realize that the poster was an exhortation to security, and not some dreadful joke about Taylor. He lifted the receiver and waited. Carol came in with a tray of papers for signature.

"How did it go?" she asked. "The Boss seems pleased." She was standing quite close to him.

"Go? There's no film. It wasn't among his things. I'm going to resign; I've decided. What the hell's wrong with this phone?"

"They probably don't know you're back. There's a thing from Accounts about your claim for a taxi. They've queried it."

"Taxi?"

"From your flat to the office. The night Taylor died. They say it's too much."

"Look, go and stir up the exchange, will you, they must be fast asleep."

Sarah answered the telephone herself.

"Oh, thank God it's you."

Avery said yes, he had got in an hour ago. "Sarah, look, I've had enough, I'm going to tell Leclerc."

But before he could finish she burst out, "John, for *God's* sake, what *have* you been doing? We had the police here, detectives; they want to talk to you about a body that's arrived at London airport; somebody called Malherbe. They say it was sent from Finland on a false passport."

He closed his eyes. He wanted to put down the receiver, he held it away from his ear but he still heard her voice, saying John, John. "They say he's your brother; it's addressed to *you*, John; some London undertaker was supposed to be doing it all for you . . . John, John are you still there?"

"Listen," he said, "it's all right. I'll take care of it now."

"I told them about Taylor: I had to."

"Sarah!"

"What else could I do? They thought I was a criminal or something; they didn't believe me, John! They asked how they could get hold of you; I had to say I didn't know; I didn't even know which country or which plane; I was ill, John, I felt awful, I've got this damn flu and I'd forgotten to take my pills. They came in the middle of the night, two of them. John, why did they come in the night?"

"What did you tell them? For Christ's sake, Sarah, what else did you say to them?"

"Don't swear at me! I should be swearing at you and your beastly Department! I said you were doing something secret; you'd had to go abroad for the Department—John, I don't even know its *name!*—that you'd been rung in the night and you'd gone away. I said it was about a courier called Taylor."

"You're mad," Avery shouted, "you're absolutely mad! I told you never to say!"

"But John, they were *policemen!* There can't be any harm in telling *them*." She was crying, he could hear the tears in her voice. "John, *please* come back. I'm so frightened. You've got to get out of this, go back to publishing; I don't care what you do but—"

"I can't. It's terribly big. More important than you can possibly understand. I'm sorry, Sarah, I just can't leave the office." He added savagely, a useful lie, "You may have wrecked the whole thing."

There was a very long silence.

"Sarah, I'll have to sort this out. I'll ring you later."

When at last she answered he detected in her voice the same flat resignation with which she had sent him to pack his things. "You took the checkbook. I've no money."

He told her he would send it around. "We've got a car," he added, "specially for this thing, chauffeur driven." As he rang off he heard her say, "I thought you'd got lots of cars."

He ran into Leclerc's room. Haldane was standing behind the desk; his coat still wet from the rain. They were bent over a file. The pages were faded and torn.

"Taylor's body!" he blurted out. "It's at London Airport. You've messed the whole thing up. They've been on to Sarah! In the middle of the night!"

"Wait!" It was Haldane who spoke. "You have no business to come running in here," he declared furiously. "Just wait." He did not care for Avery.

He returned to the file, ignoring him. "None at all," he muttered, adding to Leclerc: "Woodford has already had some success, I gather. Unarmed combat's all right; he's heard of a wireless operator, one of the best. I remember him. The garage is called the King of Hearts; it is clearly prosperous. We inquired at the bank; they were quite helpful, if not specific. He's unmarried. He has a reputation for women; the usual Polish style. No political interests, no known hobbies, no debts, no complaints. He seems to be something of a nonentity. They say he's a good mechanic. As for character—" He shrugged. "What do we know about anybody?"

"But what did they *say?* Good heavens, you can't be fifteen years in a community without leaving *some* impression. There was a grocer wasn't there—Smethwick?—he lived with them after the war."

Haldane allowed himself a smile. "They said he was a good worker and very polite. Everyone says he's polite. They remember one thing only: he has a passion for hitting a tennis ball round their back yard."

"Did you take a look at the garage?"

"Certainly not. I didn't go near it. I propose to call there this evening. I don't see that we have any other choice. After all, the man's been on our cards for twenty years."

"Is there nothing more you can find out?"

"We would have to do the rest through the Circus."

"Then let John Avery clear up the details." Leclerc seemed to have forgotten Avery was in the room. "As for the Circus, I'll deal with them myself." His interest had been arrested by a new map on the wall, a town plan of Kalkstadt showing the church and railway station. Beside it hung an older map of eastern Europe. Rocket bases whose existence had already been confirmed were here related to the putative site south of Rostock. Supply routes and chains of command, the order of battle of supporting arms, were indicated with lines of thin wool stretched between pins. A number of these led to Kalkstadt.

"It's good, isn't it? Sandford put it together last night," Leclerc said. "He does that kind of thing rather well."

On his desk lay a new whitewood pointer like a giant bodkin threaded with a loop of barrister's ribbon. He had a new telephone, green, smarter than Avery's, with a notice on it saying SPEECH ON THIS TELEPHONE IS NOT SECURE. For a time Haldane and Leclerc studied the map, referring now and then to a file of telegrams which Leclerc held open in both hands as a choirboy holds a psalter.

Finally Leclerc turned to Avery and said, "Now, John." They were waiting for him to speak.

He could feel his anger dying. He wanted to hold on to it but it was slipping away. He wanted to cry out in indignation: how dare you involve my wife? He wanted to lose control, but he could not. His eyes were on the map.

"Well?"

"The police have been round to Sarah. They woke her in the middle of the night. Two men. Her mother was there. They came about the body at the airport: Taylor's body. They knew the passport was phony and thought she was involved. They woke her up," he repeated lamely.

"We know all about that. It's straightened out. I wanted to tell you but you wouldn't let me. The body's been released."

"It was wrong to drag Sarah in."

Haldane lifted his head quickly: "What do you mean by that?"

"We're not competent to handle this kind of thing." It sounded very impertinent. "We shouldn't be doing it. We ought to give it to the Circus. Smiley or someone—they're the people, not us." He struggled on. "I don't even believe that report. I don't believe it's true! I wouldn't be surprised if that refugee never existed; if Gorton made the whole thing up. I don't believe Taylor was murdered."

"Is that all?" Haldane demanded. He was very angry.

"It's not something I want to go on with. The operation, I mean. It isn't right."

He looked at the map and at Haldane, then laughed a little stupidly. "All the time I've been chasing a dead man you've been after a live one! It's easy here, in the dream factory . . . but they're people out there, real people!"

Leclerc touched Haldane lightly on the arm as if to say he would handle this himself. He seemed undisturbed. He might almost have been gratified to recognize symptoms which he had previously diagnosed. "Go to your room, John, you're suffering from strain."

"But what do I tell Sarah?" He spoke with despair.

"Tell her she won't be troubled anymore. Tell her it was a mistake . . . tell her whatever you like. Get some hot food and come back in an hour. These airline meals are useless. Then we'll hear the rest of your news." Leclerc was smiling, the same neat, bland smile with which he had stood among the dead fliers. As Avery reached the door he heard his name called softly, with affection: he stopped and looked back.

Leclerc raised one hand from the desk and with a semicircular movement indicated the room in which they were standing.

"I'll tell you something, John. During the war we were in Baker Street. We had a cellar and the Ministry fixed it up as an emergency operations room. Adrian and I spent a lot of time down there. A *lot* of time." A glance at Haldane. "Remember how the oil lamp used to swing when the bombs fell? We had to face situations where we had one rumor, John, no more. One indicator and we'd take the risk. Send a man in, two if necessary, and maybe they wouldn't come back. Maybe there wouldn't be anything

there. Rumors, a guess, a hunch one follows up; it's easy to
forget what intelligence consists of: luck, and speculation.
Here and there a windfall, here and there a scoop. Sometimes you stumbled on a thing like this: it could be very
big, it could be a shadow. It may have been from a peasant
in Flensburg, or it may come from the Provost of King's,
but you're left with a possibility you dare not discount.
You get instructions: find a man, put him in. So we did.
And many *didn't* come back. They were sent to resolve
doubt, don't you see? We sent them because we didn't
know. All of us have moments like this, John. Don't think
it's always easy." A reminiscent smile. "Often we had scruples like you. We had to overcome them. We used to call
that the second vow." He leaned against the desk, informally. "The second vow," he repeated.

"Now, John, if you want to wait until the bombs are
falling, till people are dying in the street . . ." He was suddenly serious, as if revealing his faith. "It's a great deal
harder, I know, in peacetime. It requires courage. Courage
of a different kind."

Avery nodded. "I'm sorry," he said.

Haldane was watching him with distaste.

"What the Director means," he said acidly, "is that if
you wish to stay in the Department and do the job, do it. If
you wish to cultivate your emotions, go elsewhere and do
so in peace. We are too old for your kind here."

Avery could still hear Sarah's voice, see the rows of little
houses hanging in the rain; he tried to imagine his life
without the Department. He realized that it was too late, as
it always had been, because he had gone to them for the
little they could give him, and they had taken the little he
had. Like a doubting cleric, he had felt that whatever his
small heart contained was safely locked in the place of his
retreat; now it was gone. He looked at Leclerc, then at
Haldane. They were his colleagues. Prisoners of silence,
the three of them would work side by side, breaking the
arid land all four seasons of the year, strangers to each
other, needing each other, in a wilderness of abandoned
faith.

"Did you hear what I said?" Haldane demanded.

Avery muttered: "Sorry."

"You didn't fight in the war, John," Leclerc said kindly.

"You don't understand how these things take people. You don't understand what real duty is."

"I know," said Avery. "I'm sorry. I'd like to borrow the car for an hour . . . send something round to Sarah, if that's all right."

"Of course."

He realized he had forgotten Anthony's present. "I'm sorry," he said again.

"Incidentally—" Leclerc opened a drawer of the desk and took out an envelope. Indulgently he handed it to Avery. "That's your pass, a special one from the Ministry. To identify yourself. It's in your own name. You may need it in the weeks to come.

"Thanks."

"Open it."

It was a piece of thick pasteboard bound in cellophane, green, the color washed downward, darker at the bottom. His name was printed across it in capitals with an electric typewriter: MR. JOHN AVERY. The legend entitled the bearer to make inquiries on behalf of the Ministry. There was a signature in red ink.

"Thanks."

"You're safe with that," Leclerc said. "The Minister signed it. He uses red ink, you know. It's tradition."

He went back to his room. There were times when he confronted his own image as a man confronts an empty valley, and the vision propelled him forward again to experience, as despair compels us to extinction. Sometimes he was like a man in flight, but running toward the enemy, desperate to feel upon his vanishing body the blows that would prove his being; desperate to imprint upon his sad conformity the mark of real purpose, desperate perhaps, as Leclerc had hinted, to abdicate his conscience in order to discover God.

THREE
LEISER'S
RUN

To turn as swimmers into cleanness leaping
Glad from a world grown old and cold and
weary.

—RUPERT BROOKE
"1914"

10.

Prelude

THE HUMBER dropped Haldane at the garage.

"You needn't wait. You have to take Mr. Leclerc to the Ministry."

He picked his way reluctantly over the tarmac, past the yellow pumps and the advertisement shields rattling in the wind. It was evening; there was rain about. The garage was small but very smart; showrooms one end, workshops the other, in the middle a tower where somebody lived. Swedish timber and open plan; lights on the tower in the shape of a heart, changing color continuously. From somewhere came the whine of a metal lathe. Haldane went into the office. It was empty. There was a smell of rubber. He rang the bell and began coughing wretchedly. Sometimes when he coughed he held his chest, and his face betrayed the submissiveness of a man familiar with pain. Calendars with showgirls hung on the wall beside a small handwritten notice, like an amateur advertisement, which read, ST. CHRISTOPHER AND ALL HIS ANGELS, PLEASE PROTECT US FROM ROAD ACCIDENTS. F.L. At the window a budgerigar fluttered nervously in its cage. The first drops of rain thumped lazily against the panes. A boy came in, about eighteen, his fingers black with engine oil. He wore overalls with a red heart sewn to the breast pocket with a crown above it.

"Good evening," said Haldane. "Forgive me. I'm looking for an old acquaintance; a friend. We knew one another long ago. A Mr. Leiser. Fred Leiser. I wondered if you had any idea . . ."

"I'll get him," the boy said, and disappeared.

Haldane waited patiently, looking at the calendars and wondering whether it was the boy or Leiser who had hung them there. The door opened a second time. It was Leiser. Haldane recognized him from his photograph. There was really very little change. The twenty years were not drawn in forceful lines but in tiny webs beside each eye, in marks of discipline around the mouth. The light above him was diffuse and cast no shadow. It was a face which at first sight recorded nothing but loneliness. Its complexion was pale.

"What can I do for you?" Leiser asked. He stood almost at attention.

"Hullo, I wonder if you remember me?"

Leiser looked at him as if he were being asked to name a price, blank but wary.

"Sure it was me?"

"Yes."

"It must have been a long time ago," he said at last. "I don't often forget a face."

"Twenty years." Haldane coughed apologetically.

"In the war then, was it?"

He was a short man, very straight; in build he was not unlike Leclerc. He might have been a waiter. His sleeves were rolled up a little way, there was a lot of hair on the forearms. His shirt was white and expensive; a monogram on the pocket. He looked like a man who spent a good deal on his clothes. He wore a gold ring; a golden wristband to his watch. He took great care of his appearance; Haldane could smell the lotion on his skin. His long brown hair was full, the line along the forehead straight. Bulging a little at the sides, the hair was combed backwards. He wore no parting; the effect was definitely Slav. Though very upright he had about him a certain swagger, a looseness of the hips and shoulders, which suggested a familiarity with the sea. It was here that any comparison with Leclerc abruptly ceased. He looked, despite himself, a practical man, handy in the house or starting the car on a cold day; and he looked an innocent man, but traveled. He wore a tartan tie.

"Surely you remember me?" Haldane pleaded.

Leiser stared at the thin cheeks, touched with points of high color, at the hanging, restless body and the gently stirring hands, and there passed across his face a look of painful recognition, as if he were identifying the remains of a friend.

"You're not Captain Hawkins, are you?"

"That's right."

"God Christ," said Leiser, without moving. "You're the people who've been asking about me."

"We're looking for someone with your experience, a man like you."

"What do you want him for, sir?"

He still hadn't moved. It was very hard to tell what he was thinking. His eyes were fixed on Haldane.

"To do a job, one job."

Leiser smiled, as if it all came back to him. He nodded his head toward the window. "Over there?" He meant somewhere beyond the rain.

"Yes."

"What about getting back?"

"The usual rules. It's up to the man in the field. The war rules."

He pushed his hands into his pockets, discovered cigarettes and a lighter. The budgerigar was singing.

"The war rules. You smoke?" He gave himself a cigarette and lit it, his hands cupped around the flame as if there were a high wind. He dropped the match on the floor for someone else to pick up.

"God Christ," he repeated, "twenty years. I was a kid in those days, just a kid."

Haldane said, "You don't regret it, I trust. Shall we go and have a drink?" He handed Leiser a card. It was newly printed: CAPTAIN A. HAWKINS. Written underneath was a telephone number.

Leiser read it and shrugged. "I don't mind," he said and fetched his coat. Another smile, incredulous this time. "But you're wasting your time, Captain."

"Perhaps you know someone. Someone else from the war who might take it on."

"I don't know a lot of people," Leiser replied. He took a jacket from the peg and a nylon raincoat of dark blue.

Going ahead of Haldane to the door, he opened it elaborately as if he valued formality. His hair was laid carefully upon itself like the wings of a bird.

There was a pub on the other side of the avenue. They reached it by crossing a footbridge. The rush hour traffic thundered beneath them; the cold, plump raindrops seemed to go with it. The bridge trembled to the drumming of the cars. The pub was Tudor with new horse brasses and a ship's bell very highly polished. Leiser asked for a White Lady. He never drank anything else, he said. "Stick to one drink, Captain, that's my advice. Then you'll be all right. Down the hatch."

"It's got to be someone who knows the tricks," Haldane observed. They sat in a corner near the fire. They might have been talking about trade. "It's a very important job. They pay far more than in the war." He gave a gaunt smile. "They pay a lot of money these days."

"Still, money's not everything, is it?" A stiff phrase, borrowed from the English.

"They remembered you. People whose names you've forgotten, if you even knew them." An unconvincing smile of reminiscence crossed his thin lips: it might have been years since he had lied. "You left quite an impression behind you, Fred; there weren't many as good as you. Even after twenty years."

"They remember me then, the old crowd?" He seemed grateful for that, but shy, as if it were not his place to be held in memory. "I was only a kid then," he repeated. "Who's there still, who's left?"

Haldane, watching him, said, "I warned you, we play the same rules, Fred. *Need to know,* it's all the same." It was very strict.

"God Christ," Leiser declared. "All the same. Big as ever, then, the outfit?"

"Bigger." Haldane fetched another White Lady. "Take much interest in politics?"

Leiser lifted a clean hand and let it fall.

"You know the way we are," he said. "In Britain, you know." His voice carried the slightly impertinent assumption that he was as good as Haldane.

"I mean," Haldane prompted, "in a *broad* sense." He coughed his dusty cough. "After all, they took over your country, didn't they?" Leiser said nothing. "What did you think of Cuba, for instance?"

Haldane did not smoke, but he had bought some cigarettes at the bar, the brand Leiser preferred. He removed the cellophane with his slim, aging fingers, and offered them across the table. Without waiting for an answer, he continued, "The point was, you see, in the Cuba thing the Americans *knew*. It was a matter of information. Then they could act. Of course *they* made overflights. One can't always do that." He gave another little laugh. "One wonders what they would have done without them."

"Yes, that's right." He nodded his head like a dummy. Haldane paid no attention.

"They might have been stuck," Haldane suggested and sipped his whisky. "Are you married, by the way?"

Leiser grinned, held his hand out flat, tipped it briskly to left and right, like a man talking about airplanes. "So, so," he said. His tartan tie was fastened to his shirt with a heavy gold pin in the shape of a riding crop against a horse's head. It was very incongruous.

"How about you, Captain?"

Haldane shook his head.

"No," Leiser observed thoughtfully, "no."

"Then there have been other occasions," Haldane went on, "where very serious mistakes were made because they hadn't the *right* information, or not enough. I mean not even we can have people permanently everywhere."

"No, of course," Leiser said politely.

The bar was filling up.

"I wonder whether you know of a different place where we might talk?" Haldane inquired. "We could eat, chat about some of the old gang. Or have you another engagement?" The lower classes eat early.

Leiser glanced at his watch. "I'm all right till eight," he said. "You want to do something about that cough, sir. It can be dangerous, a cough like that." The watch was of gold; it had a black face and a compartment for indicating phases of the moon.

The Under Secretary, similarly conscious of the time, was bored to be kept so late.

"I think I mentioned to you," Leclerc was saying, "that

the Foreign Office has been awfully sticky about providing operational passports. They've taken to consulting the Circus in every case. We have no status, you understand; it's hard for me to make myself unpleasant about these things —they have only the vaguest notion of how we work. I wondered whether the best system might not be for my Department to route passport requisitions through your Private Office. That would save the bother of going to the Circus every time."

"What do you mean, sticky?"

"You will remember we sent poor Taylor out under another name. The Office revoked his operational passport a matter of hours before he left London. I fear the Circus made an administrative blunder. The passport which accompanied the body was therefore challenged on arrival in the United Kingdom. It gave us a lot of trouble. I had to send one of my best men to sort it out," he lied. "I'm sure that if the Minister insisted, Control would be quite agreeable to a new arrangement."

The Under Secretary jabbed a pencil at the door which led to his Private Office. "Talk to them in there. Work something out. It sounds very stupid. Who do you deal with at the Office?"

"De Lisle," said Leclerc with satisfaction, "in General Department. He's the Assistant. And Guillam at the Circus."

The Under Secretary wrote it down. "One never knows *who* to talk to in that place; they're so top-heavy."

"Then I may have to approach the Circus for technical resources. Wireless and that kind of thing. I propose to use a cover story for security reasons: a pretended training scheme is the most appropriate."

"Cover story? Ah yes: a lie. You mentioned it."

"It's a precaution, no more."

"You must do as you think fit."

"I imagined you would prefer the Circus not to know. You said yourself: no monolith. I have proceeded on that assumption."

The Under Secretary glanced again at the clock above the door. "He's been in a rather difficult mood: a dreary day with the Yemen. I think it's partly the Woodbridge by-election: he gets so upset about the marginals. How's this thing going, by the way? It's been very worrying for him, you know. I mean, what's he to believe?" He paused. "It's these Germans who terrify me. . . . You mentioned you'd found a fellow who fitted the bill." They moved to the corridor.

"We're onto him now. We've got him in play. We shall know tonight."

The Under Secretary wrinkled his nose very slightly, his hand on the Minister's door. He was a churchman and disliked irregular things.

"What makes a man take on a job like that? Not you; him, I mean."

Leclerc shook his head in silence, as if the two of them were in close sympathy. "Heaven knows. It's something we don't even understand ourselves."

"What kind of person is he? What sort of class? Only generally, you appreciate."

"Intelligent. Self-educated. Polish extraction."

"Oh, I see." He seemed relieved. "We'll keep it gentle, shall we? Don't paint it too black. He loathes drama. I mean, any fool can see what the *dangers* are."

They went in.

Haldane and Leiser took their places at a corner table, like early lovers in a coffee bar. It was one of those restaurants which rely on empty Chianti bottles for their charm and on very little else for their custom. It would be gone tomorrow, or the next day, and scarcely anyone would notice, but while it was there and new and full of hope, it was not at all bad. Leiser had steak, it seemed to be habit, and sat primly while he ate it, his elbows firmly at his sides.

At first Haldane pretended to ignore the purpose of his visit. He talked badly about the war and the Department; about operations he had half forgotten until that afternoon, when he had refreshed his memory from the files. He spoke—no doubt it seemed desirable—mainly of those who had survived.

He referred to the courses Leiser had attended; had he kept up his interest in radio at all? Well, no, as a matter of fact. How about unarmed combat? There hadn't been the opportunity, really.

"You had one or two rough moments in the war, I remember," Haldane prompted. "Didn't you have some trouble in Holland?" They were back to vanity and old times' sake.

A stiff nod. "I had a spot of trouble," he conceded. "I was younger then."

"What happened exactly?"

Leiser looked at Haldane, blinking, as if the other had waked him, then began to talk. It was one of those wartime stories which have been told with variations since war began, as remote from the neat little restaurant as hunger or poverty, less credible for being articulate. He seemed to tell it at second hand. It might have been a big fight he had heard on the wireless. He had been caught, he had escaped, he had lived for days without food, he had killed, been taken into refuge and smuggled back to England. He told it well; perhaps it was what the war meant to him now, perhaps it was true, but as with a Latin widow relating the manner of her husband's death, the passion had gone out of his heart and into the telling. He seemed to speak because he had been told to; his affectations, unlike Leclerc's, were designed less to impress others than to protect himself. He seemed a very private man whose speech was exploratory; a man who had been a long time alone and had not reckoned with society; poised, not settled. His accent was good but exclusively foreign, lacking the slur and the elision which escapes even gifted imitators; a voice familiar with its environment, but not at home there.

Haldane listened courteously. When it was over he asked, "How did they pick you up in the first place, do you know?" The space between them was very great.

"They never told me," he said blankly, as if it were not proper to inquire.

"Of course you *are* the man we need. You've got the German background, if you understand me. You know them, don't you? You have the German experience."

"Only from the war," Leiser said.

They talked about the training school. "How's that fat one? George somebody. Little sad bloke."

"Oh . . . he's well, thank you."

"He married a pretty girl." He laughed obscenely, raising his right forearm in an Arab gesture of sexual prowess. "God Christ," he said, laughing again. "Us little blokes! Go for anything."

It was an extraordinary lapse. It seemed to be what Haldane had been waiting for. He watched him coolly for a long time. The silence became remarkable. Deliberately he stood up; he seemed suddenly very angry; angry at Leiser's silly grin and this whole cheap, incompetent flirtation; at these meaningless repetitive blasphemies and this squalid derision of a person of quality.

"Do you mind not saying that? George Smiley happens to be a friend of mine."

He called the waiter and paid the bill, stalked quickly from the restaurant, leaving Leiser bewildered and alone, his White Lady held delicately in his hand, his brown eyes turned anxiously toward the doorway through which Haldane had so abruptly vanished.

Eventually he left, making his way back by the footbridge, slowly through the dark and the rain, staring down on the double alley of streetlights and the traffic passing between them. Across the road was his garage, the line of illuminated pumps, the tower crowned with its neon heart of sixty-watt bulbs alternating green and red. He entered the brightly lit office, said something to the boy, walked slowly upstairs toward the blare of music.

Haldane waited till he had disappeared from sight, then hurried back to the restaurant to order a taxi.

She had turned the phonograph on. She was listening to dance music, sitting in his chair, drinking.

"Christ, you're late," she said. "I'm starving."

He kissed her.

"You've eaten," she said. "I can smell the food."

"Just a snack, Bett. I had to. A man called; we had a drink."

"Liar."

He smiled. "Come off it, Betty. We've got a dinner date, remember?"

"What man?"

The flat was very clean. Curtains and carpets were flowered, the polished surfaces protected with lace. Everything was protected; vases, lamps, ashtray, all were carefully

guarded, as if Leiser expected nothing from nature but
stark collision. He favored a suggestion of the antique: it
was reflected in the scrolled woodwork of the furniture and
the wrought iron of the lamp brackets. He had a mirror
framed in gold and a picture made of fretwork and plaster;
a new clock with weights which turned in a glass case.

When he opened the cocktail cabinet it played a brief
tune on a music box.

He mixed himself a White Lady, carefully, like a man
making up medicine. She watched him, moving her hips to
the record, holding her glass away to one side as if it were
her partner's hand, and the partner were not Leiser.

"What man?" she repeated.

He stood at the window, straight-backed like a soldier.
The flashing heart on the roof played over the houses,
caught the staves of the bridge and quivered in the wet surface of the Avenue. Beyond the houses was the church,
like a cinema with a spire, fluted brick with vents where
the bells rang. Beyond the church was the sky. Sometimes
he thought the church was all that remained, and the
London sky was lit with the glow of a burning city.

"Christ, you're really gay tonight."

The church bells were recorded, much amplified to
drown the noise of traffic. He sold a lot of petrol on Sundays. The rain was running harder against the road; he
could see it shading the beams of the car lights, dancing
green and red on the tarmac.

"Come on, Fred, dance."

"Just a minute, Bett."

"Oh, for Christ's sake what's the matter with you? Have
another drink and forget it."

He could hear her feet shuffling across the carpet to the
music; the tireless jingle of her charm bracelet.

"Dance, for Christ's sake."

She had a slurred way of talking, slackly dragging the
last syllable of a sentence beyond its natural length; it was
the same calculated disenchantment with which she gave
herself, sullenly, as if she were giving money, as if men
had all the pleasure and women the pain.

She stopped the record, careless as she pulled the arm.
The needle scratched in the loudspeaker.

"Look, what the hell goes on?"

"Nothing I tell you. I've just had a hard day, that's all. Then this man called, somebody I used to know."

"I keep asking you: who? Some woman, wasn't it? Some tart."

"No, Betty, it was a man."

She came to the window, nudging him indifferently. "What's so bloody marvelous about the view anyway? Just a lot of rotten little houses. You always said you hated them. Well, who was it?"

"He's from one of the big companies."

"And they want you?"

"Yes . . . they want to make me an offer."

"Christ, who'd want a bloody Pole?"

He hardly stirred. "They do."

"Someone came to the bank, you know, asking about you. They all sat together in Mr. Dawnay's office. You're in trouble, aren't you?"

He took her coat and helped her into it, very correct, elbows wide.

She said: "Not that new place with waiters, for Christ's sake."

"It's nice there, isn't it? I thought you fancied it there. You can dance too; you like that. Where do you want to go then?"

"With you? For Christ's sake! Somewhere where there's a bit of life, that's all."

He stared at her. He was holding the door open. Suddenly he smiled.

"O. K. Bett. It's your night. Slip down and start the car, I'll book a table." He gave her the key. "I know a place, a real place."

"What the hell's come over you now?"

"You can drive. We'll have a night out." He went to the telephone.

It was shortly before eleven when Haldane returned to the Department. Leclerc and Avery were waiting for him. Carol was typing in the private office.

"I thought you'd be here earlier," Leclerc said.

"It's no good. He said he wouldn't play. I think you'd

better try the next one yourself. It's not my style any-more." He seemed undisturbed. He sat down. They stared at him incredulously.

"Did you offer money?" Leclerc asked finally. "We have clearance for five thousand pounds."

"Of course I offered money. I tell you he's just not inter-ested. He was a singularly unpleasant person."

"I'm sorry." He didn't say why.

They could hear the tapping of Carol's typewriter. Le-clerc said, "Where do we go from here?"

"I have no idea." He glanced restlessly at his watch.

"There must be others, there must be."

"Not on our cards. Not with his qualifications. There are Belgians, Swedes, Frenchmen. But Leiser was the only Ger-man speaker with technical experience. On paper, he's the only one."

"Still young enough. Is that what you mean?"

"I suppose so. It would have to be an old hand. We haven't the time to train a new man, nor the facilities. We'd better ask the Circus. They'll have someone."

"We can't do that," Avery said.

"What kind of man was he?" Leclerc persisted, reluctant to abandon hope.

"Common, in a Slav way. Small. He plays the Rittmeist-er. It's most unattractive." He was looking in his pockets for the bill. "He dresses like a bookie, but I suppose they all do that. Do I give this to you or Accounts?"

"Secure?"

"I don't see why not."

"And you spoke about the urgency? New loyalties and that kind of thing?"

"He found the old loyalties more attractive." He put the bill on the table.

"And politics . . . some of these exiles are very . . ."

"We spoke about politics. He's not that sort of exile. He considers himself integrated, naturalized British. What do you expect him to do? Swear allegiance to the Polish royal house?" Again he looked at his watch.

"You never wanted to recruit him!" Leclerc cried, an-gered by Haldane's indifference. "You're pleased, Adrian, I can see it in your face! Good God, what about the De-partment! Didn't that mean anything to him? You don't believe in it any more, you don't care! You're sneering at me!"

"Who of us does believe?" asked Haldane with contempt. "You said yourself: we do the job."

"I believe," Avery declared.

Haldane was about to speak when the green telephone rang.

"That will be the Ministry," Leclerc said. "Now what do I tell them?" Haldane was watching him.

He picked up the receiver, put it to his ear then handed it across the table. "It's the exchange. Why on earth did they come through on green? Somebody asking for Captain Hawkins. That's you, isn't it?"

Haldane listened, his thin face expressionless. Finally he said, "I imagine so. We'll find someone. There should be no difficulty. Tomorrow at eleven. Kindly be punctual," and rang off. The light in Leclerc's room seemed to ebb toward the thinly curtained window. The rain fell ceaselessly outside.

"That was Leiser. He's decided he'll do the job. He wants to know whether we can find someone to take care of his garage while he's away."

Leclerc looked at him in astonishment. Pleasure spread comically over his face. "You expected it!" he cried. He stretched out his small hand. "I'm sorry, Adrian. I misjudged you. I congratulate you warmly."

"Why did he accept?" Avery asked excitedly. "What made him change his mind?"

"Why do agents ever do anything? Why do any of us?" Haldane sat down. He looked old but inviolate, like a man whose friends had already died. "Why do they consent or refuse, why do they lie or tell the truth? Why do any of us?" He began coughing again. "Perhaps he's underemployed. It's the Germans: he hates them. That's what he says. I place no value on that. Then he said he couldn't let us down. I assume he means himself."

To Leclerc he added, "The war rules: that was right, wasn't it?"

But Leclerc was dialing the Ministry.

Avery went into the Private Office. Carol was standing up.

"What's going on?" she said quickly. "What's the excitement?"

"It's Leiser." Avery closed the door behind him. "He's agreed to go." He stretched out his arms to embrace her. It would be the first time.

"Why?"

"Hatred of the Germans, he says. My guess is money."

"Is that a good thing?"

Avery grinned knowingly. "As long as we pay him more than the other side."

"Shouldn't you go back to your wife?" she said sharply. "I can't believe you need to sleep here."

"It's operational." Avery went to his room. She did not say good night.

Leiser put down the telephone. It was suddenly very quiet. The lights on the roof went out, leaving the room in darkness. He went quickly downstairs. He was frowning, as if his entire mental force were concentrated on the prospect of eating a second dinner.

11.

THEY CHOSE OXFORD as they had done in the war. The variety of nationalities and occupations, the constant coming and going of visiting academics and the resultant anonymity, the proximity of open country, all perfectly suited their needs. Besides, it was a place they could understand. The morning after Leiser had rung, Avery went ahead to find a house. The following day he telephoned Haldane to say he had taken one for a month in the north of the town, a large Victorian affair with four bedrooms and a garden. It was very expensive. It was known in the Department as the Mayfly house and carded under Live Amenities.

As soon as Haldane heard, he told Leiser. At Leiser's suggestion it was agreed that he should put it about that he was attending a course in the Midlands.

"Don't give any details," Haldane had said. "Have your mail sent poste restante to Coventry. We'll get it picked up from there." Leiser was pleased when he heard it was Oxford.

Leclerc and Woodford had searched desperately for someone to run the garage in Leiser's absence; suddenly they thought of McCulloch. Leiser gave him power of attorney and spent a hasty morning showing him the ropes. "We'll offer you some kind of guarantee in return," Haldane said.

"I don't need it," Leiser replied, explaining quite seriously. "I'm working for English gentlemen."

On Friday night, Leiser had telephoned his consent; by Wednesday, preparations were sufficiently advanced for Leclerc to convene a meeting of Special Section and outline his plans. Avery and Haldane were to be with Leiser in Oxford; the two of them would leave the following evening by which time he understood that Haldane would be ready with his syllabus. Leiser would arrive in Oxford a day or two later, as soon as his own arrangements were complete. Haldane was to supervise his training, Avery to act as Haldane's assistant. Woodford would remain in London. Among his tasks was that of consulting with the Ministry (and Sandford of Research) in order to assemble instructional material on the external specifications of short- and medium-range rockets, and thus provided come himself to Oxford.

Leclerc had been tireless, now at the Ministry to report on progress, now at the Treasury to argue the case for Taylor's widow, now, with Woodford's aid, engaging former instructors in wireless transmission, photography and unarmed combat.

Such time as remained to Leclerc he devoted to Mayfly Zero: the moment at which Leiser was to be infiltrated into eastern Germany. At first he seemed to have no firm idea of how this was to be done. He talked vaguely of a sea operation from Denmark; small fishing craft and a rubber dinghy to evade radar detection. He discussed illegal frontier crossing with Sandford and telegraphed Gorton for information on the border area round Lübeck. In veiled terms he even consulted the Circus. Control was remarkably helpful.

All this took place in that atmosphere of heightened activity and optimism which Avery had observed on his return. Even those who were kept, supposedly, in ignorance of the operation were infected by the air of crisis. The little lunch group that gathered daily at a corner table of the Cadena café was alive with rumors and speculation. It was said, for instance, that a man named Johnson, known in the war as Jack Johnson, a wireless instructor, had been taken on to the strength of the Department. Accounts had paid him subsistence and—most intriguing of all—they had been asked to draft a three-month contract for submission to the Treasury. Who ever heard, they asked, of a three-month contract? Johnson had been concerned with the French drops during the war; a senior girl remembered him. Berry, the cipher clerk, had asked Mr. Woodford what Johnson was up to (Berry was always the cheeky one) and Mr. Woodford had grinned and told him to mind his own business, but it was for an operation, he'd said, a very secret one they were running in Europe . . . Northern Europe, as a matter of fact, and it might interest Berry to know that poor Taylor had not died in vain.

There was now a ceaseless traffic of cars and Ministry messengers in the front drive; Pine requested and received from another Government establishment a junior whom he treated with sovereign brutality. In some oblique way he had learned that Germany was the target, and the knowledge made him diligent.

It was even rumored among the local tradesmen that the Ministry House was changing hands; private buyers were named and great hopes placed upon their custom. Meals were sent for at all hours, lights burned day and night; the front door, hitherto permanently sealed for reasons of security, was opened; and the sight of Leclerc with bowler hat and briefcase entering his black Humber became a familiar one in Blackfriars Road.

And Avery, like an injured man who would not look at his own wound, slept within the walls of his little office, so that they became the boundary of his life. Once he sent Carol out to buy Anthony a present. She came back with a toy milk lorry with plastic bottles. You could lift the caps off and fill the bottles with water. They tried it out one evening, then sent it round to Battersea in the Humber.

When all was ready, Haldane and Avery traveled to Oxford first class on a Ministry Warrant. At dinner on the train they had a table to themselves. Haldane ordered half a bottle of wine and drank it while he completed the *Times* crossword. They sat in silence, Haldane occupied, Avery too diffident to interrupt him.

Suddenly Avery noticed Haldane's tie; before he had time to think, he said, "Good Lord, I never knew you were a cricketer."

"Did you expect me to tell you?" Haldane snapped. "I could hardly wear it in the Office."

"I'm sorry."

Haldane looked at him closely. "You shouldn't apologize so much," he observed. "You both do it." He helped himself to some coffee and ordered a brandy. Waiters noticed Haldane.

"Both?"

"You and Leiser. He does it by implication."

"It's going to be different with Leiser, isn't it?" Avery said quickly. "Leiser's a professional."

"Leiser is not one of us. Never make that mistake. We touched him long ago, that's all."

"What's he like? What sort of man is he?"

"He's an agent. He's a man to be handled, not known."

He returned to his crossword.

"He must be loyal," Avery said. "Why else would he accept?"

"You heard what the Director said: the two vows. The first is often quite frivolously taken."

"And the second?"

"Ah, that is different. We shall be there to help him take it."

"But why did he accept the first time?"

"I mistrust reasons. I mistrust words like loyalty. And above all," Haldane declared, "I mistrust *motive*. We're running an agent; the arithmetic is over. You read German, didn't you? In the beginning was the deed."

Shortly before they arrived, Avery ventured one more question.

"Why *was* that passport out of date?"

Haldane had a way of inclining his head when addressed.

"The Foreign Office used to allocate a series of passport numbers to the Department for operational purposes. The arrangement ran from year to year. Six months ago the Office said they wouldn't issue any more without reference to the Circus. It seems Leclerc had been making insufficient claims on the facility and Control cut him out of the market. Taylor's passport was one of the old series. They revoked the whole lot three days before he left. There was no time to do anything about it. It might never have been noticed. The Circus has been very devious." A pause. "Indeed, I find it hard to understand what Control *is* up to."

They took a taxi to North Oxford and got out at the corner of the road. As they walked along the pavement Avery looked at the houses in the half-darkness, glimpsed gray-haired figures moving across lighted windows, velvet-covered chairs trimmed with lace, Chinese screens, music stands and a bridge-four sitting like bewitched courtiers in a castle. It was a world he had known about once; for a time he had almost fancied he was part of it; but that was long ago.

They spent the evening preparing the house. Haldane said Leiser should have the rear bedroom overlooking the garden, they themselves would take the rooms on the street side. He had sent some academic books in advance, a typewriter and some imposing files. These he unpacked and arranged on the dining room table for the benefit of the landlord's housekeeper who would come each day. "We shall call this room the study," he said. In the drawing room he installed a tape recorder.

He had some tapes which he locked in a cupboard, meticulously adding the key to his key ring. Other luggage was still waiting in the hall: a projector, Air Force issue; a screen; and a suitcase of green canvas securely fastened, with leather corners.

The house was spacious and well kept; the furniture was of mahogany, with brass inlay. The walls were filled with pictures of some unknown family: sketches in sepia, miniatures, photographs faded with age. There was a bowl of potpourri on the sideboard and a palm cross pinned to the mirror; chandeliers hung from the ceiling, clumsy, but inoffensive; in one corner, a Bible table; in another a small cupid, very ugly, its face turned to the dark. The whole house gently asserted an air of old age; it had a quality, like incense, of courteous but inconsolable sadness.

By midnight they had finished unpacking. They sat down in the drawing room. The marble fireplace was supported by blackamoors of ebony; the light of the gas fire played over the gilded rose-chains which linked their thick ankles. The fireplace came from an age, it might have been

the seventeenth century, it might have been the nineteenth,
when blackamoors had briefly replaced Borzois as the decorative beasts of society; they were quite naked, as a dog
might be, and chained with golden roses. Avery gave himself
a whisky, then went to bed, leaving Haldane sunk in his
own thoughts.

His room was large and dark. Above the bed hung a
light shade of blue china; there were embroidered covers
on the bedside tables and a small enameled notice saying,
GOD'S BLESSING ON THIS HOUSE; beside the window hung
a picture of a child saying its prayers while her sister ate
breakfast in bed.

He lay awake, wondering about Leiser; it was like waiting for a girl. From across the passage he could hear Haldane's solitary cough, on and on. It had not ended when he
fell asleep.

Leclerc thought Smiley's club a very strange place; not
at all the kind of thing he had expected. Two half-base-
ment rooms and a dozen people dining at separate tables
before a large fire. Some of them were vaguely familiar.
He suspected they were connected with the Circus.

"This is a rather good spot. How do you join?"

"Oh, you don't," said Smiley apologetically, then
blushed and continued, "I mean they don't have new members. Just one generation . . . several went in the war, you
know, some have died or gone abroad. What was it you
had in mind, I wonder?"

"You were good enough to help young Avery out."

"Yes . . . yes of course. How did that go, by the way? I
never heard."

"It was just a training run. There was no film in the
end."

"I'm sorry." Smiley spoke hastily, covering up, as if
someone were dead and he had not known.

"We didn't really expect there would be. It was just a
precaution. How much did Avery tell you, I wonder?
We're training up one or two of the old hands . . . and
some of the new boys too. It's something to do," Leclerc
explained, "during the slack season. . . . Christmas, you
know. People on leave."

"I know."

Leclerc noticed that the claret was very good. He wished he had joined a smaller club; his own had gone off terribly. They had such difficulty with staff.

"You have probably heard," Leclerc added, officially as it were, "that Control has offered me full assistance for training purposes."

"Yes, yes, of course."

"My Minister was the moving spirit. He likes the idea of a pool of trained agents. When the plan was first mooted I went and spoke to Control myself. Later, Control called on me. You knew that, perhaps?"

"Yes. Control wondered . . ."

"He has been most helpful. Don't think I am unappreciative. It has been agreed—I think I should give you the background, your own office will confirm it—that if the training is to be effective, we must create as nearly as possible an operational atmosphere. What we used to call battle conditions." An indulgent smile. "We've chosen an area in western Germany. It's bleak and unfamiliar ground, ideal for frontier crossing exercises and that kind of thing. We can ask for the Army's cooperation if we need it."

"Yes indeed. What a good idea."

"For elementary reasons of security, we all accept that your office should only be briefed in the aspects of this exercise in which you are good enough to help."

"Control told me," said Smiley. "He wants to do whatever he can. He didn't know you touched this kind of thing anymore. He was pleased."

"Good," Leclerc said shortly. He moved his elbows forward a little across the polished table. "I thought I might pick your brains . . . quite informally. Rather as you people from time to time have made use of Adrian Haldane."

"Of course."

"The first thing is false documents. I looked up our old forgers in the index. I see Hyde and Fellowby went over to the Circus some years ago."

"Yes. It was the change in emphasis."

"I've written down a personal description of a man in our employment; he is supposedly resident at Magdeburg for the purposes of the scheme. One of the men under training. Do you think they could prepare documents, Identity Card, Party Membership and that kind of thing? Whatever is necessary."

"The man would have to sign them," Smiley said. "We would then stamp on top of his signature. We'd need photographs, too. He'd have to be briefed on how the documents worked; perhaps Hyde could do that on the spot with your agent?"

A slight hesitation. "No doubt. I have selected a cover name. It closely approximates his own; we find that a useful technique."

"I might just make the point," Smiley said, with a rather comic frown, "since this is such an *elaborate* exercise, that forged papers are of very *limited* value. I mean, one telephone call to the Magdeburg Town Administration and the best forgery in the world is blown sky high . . ."

"I think we know about that. We want to teach them cover, submit them to interrogation . . . you know the kind of thing."

Smiley sipped his claret. "I just thought I'd make the point. It's so easy to get hypnotized by *technique*. I didn't mean to imply . . . How is Haldane, by the way? He read Greats, you know. We were up together."

"Adrian is well."

"I liked your Avery," Smiley said politely. His heavy small face contracted in pain. "Do you realize," he asked impressively, "they *still* don't include the Baroque period in the German syllabus? They call it a special subject."

"Then there is the question of a clandestine wireless. We haven't used that kind of thing much since the war. I understand it has all become a great deal more sophisticated. High-speed transmission and so on. We want to keep up with the times."

"Yes. Yes, I believe the message is taped on a miniature recorder and sent over the air in a matter of seconds." He sighed. "But no one really tells us much. The technical people hold their cards very close to their chests."

"Is that a method in which our people could profitably be trained . . . in a month, say?"

"And use under operational conditions?" Smiley asked in astonishment. "Straightaway, after a month's training?"

"Some are technically minded, you understand. People with wireless experience."

Smiley was watching Leclerc incredulously. "Forgive me. Would he, would they," he inquired, "have *other* things to learn in that month as well?"

"For some it's more a refresher course."

"Ah."

"What do you mean?"

"Nothing, nothing," Smiley said vaguely and added, "I don't *think* our technical people would be very keen to part with this kind of equipment unless . . ."

"Unless it were their own training operation?"

"Yes." Smiley blushed. "Yes, that's what I mean. They're very particular, you know; jealous."

Leclerc lapsed into silence, lightly tapping the vase of his wine glass on the polished surface of the table. Suddenly he smiled and said, as if he had shaken off depression, "Oh well. We shall just have to use a conventional set. Have direction-finding methods also improved since the war? Interception, location of an illegal transmitter?"

"Oh yes. Yes, indeed."

"We would have to incorporate that. How long can a man remain on the air before they spot him?"

"Two or three minutes, perhaps. It depends. Often it's a matter of luck how soon they hear him. They can only pin him down while he's transmitting. Much depends on the frequency. Or so they tell me."

"In the war," said Leclerc reflectively, "we gave an agent several crystals. Each vibrated at a fixed frequency. Every so often he changed the crystal; that was usually a safe enough method. We could do that again."

"Yes. Yes, I remember that. But there was the headache of retuning the transmitter . . . possibly changing the coil . . . matching the aerial."

"Suppose a man is used to a conventional set? You tell me the chances of interception are greater now than they were in the war? You say allow two or three minutes?"

"Or less," said Smiley, watching him. "It depends on a lot of things . . . luck, reception, amount of signal traffic, density of population. . . ."

"Supposing he changed his frequency after every two and a half minutes on the air. Surely that would meet the case?"

"It could be a slow business." His sad, unhealthy face

was wrinkled in concern. "You're quite sure this *is* only training?"

"As far as I remember," Leclerc persisted, courting his own idea, "these crystals are the size of a small matchbox. We could give them several. We're only aiming at a few transmissions; perhaps only three or four. Would you consider my suggestion impractical?"

"It's hardly my province."

"What is the alternative? I asked Control; he said speak to you. He said you'd help, find me the equipment. What else can I do? Can I *talk to* your technical people?"

"I'm sorry. Control rather agreed with the technical side, that we should give all the help we can, but not compromise new equipment. *Risk* compromising it, I mean. After all, it *is* only training. I think he felt that if you hadn't full technical resources you should . . ."

"Hand over the commitment?"

"No, no," Smiley protested, but Leclerc interrupted him.

"These people would eventually be used against military targets," he said angrily. "Purely military. Control accepts that."

"Oh quite." Smiley seemed to have given up. "And if you want a conventional set, no doubt we can dig one up."

The waiter brought a decanter of port. Leclerc watched Smiley pour a little into his glass, then slide the decanter carefully across the polished table.

"It's quite good, but I'm afraid it's nearly finished. When this is gone we shall have to break into the younger ones. I'm seeing Control first thing tomorrow. I'm sure he'll have no objection. About the documents, I mean. And crystals. We could advise you on frequencies, I'm sure. Control made a point of that."

"Control's been very good," Leclerc confessed. He was slightly drunk. "It puzzles me sometimes."

12.

Two DAYS LATER, Leiser arrived at Oxford. They waited anxiously for him on the platform, Haldane peering among the hurrying faces in the crowd. It was Avery, curiously, who saw him first: a motionless figure in a camel's hair coat at the window of an empty compartment.

"Is that he?" Avery asked.

"He's traveling first class. He must have paid the difference." Haldane spoke as if it were an affront.

Leiser lowered the window and handed out two pigskin cases shaped for the trunk of a car, a little too orange for nature. They greeted one another briskly, shaking hands for everyone to see. Avery wanted to carry the luggage to the taxi, but Leiser preferred to take it himself, a piece in each hand, as if it were his duty. He walked a little away from them, shoulders back, staring at the people as they went by, startled by the crowd. His long hair bounced with each step.

Avery, watching him, felt suddenly disturbed.

He was a man; not a shadow. A man with force to his body and purpose to his movement, but somehow theirs to direct. There seemed to be nowhere he would not walk. He was recruited; and had assumed already the anxious, brisk manner of an enlisted man. Yet, Avery accepted, no single factor wholly accounted for Leiser's recruitment. Avery was already familiar, during his short association with the Department, with the phenomenon of organic motivation; with operations which had no discernible genesis and no conclusion, which formed part of an unending pattern of activity until they ceased to have any further identity; with that progress of fruitless courtships which, in the aggregate, passed for an active love life. But as he observed this man bobbing beside him, animate and quick, he recognized that hitherto they had courted ideas, incestuously among themselves; now they had a human being upon their hands, and this was he.

They climbed into the taxi, Leiser last because he insisted. It was midafternoon, a slate sky behind the plane trees. The smoke rose from the North Oxford chimneys in ponderous columns like proof of a virtuous sacrifice. The houses were of a modest stateliness; romantic hulls redecked, each according to a different legend. Here the turrets of Avalon, there the carved trellis of a pagoda; between them the monkey-puzzle trees, and the half-hidden washing like butterflies in the wrong season. The houses sat decently in their own gardens, the curtains drawn, first lace and then brocade, petticoats and skirts. It was like a bad watercolor, the dark things drawn too heavy, the sky gray and soiled in the dusk, the paint too worked.

They dismissed the taxi at the corner of the street. A smell of leaf-mold lingered in the air. If there were children they made no noise. The three men walked to the gate. Leiser, his eyes on the house, put down his suitcases.

"Nice place," he said with appreciation. He turned to Avery: "Who chose it?"

"I did."

"That's nice." He patted his shoulder. "You did a good job." Avery, pleased, smiled and opened the gate; again Leiser was determined that the others should pass through first. They took him upstairs and showed him his room. He still carried his own luggage.

"I'll unpack later," he said. "I like to make a proper job of it."

He walked through the house in a critical way, picking things up and looking at them; he might have come to bid for the place.

"It's a nice spot," he repeated finally; "I like it."

"Good," said Haldane, as if he didn't give a damn.

Avery went with him to his room to see if he could help.

"What's your name?" Leiser asked. He was more at ease with Avery; more vulgar.

"John."

They shook hands again.

"Well, hello, John; glad to meet you. How old are you?"

"Thirty-four," he lied.

A wink. "Christ, I wish I was thirty-four. Done this kind of thing before, have you?"

"I finished my own run last week."

"How did it go?"

"Fine."

"That's the boy. Where is your room?"

Avery showed him.

"Tell me, what's the setup here?"

"What do you mean?"

"Who's in charge?"

"Captain Hawkins."

"Anyone else?"

"Not really. I shall be around."

"All the time?"

"Yes."

He began unpacking. Avery watched. He had brushes backed with leather, hair lotion, a whole range of little bottles of things for men, an electric shaver of the newest kind and ties, some in tartan, others in silk, to match his costly shirts. Avery went downstairs. Haldane was waiting. He smiled as Avery came in. "Well?"

Avery shrugged, too big a gesture. He felt elated, ill at ease. "What do *you* make of him?" he asked.

"I hardly know him," Haldane said drily. He had a way of terminating conversations. "I want you to be always in his company. Walk with him, shoot with him, drink with him if you must. He's not to be alone."

"What about his leave in between?"

"We'll see about that. Meanwhile do as I say. You will find he enjoys your company. He's a very *lonely* man. And remember, he's British: British to the core. One more thing —this is most important—do not let him think we have changed since the war. The Department has remained exactly as it was: that is an illusion you must foster even"— he did not smile—"even though you are too young to make the comparison."

They began next morning. Breakfast over, they assembled in the drawing room and Haldane addressed them.

The training would be divided into two periods of a fortnight each, with a short rest in between. The first was to be a refresher course; in the second, old skills, now revived, would be related to the task which lay ahead. Not until the second period would Leiser be told his operational name, his cover and the nature of his mission; even then, the information would reveal neither the target area nor the means by which he was to be infiltrated.

In communications as in all other aspects of his training he would graduate from the general to the particular. In the first period he would familiarize himself once more with the technique of ciphers, signal plans and schedules. In the second he would spend much time actually transmitting under semi-operational conditions. The instructor would arrive during that week.

Haldane explained all this with a certain pedagogic acrimony while Leiser listened carefully, now and then briskly nodding his assent. Avery found it strange that Haldane took so little care to conceal his distaste.

"In the first period we shall see what you remember. We shall give you a lot of running about, I'm afraid. We want to get you fit. There'll be small arms training, unarmed combat, mental exercises, tradecraft. We shall try to take you walking in the afternoons."

"Who with? Will John come?"

"Yes. John will take you. You should regard John as your adviser on all minor matters. If there is anything you wish to discuss, any complaint or anxiety, I trust you will not hesitate to mention it to either one of us."

"All right."

"On the whole, I must ask you not to venture out alone. I should prefer John to accompany you if you wish to go to the cinema, do some shopping or whatever else the time allows. But I fear you may not have much chance of recreation."

"I don't expect it," Leiser said. "I don't need it." He seemed to mean he didn't want it.

"The wireless instructor, when he comes, will not know your name. That is a customary precaution: please observe it. The daily woman believes we are participating in an academic conference. I cannot imagine you will have occasion to talk to her, but if you do, remember that. If you wish to make inquiries about your business, kindly consult me first. You should not telephone without my consent. Then there will be other visitors: photographers, medical people, technicians. They are what we call ancillaries and are not in the picture. Most of them believe you're here as part of a wider training scheme. Please remember this."

"O.K.," said Leiser. Haldane looked at his watch.

"Our first appointment is at ten o'clock. A car will collect us from the corner of the road. The driver is not one of us: no conversation on the journey, please. Have you no other clothes?" he asked. "Those are scarcely suitable for the range."

"I've got a sports coat and a pair of flannels."

"I could wish you less conspicuous."

As they went upstairs to change, Leiser smiled wryly at Avery. "He's a real boy, isn't he? The old school."

"But good," Avery said.

Leiser stopped. "Of course. Here, tell me something. Was this place always here? Have you used it for many people?"

"You're not the first," Avery said.

"Look, I know you can't tell me much. Is the outfit still like it was . . . people everywhere . . . the same setup?"

"I don't think you'd find much difference. I suppose we've expanded a bit."

"Are there many young ones like you?"

"Sorry, Fred."

Leiser put his open hand on Avery's back. He used his hands a lot.

"You're good, too," he said. "Don't bother about me. Not to worry, eh, John?"

They went to Abingdon: the Ministry had made arrangements with the parachute base. The instructor was expecting them.

"Used to any particular gun, are you?"

"Browning three eight automatic, please," Leiser said, like a child ordering groceries.

"We call it the nine millimeter now. You'll have had the Mark One."

Haldane stood in the gallery at the back while Avery helped wind in the man-sized target to a distance of ten yards and pasted squares of gum-strip over the old holes.

"You call me 'Staff,'" the instructor said and turned to Avery. "Like to have a go as well, sir?"

Haldane put in quickly, "Yes, they are both shooting, please, Staff."

Leiser took first turn. Avery stood beside Haldane while Leiser, his long back toward them, waited in the empty range, facing the plywood figure of a German soldier. The target was black, framed against the crumbling whitewash of the walls; over its belly and groin a heart had been crudely described in chalk, its interior extensively repaired with fragments of paper. As they watched, he began testing the weight of the gun, raising it quickly to the level of his eye, then lowering it slowly; pushing home the empty magazine, taking it out and thrusting it in again. He glanced over his shoulder at Avery, with his left hand brushing from his forehead a strand of brown hair which threatened to impede his view. Avery smiled encouragement, then said quickly to Haldane, talking business, "I still can't make him out."

"Why not? He's a perfectly ordinary Pole."

"Where does he come from? What part of Poland?"

"You've read the file. Danzig."

"Of course."

The instructor began. "We'll just try it with the empty gun first, both eyes open, and look along the line of sight, feet nicely apart now thank you, that's lovely. Relax now, be nice and comfy, it's not a drill movement, it's a firing position, oh yes, we've done *this* before! Now traverse the gun, point it but never aim. Right!" The instructor drew breath, opened a wooden box and took out four magazines. "One in the gun and one in the left hand," he said and handed the other two up to Avery, who watched with fascination as Leiser deftly slipped a full magazine into the butt of the automatic and advanced the safety catch with his thumb.

"Now cock the gun, pointing it at the ground three yards ahead of you. Now take up a firing position, keeping the arm straight. Pointing the gun but not aiming it, fire off one magazine, two shots at a time, remembering that we don't regard the automatic as a weapon of science but more in the order of a stopping weapon for close combat. Now slowly, very slowly . . ."

Before he could finish, the range was vibrating with the sound of Leiser's shooting—he shot fast, standing very stiff, his left hand holding the spare magazine precisely at his side like a grenade. He shot angrily, a mute man finding expression. Avery could feel with rising excitement the fury and purpose of his shooting; now two shots, and another two, then three, then a long volley, while the haze gathered around him and the plywood soldier shook and Avery's nostrils filled with the sweet smell of cordite.

"Eleven out of thirteen on the target," the instructor declared. "Very nice, very nice indeed. Next time, stick to two shots at a time please, and wait till I give the fire order." To Avery, the subaltern, he said, "Care to have a go, sir?"

Leiser had walked up to the target and was lightly tracing the bullet holes with his slim hands. The silence was suddenly oppressive. He seemed lost in meditation, feeling the plywood here and there, running a finger thoughtfully along the outline of the German helmet, until the instructor called, "Come on, we haven't got all day."

Avery stood on the gym mat, measuring the weight of the gun. With the instructor's help he inserted one magazine, clutching the other nervously in his left hand. Haldane and Leiser looked on.

Avery fired, the heavy gun thudding in his ears, and he felt his young heart stir as the silhouette flicked passively to his shooting.

"Good shot, John, good shot!"

"Very good," said the instructor automatically. "A very good first effort, sir." He turned to Leiser: "Do you mind not shouting like that?" He knew a foreigner when he saw one.

"How many?" Avery asked eagerly, as he and the sergeant gathered round the target, touching the blackened perforations scattered thinly over the chest and belly. "How many, Staff?"

"You'd better come with me, John," Leiser whispered, throwing his arm over Avery's shoulder. "I could do with you over there." For a moment Avery recoiled. Then, with

a laugh, he put his own arm around Leiser, feeling the
warm, crisp cloth of his sports jacket in the palm of his
hand.

The instructor led them across the parade ground to a
brick barrack like a theatre with no windows, tall at one
end. There were walls half crossing one another like the
entrance to a public lavatory.

"Moving targets," Haldane said. "And shooting in the
dark."

At lunch they played the tapes.

The tapes were to run like a theme through the first two
weeks of his training. They were made from old phonograph records; there was a crack in one which recurred
like a metronome. Together, they comprised a massive par-
lor game in which things to be remembered were not listed
but mentioned, casually, obliquely, often against a distract-
ing background of other noises, now contradicted in conversation, now corrected or contested. There were three
principal voices, one female and two male. Others would
interfere. It was the woman who got on their nerves.

She had that antiseptic voice which air hostesses seem to
acquire. In the first tape she read from lists, quickly. First
it was a shopping list, two pounds of this, one kilo of that;
without warning she was talking about colored skittles—so
many green, so many ochre; then it was weapons, guns,
torpedoes, ammunition of this and that caliber; then a factory with capacity, waste and production figures, annual
targets and monthly achievements. In the second tape she
had not abandoned these topics, but strange voices distracted her and led the dialogue into unexpected paths.

While shopping she entered into an argument with the
grocer's wife about certain merchandise which did not
meet with her approval; eggs that were not sound, the outra-
geous cost of butter. When the grocer himself attempted to
mediate he was accused of favoritism; there was talk of
points and ration cards, the extra allowance of sugar for
jam-making; a hint of undisclosed treasures under the
counter. The grocer's voice was raised in anger but he
stopped when the child intervened, talking about skittles. "Mummy, Mummy, I've knocked over the three green
ones, but when I tried to put them up, seven black ones fell
down; Mummy, why are their only eight black ones left?"

The scene shifted to a public house. It was the woman again. She was reciting armaments statistics; other voices joined in. Figures were disputed, new targets stated, old ones recalled; the performance of a weapon—a weapon unnamed, undescribed—was cynically questioned and heatedly defended.

Every few minutes a voice shouted "Break!" It might have been a referee—and Haldane stopped the tape and made Leiser talk about football or the weather, or read aloud from a newspaper for five minutes by his watch (the clock on the mantelpiece was broken). The tape recorder was switched on again, and they heard a voice, vaguely familiar, trailing a little like a parson's; a young voice, deprecating and unsure, like Avery's: "Now here are the four questions. Discounting those eggs which were not sound, how many has she bought in the last three weeks? How many skittles are there altogether? What was the annual overall output of proved and calibrated gun barrels for the years 1937 and 1938? Finally, put in telegraph form any information from which the length of the barrels might be computed."

Leiser rushed to the study—he seemed to know the game—to write down his answers. As soon as he had left the room Avery said accusingly, "That was you. That was your voice speaking at the end."

"Was it?" Haldane replied. He might not have known.

There were other tapes too, and they had the smell of death; the running of feet on a wooden staircase, the slamming of a door, a click, and a girl's voice asking—she might have been offering lemon or cream—"Catch of a door? Cocking of a gun?"

Leiser hesitated. "A door," he said. "It was just the door."

"It was a gun," Haldane retorted. "A Browning nine millimeter automatic. The magazine was being slid into the butt."

In the afternoon they went for their first walk, the two of them, Leiser and Avery, through Port Meadow and into the country beyond. Haldane had sent them. They walked fast, striding over the whip grass, the wind catching at Leiser's hair and throwing it wildly about his head. It was cold but there was no rain; a clear, sunless day when the sky above the flat fields was darker than the earth.

"You know your way around here, don't you?" Leiser asked. "Were you at school here?"

"I was an undergraduate here, yes."

"What did you study?"

"I read languages. German principally."

They climbed a stile and emerged in a narrow lane.

"You married?" he asked.

"Yes."

"Kids?"

"One."

"Tell me something, John. When the Captain turned up my card . . . what happened?"

"What do you mean?"

"What does it look like, an index for so many? It must be a big thing in an outfit like ours."

"It's in alphabetical order," Avery said helplessly. "Just cards. Why?"

"He said they remembered me: the old hands. I was the best, he said. Well, *who* remembered?"

"They all did. There's a special index for the best people. Practically everyone in the Department knows Fred Leiser. Even the new ones. You can't have a record like yours and get forgotten, you know." He smiled. "You're part of the furniture, Fred."

"Tell me something else, John. I don't want to rock the boat, see, but tell me this . . . Would I be any good on the inside?"

"The inside?"

"In the Office, with you people. I suppose you've got to be born to it really, like the Captain."

"I'm afraid so, Fred."

"What cars do you use up there, John?"

"Humbers."

"Hawk or Snipe?"

"Hawk."

"Only four-cylinder? The Snipe's a better job, you know."

"I'm talking about nonoperational transport," Avery said. "We've a whole range of stuff for the special work."

"Like the van?"

"That's it."

"How long before . . . how long does it take to train you? You, for instance; you just did a run. How long before they let you go?"

"Sorry, Fred. I'm not allowed . . . not even you."

"Not to worry."

They passed a church set back on a rise above the road, skirted a plowed field and returned, tired and radiant, to the cheerful embrace of the Mayfly house and the gas fire playing on the golden roses.

In the evening, they had the projector for visual memory: they would be in a car, passing a marshaling yard; or in a train beside an airfield; they would be taken on a walk through a town, and suddenly they would become aware that a vehicle or a face had reappeared, and they had not remembered its features. Sometimes a series of disconnected objects were flashed in rapid succession on the screen, and there would be voices in the background, like the voices on the tape, but the conversation was not related to the film, so that the student must consult both his senses and retain what was valuable from each.

Thus the first day ended, setting the pattern for those that followed: carefree, exciting days for them both, days of honest labor and cautious but deepening attachment as the skills of boyhood became once more the weapons of war.

For the unarmed combat they had rented a small gymnasium near Headington which they had used in the war. An instructor had come by train. They called him Sergeant.

"Will he be carrying a knife at all? Not wanting to be curious," he asked respectfully. He had a Welsh accent.

Haldane shrugged. "It depends what he likes. We don't want to clutter him up."

"There's a lot to be said for a knife, sir." Leiser was still in the changing room. "If he knows how to use it. And the Jerries don't like them, not one bit." He had brought some knives in a handcase, and he unpacked them in a private way, like a salesman unpacking his samples. "They never could take cold steel," he explained. "Nothing too long, that's the trick of it, sir. Something flat with the two cutting edges." He selected one and held it up. "You can't do much better than this as a matter of fact." It was wide and flat like a laurel leaf, the blade unpolished, the handle waisted like an hourglass, crosshatched to prevent slip. Leiser was walking toward them, smoothing a comb through his hair.

"Used one of these, have you?"

Leiser examined the knife and nodded. The sergeant looked at him carefully. "I know you, don't I? My name's Sandy Lowe. I'm a bloody Welshman."

"You taught me in the war."

"Christ," said Lowe softly, "so I did. You haven't changed much, have you?" They grinned shyly at one another, not knowing whether to shake hands. "Come on then, see what you remember." They walked to the coconut matting in the center of the floor. Lowe threw the knife at Leiser's feet and he snatched it up, grunting as he bent.

Lowe wore a jacket of torn tweed, very old. He stepped quickly back, took it off and with a single movement wrapped it around his left forearm, like a man preparing to fight a dog. Drawing his own knife he moved slowly around Leiser, keeping his weight steady but riding a little from one foot to the other. He was stooping, his bound arm held loosely in front of his stomach, fingers outstretched, palm facing the ground. He had gathered his body behind the guard, letting the blade play restlessly in front of it while Leiser kept steady, his eyes fixed upon the sergeant. For a time they feinted back and forth; once Leiser lunged and Lowe sprang back, allowing the knife to cut the cloth of the jacket on his arm. Once Lowe dropped to his knees, as if to drive the knife upward beneath Leiser's guard, and it was Leiser's turn to spring back, but too slowly it seemed, for Lowe shook his head, shouted "Halt!" and stood upright.

"Remember that?" He indicated his own belly and groin, pressing his arms and elbows in as if to reduce the width of his body. "Keep the target small." He made Leiser put his knife away and showed him holds, crooking his left arm around Leiser's neck and pretending to stab him in the kidneys or the stomach. Then he asked Avery to stand as a dummy, and the two of them moved around him with detachment, Lowe indicating the places with his knife and Leiser nodding, smiling occasionally when a particular trick came back to him.

"You didn't weave with the blade enough. Remember, thumb on top, blade parallel to the ground, forearm stiff, wrist loose. Don't let his eye settle on it, not for a moment. And left hand in over your own target, whether you've got the knife or not. Never be generous about offering the body, that's what I say to my daughter." They laughed dutifully, all but Haldane.

After that, Avery had a turn. Leiser seemed to want it. Removing his glasses, he held the knife as Lowe showed him, hesitant, alert, while Leiser trod crabwise, feinted and darted lightly back, the sweat running off his face, his small eyes alight with concentration. All the time Avery was conscious of the sharp grooves of the haft against the flesh of his palm, the aching in his calves and buttocks as he kept his weight forward on his toes, and Leiser's angry eyes searching his own. Then Leiser's foot had hooked around his ankle; as he lost balance he felt the knife being wrenched from his hand; he fell back, Leiser's full weight upon him, Leiser's hand clawing at the collar of his shirt.

They helped him up, all laughing, while Leiser brushed the dust from Avery's clothes. The knives were put away while they did physical training; Avery took part.

When it was over, Lowe said, "We'll just have a spot of unarmed combat and that will do nicely."

Haldane glanced at Leiser. "Have you had enough?"

"I'm all right."

Lowe took Avery by the arm and stood him in the center of the gym mat. "You sit on the bench," he called to Leiser, "while I show you a couple of things."

He put a hand on Avery's shoulder. "We're only concerned with five marks, whether we got a knife or not. What are they?"

"Groin, kidneys, belly, heart and throat," Leiser replied wearily.

"How do you break a man's neck?"

"You don't. You smash his windpipe at the front."

"What about a blow on the back of the neck?"

"Not with the bare hand. Not without a weapon." He had put his face in his hands.

"Correct." Lowe moved his open palm in slow motion toward Avery's throat. "Hand open, fingers straight, right?"

"Right," Leiser said.

"What else do you remember?"

A pause. "Tiger's Claw. An attack on the eyes."

"Never use it," the sergeant replied shortly. "Not as an attacking blow. You leave yourself wide open. Now for the strangleholds. All from behind, remember? Bend the head back, so, hand on the throat, so, and *squeeze*." Lowe looked over his shoulder: "Look this way, please, I'm not doing this for my own benefit. . . . Come on, then, if you know it all, show us some throws!"

Leiser stood up, locking arms with Lowe, and for a while they struggled back and forth, each waiting for the other to offer an opening. Then Lowe gave way, Leiser toppled and Lowe's hand slapped the back of his head, thrusting it down so that Leiser fell face forward heavily on to the mat.

"You fall a treat," said Lowe with a grin, and then Leiser was upon him, twisting Lowe's arm savagely back and throwing him very hard so that his little body hit the carpets like a bird hitting the windshield of a car.

"You play fair!" Leiser demanded, "or I'll damn well hurt you."

"Never lean on your opponent," Lowe said shortly. "And don't lose your temper in the gym." He called across to Avery. "You have a turn now, sir; give him some exercise."

Avery stood up, took off his jacket and waited for Leiser to approach him. He felt the strong grasp upon his arms and was suddenly conscious of the frailty of his body when matched against this adult force. He tried to seize the forearms of the older man, but his hands could not encompass them; he tried to break free, but Leiser held him; Leiser's head was against his own, filling his nostrils with the smell of hair oil. He felt the damp stubble of his cheek and the close, rank heat of his thin, straining body. Putting his hands on Leiser's chest he forced himself back, throwing all his energy into one frantic effort to escape the suffocating constriction of the man's embrace. As he drew away they caught sight of one another, it might have been for the first time, across the heaving cradle of their entangled arms; Leiser's face, contorted with exertion, softened into a smile; the grip relaxed.

Lowe walked over to Haldane. "He's foreign, isn't he?"

"A Pole. What's he like?"

"I'd say he was quite a fighter in his day. Nasty. He's a good build. Fit too, considering."

"I see," Haldane said.

"How are you these days, sir, in yourself? All right, then?"

"Yes, thank you."

"That's right. Twenty years. Amazing, really. Kiddies all grown up."

"I'm afraid I have none."

"Mine, I mean."

"Ah."

"See any of the old crowd, then, sir? How about Mr. Smiley?"

"I'm afraid I have not kept in touch. I am not a gregarious kind of person. Shall we settle up?"

Lowe stood lightly to attention while Haldane prepared to pay him: traveling money, salary, and thirty-seven and six for the knife, plus twenty-two shillings for the sheath, a flat metal one with a spring to facilitate extraction. Lowe wrote him a receipt, signing it S.L. for reasons of security. "I got the knife at cost," he explained. "It's a fiddle we work through the Sports Club." He seemed proud of that.

Haldane gave Leiser a trench coat and Wellingtons and Avery took him for a walk. They went by bus as far as Headington, sitting on the top deck.

"What happened this morning?" Avery asked.

"I thought we were fooling about, that's all. Then he threw me."

"He remembered you, didn't he?"

"Of course he did: then why did he hurt me?"

"He didn't mean to."

"Look, it's all right, see." He was still upset.

They got out at the end of the line and began trudging through the rain. Avery said, "It's because he wasn't one of us; that's why you didn't like him."

Leiser laughed, slipped his arm through Avery's. The rain, drifting in slow waves across the empty street, ran down their faces and trickled into the collars of their mackintoshes. Avery pressed his arm to his side, holding

Leiser's hand captive, and they continued their walk in shared contentment, forgetting the rain, or playing with it, treading in the deepest parts and not caring about their clothes.

"Is the Captain pleased, John?"

"Very. He says it's going fine. We begin the wireless soon, just the elementary stuff. Jack Johnson's expected tomorrow."

"It's coming back to me, John, the shooting and that. I hadn't forgotten." He smiled. "The old three eight."

"Nine millimeter. You're doing fine, Fred. Just fine. The Captain said so."

"Is that what he said, John, the Captain?"

"Of course. And he's told London. London's pleased too. We're only afraid you're a bit too . . ."

"Too what?"

"Well—too English."

Leiser laughed. "Not to worry, John."

The inside of Avery's arm, where he held Leiser's hand, felt dry and warm.

They spent a morning on ciphers. Haldane acted as instructor. He had brought pieces of silk cloth imprinted with a cipher of the type Leiser would use, and a chart backed with cardboard for converting letters into numerals. He put the chart on the mantelpiece, wedging it behind the marble clock, and lectured them rather as Leclerc would have done, but without affectation. Avery and Leiser sat at the table, pencil in hand, and under Haldane's tuition converted one passage after another into numbers according to the chart, deducted the result from figures on the silk cloth, finally retranslating into letters. It was a process which demanded application rather than concentration, and perhaps because Leiser was trying too hard he became bothered and erratic.

"We'll have a timed run over twenty groups," Haldane said, and dictated from the sheet of paper in his hand a message of eleven words with the signature Mayfly. "From next week you will have to manage without the chart. I shall put it in your room and you must commit it to memory. Go!"

He pressed the stopwatch and walked to the window

while the two men worked feverishly at the table, muttering almost in unison while they jotted elementary calcula-
tions on the scrap paper in front of them. Avery could detect the increasing flurry of Leiser's movements, the sup-
pressed sighs and imprecations, the angry erasures; deliberately slowing down, he glanced over the other's arm to ascertain his progress and noticed that the stub of pencil buried in his little hand was smeared with sweat. Without a
word, he silently changed his paper for Leiser's. Haldane,
turning around, might not have seen.

Even in these first few days, it had become apparent that
Leiser looked to Haldane as an ailing man looks to his doctor; a sinner to his priest. There was something terrible
about a man who derived his strength from such a sickly
body.

Haldane affected to ignore him. He adhered stubbornly
to the habits of his private life. He never failed to complete
his crossword. A case of Burgundy was delivered from the
town, half bottles, and he drank one alone at each meal
while they listened to the tapes. So complete, indeed, was
his withdrawal that one might have thought him revolted
by the man's proximity. Yet the more elusive, the more
aloof Haldane became, the more surely he drew Leiser after him. Leiser, by some obscure standards of his own, had
cast him as the English gentleman, and whatever Haldane
did or said only served, in the eyes of the other, to fortify
him in the part.

Haldane grew in stature. In London he was a slow-walk-
ing man; he picked his way pedantically along the corridors
as if he were looking for footholds; clerks and secretaries
would hover impatiently behind him, lacking the courage
to pass. In Oxford he betrayed an agility which would have
astonished his London colleagues. His parched frame had
revived, he held himself erect. Even his hostility acquired
the mark of command. Only the cough remained, that
racked, abandoned sob too heavy for such a narrow chest,
bringing dabs of red to his thin cheeks and causing Leiser
the mute concern of a pupil for his admired master.

"Is the Captain sick?" he once asked Avery, picking up
an old copy of Haldane's *Times*.

"He never speaks of it."

"I suppose that would be bad form." His attention was suddenly arrested by the newspaper. It was unopened. Only the crossword had been done, the margins around it sparsely annotated with permutations of a nine-letter anagram. He showed it to Avery in bewilderment.

"He doesn't read it," he said. "He's only done the competition."

That night, when they went to bed, Leiser took it with him, furtively as if it contained some secret which study could reveal.

So far as Avery could judge, Haldane was content with Leiser's progress. In the great variety of activities to which Leiser was now subjected, they had been able to observe him more closely; with the corrosive perception of the weak they discovered his failing and tested his power. He acquired, as they gained his trust, a disarming frankness; he loved to confide. He was their creature; he gave them everything, and they stored it away as the poor do. They saw that the Department had provided direction for his energy: like a man of uncommon sexual appetite, Leiser had found in his new employment a love which he could illustrate with his gifts. They saw that he took pleasure in their command, giving in return his strength as homage for fulfillment. They even knew perhaps that between them they constituted for Leiser the poles of absolute authority: the one by his bitter adherence to standards which Leiser could never achieve; the other by his youthful accessibility, the apparent sweetness and dependence of his nature.

He liked to talk to Avery. He talked about his women or the war. He assumed—it was irritating for Avery, but nothing more—that a man in his middle thirties, whether married or not, led an intense and varied love life. Later in the evening when the two of them had put on their coats and hurried to the pub at the end of the road, he would lean his elbows on the small table, thrust his bright face forward and relate the smallest detail of his exploits, his hand beside his chin, his slim fingertips rapidly parting and closing in unconscious imitation of his mouth. It was not vanity which made him thus, but friendship. These betrayals and confessions, whether truth or fantasy, were the simple coinage of their intimacy. He never mentioned Betty.

Avery came to know Leiser's face with an accuracy no

longer related to memory. He noticed how its features seemed structurally to alter shape according to his mood, how when he was tired or depressed at the end of a long day the skin on his cheekbones was drawn upward rather than down, and the corners of his eyes and mouth rose tautly so that his expression was at once more Slav and less familiar.

He had acquired from his neighborhood or his clients certain turns of phrase which, though wholly without meaning, impressed his foreign ear. He would speak, for instance, of "some measure of satisfaction," using an impersonal construction for the sake of dignity. He had assimilated also a variety of clichés. Expressions like "not to worry," "don't rock the boat," "let the dog see the rabbit," came to him continually, as if he were aspiring after a way of life which he only imperfectly understood, and these were the offerings that would buy him in. Some expressions, Avery remarked, were out of date.

Once or twice Avery suspected that Haldane resented his intimacy with Leiser. At other times it seemed that Haldane was deploying emotions in Avery over which he himself no longer disposed. One evening at the beginning of the second week, while Leiser was engaged in that lengthy toilet which preceded almost any recreational engagement, Avery asked Haldane whether he did not wish to go out himself.

"What do you expect me to do? Make a pilgrimage to the shrine of my youth?"

"I thought you might have friends there; people you still know."

"If I do, it would be insecure to visit them. I am here under another name."

"I'm sorry. Of course."

"Besides"—a dour smile—"we are not all so prolific in our friendships."

"You told me to stay with him!" Avery said hotly.

"Precisely; and you have. It would be churlish of me to complain. You do it admirably."

"Do what?"

"Obey instructions."

At that moment the doorbell rang and Avery went downstairs to answer it. By the light of the streetlight he

could see the familiar shape of a Department van parked
in the road. A small, homely figure stood on the doorstep.
He was wearing a brown suit and overcoat. There was a
high shine on the toes of his brown shoes. He might have
come to read the meter.

"Jack Johnson's my name," he said uncertainly. "Johnson's Fair Deal, that's me."

"Come in," Avery said.

"This is the right place, isn't it? Captain Hawkins . . .
and all that?"

He carried a soft leather bag which he laid carefully on
the floor as if it contained all he possessed. Half closing his
umbrella he shook it expertly to rid it of the rain, then
placed it on the stand beneath his overcoat.

"I'm John."

Johnson took his hand and squeezed it warmly.

"Very pleased to meet you. The boss has talked a lot
about you. You're quite the blue-eyed boy, I hear."

They laughed.

He took Avery by the arm in a quick confiding gesture.
"Using your own name, are you?"

"Yes. Christian name."

"And the Captain?"

"Hawkins."

"What's he like, Mayfly? How's he bearing up?"

"Fine. Just fine."

"I hear he's quite a one for the girls."

While Johnson and Haldane talked in the drawing room,
Avery slipped upstairs to Leiser.

"It's no go, Fred. Jack's come."

"Who's Jack?"

"Jack Johnson, the wireless chap."

"I thought we didn't start that till next week."

"Just the elementary this week, to get your hand in.
Come down and say hello."

He was wearing a dark suit and held a nail file in one
hand.

"What about going out, then?"

"I told you; we can't tonight, Fred; Jack's here."

Leiser went downstairs and shook Johnson briefly by the
hand, without formality, as if he did not care for latecom-
ers. They talked awkwardly for a quarter of an hour until

Leiser, protesting tiredness, went sullenly to bed.

Johnson made his first report. "He's slow," he said. "He hasn't worked a key for a long time, mind. But I daren't try him on a set till he's quicker on the key. I know it's all of twenty years, sir; you can't blame him. But he *is* slow, sir, very." He had an attentive, nursery-rhyme way of talking as if he spent much time in the company of children. "The Boss says I'm to play him all the time—when he starts the job, too. I understand we're all going over to Germany, sir."

"Yes."

"Then we shall have to get to know each other," he insisted, "Mayfly and me. We ought to be together a lot, sir, the moment I begin working him on the set. It's like handwriting, this game, we've got to get used to one another's handwriting. Then there's schedules, times for coming up and that; signal plans for his frequencies. Safety devices. That's a lot to learn in a fortnight."

"Safety devices?" Avery asked.

"Deliberate mistakes, sir; like a misspelling in a particular group, an E for an A or something of that kind. If he wants to tell us he's been caught and is transmitting under control, he'll miss the safety device." He turned to Haldane. "You know the kind of thing, Captain."

"There was talk in London of teaching him high-speed transmission on tape. Do you know what became of that idea?"

"The Boss did mention it to me, sir. I understand the equipment wasn't available. I can't say I know much about it, really; since my time, the transistorized stuff. The Boss said we were to stick to the old methods but change the frequency every two and a half minutes, sir; I understand the Jerries are very hot on the direction finding these days."

"What set did they send down? It seemed very heavy for him to carry about."

"It's the kind Mayfly used in the war, sir, that's the beauty of it. The old B2 in the waterproof casing. If we've only got a couple of weeks, there doesn't hardly seem time to go over anything else. Not that he's ready to work it yet—"

"What does it weigh?"

"About fifty pounds, sir, in all. The ordinary suitcase set. It's the waterproofing that adds the weight, but he's got to have it if he's going over rough country. Specially at this time of year." He hesitated. "But he's slow on his Morse, sir."

"Quite. Do you think you can bring him up to scratch in the time?"

"Can't tell yet, sir. Not till we really get cracking on the set. Not till the second period, when he's had his little bit of leave. I'm just letting him handle the buzzer at present."

"Thank you," said Haldane.

13.

AT THE END of the first two weeks they gave him forty-eight hours' leave of absence. He had not asked for it and when they offered it to him, he seemed puzzled. In no circumstances was he to visit his own neighborhood. He could depart for London on Friday but he said he preferred to go on Saturday. He could return Monday morning but he said it depended and he might come back late on Sunday. They stressed that he was to keep clear of anyone who might know him, and in some curious fashion this seemed to console him.

Avery, worried, went to Haldane.

"I don't think we should send him off into the blue. You've told him he can't go back to South Park, or visit his friends, even if he's got any. I don't see quite where he can go."

"You think he'll be lonely?"

Avery blushed. "I think he'll just want to come back all the time."

"We can hardly object to that."

They gave him subsistence money in old notes, fives and ones. He wanted to refuse it, but Haldane pressed it on him as if a principle were involved. They offered to book him a room but he declined. Haldane assumed he was going to London so in the end he went, as if he owed it to them.

"He's got some woman," said Johnson with satisfaction.

He left on the midday train, carrying one pigskin suitcase and wearing his camel's hair coat; it had a slightly

military cut, and leather buttons but no person of breeding
could ever have mistaken it for a British officer's coat.

He handed in his suitcase to the checkroom at Padding-
ton Station and wandered out into Praed Street because he
had nowhere to go. He walked about for half an hour,
looking at the shopwindows and reading the tarts' adver-
tisements on the glazed notice boards. It was Saturday afternoon: a handful of old men in trilby hats and raincoats
hovered between the pornography shops and the pimps on
the corner. There was very little traffic: an atmosphere of
hopeless recreation filled the street.

The cinema club charged a pound and gave him a pre-
dated membership card because of the law. He sat among
ghost figures on a kitchen chair. The film was very old; it
might have come over from Vienna when the persecutions
began. Two girls, quite naked, took tea. There was no
sound track and they just went on drinking tea, changing
position a little as they passed their cups. They would be
sixty by now if they had survived the war. He got up to go
because it was after half past five and the pubs were open.
As he passed the kiosk at the doorway, the manager
said: "I know a girl who likes a gay time. Very young."

"No thanks."

"Two and a half quid; she likes foreigners. She gives it
foreign if you like. French."

"Run away."

"Don't you tell me to run away."

"Run away." Leiser returned to the kiosk, his small eyes
suddenly alight. "Next time you offer me a girl, make it
something English, see."

The air was warmer, the wind had dropped, the street
emptied; pleasures were indoors now. The woman behind
the bar said, "Can't mix it for you now, dear. Not till the
rush dies down. You can see for yourself."

"It's the only thing I drink."

"Sorry, dear."

He ordered gin and Italian instead and got it warm with
no cherry. Walking had made him tired. He sat on the
bench which ran along the wall, watching the darts four-
some. They did not speak, but pursued their game with
quiet devotion, as if they were deeply conscious of tradi-

tion. It was like the film club. One of them had a date, and they called to Leiser, "Make a four, then?"

"I don't mind," he said, pleased to be addressed, and stood up; but a friend came in, a man called Henry, and Henry was preferred. Leiser was going to argue but there seemed no point.

Avery too had gone out alone. To Haldane he had said he was taking a walk, to Johnson that he was going to the cinema. Avery had a way of lying which defied rational explanation. He found himself drawn to the old places he had known: his college in the Turl; the bookshops, pubs and libraries. The term was just ending. Oxford had a smell of Christmas about it, and acknowledged it with prudish ill will, dressing the shopwindows with last year's tinsel.

He took the Banbury Road until he reached the street where he and Sarah had lived for the first year of marriage. The flat was in darkness. Standing before it, he tried to detect in the house, in himself, some trace of the sentiment, or affection, or love, or whatever it was that explained their marriage, but it was not to be found and he supposed it had never been. He sought desperately, wanting to find the motive of youth; but there was none. He was staring into an empty house. He hastened home to the place where Leiser lived.

"Good film?" Johnson asked.

"Fine."

"I thought you were going for a walk," Haldane complained, looking up from his crossword.

"I changed my mind."

"Incidentally," Haldane said, "Leiser's gun. I understand he prefers the three eight."

"Yes. They call it the nine millimeter now."

"When he returns he should start to carry it with him; take it everywhere, unloaded of course." A glance at Johnson. "Particularly when he begins transmission exercises of any scale. He must have it on him all the time; we want him to feel lost without it. I have arranged for one to be issued; you'll find it in your room, Avery, with various holsters. Perhaps you'd explain it to him, would you?"

"Won't you tell him yourself?"

"You do it. You get on with him so nicely."

Avery went upstairs to telephone Sarah. She had gone to stay with her mother. The conversation was very formal.

Leiser dialed Betty's number, but there was no reply.

Relieved, he went to a cheap jeweler's near the station, which was open on Saturday afternoon, and bought a gold coach and horses for a charm bracelet. It cost eleven pounds which was what they had given him for subsistence. He asked them to send it by registered mail to her address in South Park. He put a note in saying *Back in two weeks. Be good*, signing it, in a moment of aberration, *F. Leiser*. So he crossed it out and wrote *Fred*.

He walked for a bit, thought of picking up a girl, and finally booked in at the hotel near the station. He slept badly because of the noise of the traffic. In the morning he rang her number again; there was no reply. He replaced the receiver quickly; he might have waited a little longer. He had breakfast, went out and bought the Sunday papers, took them to his room and read the football reports till lunch time. In the afternoon he went for a walk; it had become a habit, right through London, he hardly knew where. He followed the river as far as Charing Cross and found himself in an empty garden filled with drifting rain. The tarmac paths were strewn with yellow leaves. An old man sat on the bandstand, quite alone. He wore a black overcoat and a rucksack of green webbing like the case of a gas mask. He was asleep, or listening to music.

He waited till evening in order not to disappoint Avery, then caught the last train home to Oxford.

Avery knew a pub behind Balliol where they let you play bar billiards on Sundays. Johnson liked a game of bar billiards. Johnson was on Guinness, Avery was on whisky. They were laughing a good deal; it had been a tough week. Johnson was winning; he went for the lower numbers, methodically, while Avery tried cushion shots at the hundred pocket.

"I wouldn't mind a bit of what Fred's having," Johnson said with a snigger. He played a shot; a white ball dropped dutifully into its hole. "Poles are dead randy. Go up anything, a Pole will. Specially Fred, he's a real terror. He's got the walk."

"Are you that way, Jack?"

"When I'm in the mood. I wouldn't mind a little bit now, as a matter of fact."

They played a couple of shots, each lost in an alcoholic euphoria of erotic fancy.

"Still," said Johnson gratefully, "I'd rather be in our shoes, wouldn't you?"

"Any day."

"You know," Johnson said, chalking his cue, "I shouldn't be speaking to you like this, should I? You've had college and that. You're different class, John."

They drank to each other, both thinking of Leiser.

"For Christ's sake," Avery said, "we're fighting the same war, aren't we?"

"Quite right."

Johnson poured the rest of the Guinness out of the bottle. He took great care, but a little ran over the side onto the table.

"Here's to Fred," Avery said.

"To Fred. On the nest. And bloody good luck to him."

"Good luck, Fred."

"I don't know how he'll manage the B2," Johnson murmured. "He's got a long way to go."

"Fred. He's a lovely boy. Here: do you know this bloke Woodford, the one who picked me up?"

"Of course. He'll be coming down next week."

"Met his wife at all; Babs? She was a girl, she was; give it to anyone. . . . Christ! Past it now, I suppose. Still, many a good tune, eh?"

"That's right."

"To him that hath shall be given," Johnson declared.

They drank; that joke went astray.

"She used to go with the admin bloke, Jimmy Gorton. What happened to him then?"

"He's in Hamburg. Doing very well."

They got home before Leiser. Haldane was in bed.

It was after midnight when Leiser hung his wet camel's hair coat in the hall, on a hanger because he was a precise man: tiptoed to the drawing room and put on the light. His eye ran fondly over the heavy furniture, the tallboy elaborately decorated with fretwork and heavy brass handles; the escritoire and the Bible table. Lovingly he revisited the handsome women at croquet, handsome men at war, disdainful boys in boaters, girls at Cheltenham; a whole long history of discomfort and not a breath of passion. The clock on the mantelpiece was like a pavilion in blue marble. The hands were of gold, so ornate, so fashioned, so flowered and spreading that you had to look twice to see where the points of them lay. They had not moved since he went away, perhaps not since he was born, and somehow that was a great achievement for an old clock.

He picked up his suitcase and went upstairs. Haldane was coughing but no light came from his room. He tapped on Avery's door.

"You there, John?"

After a moment he heard him sit up. "Nice time, Fred?"

"You bet."

"Woman all right?"

"Just the job. See you tomorrow, John."

"See you in the morning. Night, Fred. Fred . . ."

"Yes, John?"

"Jack and I had a bit of a session. You should have been there."

"That's right, John."

Slowly he made his way along the corridor, content in his weariness, entered his room, took off his jacket, lit a cigarette and threw himself gratefully into the armchair. It was tall and very comfortable with wings on the side. As he did so he caught sight of something. A chart hung on the wall for turning letters into figures and beneath it, on the bed, lying in the middle of the eiderdown was an old suitcase of continental pattern, dark green canvas with leather on the corners. It was open; inside were two boxes of gray steel. He got up, staring at them in mute recognition; reached out and touched them, wary, as if they might be hot; turned the dials, stooped and read the legend by the switches. It could have been the set he had in Holland: transmitter and receiver in one box; power unit, key and earphones in the other. Crystals, a dozen of them, in a bag of parachute silk with a green drawstring threaded through the top. He tested the key with his finger; it seemed much smaller than he remembered.

He returned to the armchair, his eyes still fixed upon the suitcase; sat there, stiff and sleepless, like a man conducting a wake.

He was late for breakfast. Haldane said, "You spend all day with Johnson. Morning and afternoon."

"No walk?" Avery was busy with his egg.

"Tomorrow perhaps. From now on we're concerned with technique. I'm afraid walks take second place."

Control quite often stayed in London on Monday nights, which he said was the only time he could get a chair at his club; Smiley suspected he wanted to get away from his wife.

"I hear the flowers are coming out in Blackfriars Road," he said. "Leclerc's driving around in a Rolls Royce."

"It's a perfectly ordinary Humber," Smiley retorted. "From the Ministry pool."

"Is that where it comes from?" Control asked, his eyebrows very high. "Isn't it fun? So the blackfriars have won the pools."

14.

"You know the set, then?" Johnson asked.

"The B2."

"O.K. Official title, Type three, Mark two; runs on AC or six-volt car battery, but you'll be using the mains, right? They've queried the current where you're going and it's AC. Your mains consumption with this set is fifty-seven watts on transmit and twenty-five on receive. So if you *do* end up somewhere and they've only got DC, you're going to have to borrow a battery, right?"

Leiser did not laugh.

"Your mains lead is provided with adapters for all continental sockets."

"I know."

Leiser watched Johnson prepare the set for operation. First he linked the transmitter and receiver to the power pack by means of six-pin plugs, adjusting the twin claws to the terminals; having plugged in the set and turned it on, he joined the miniature Morse key to the transmitter and the earphones to the receiver.

"That's a smaller key than we had in the war," Leiser objected. "I tried it last night. My fingers kept slipping."

Johnson shook his head.

"Sorry, Fred; same size." He winked. "Perhaps your finger's grown."

"All right, come on."

Now he extracted from the spares box a coil of multi-stranded wire, plastic covered, attaching one end to the aerial terminals. "Most of your crystals will be around the three-megacycle mark, so you may not have to change your coil —get a nice stretch on your aerial and you'll be a hundred percent, Fred; specially at night. Now watch the tuning. You've connected up your aerial, earth, key, headphones and power pack. Look at your signal plan and see what frequency you're on; fish out the corresponding crystal, right?" He held up a small capsule of black bakelite, guided the pins into the double socket. "Shoving the male ends into the doodahs, like so. All right so far, Fred? Not hurrying you, am I?"

"I'm watching. Don't keep asking."

"Now turn the Crystal Selector dial to 'fundamental all crystals,' and adjust your wave band to match your frequency. If you're on three and a half megs you want the wave-band knob on three to four, like so. Now insert your plug-in coil either way around, Fred; you've got a nice overlap there."

Leiser's head was supported in his hand as he tried desperately to remember the sequence of movements which once had come so naturally to him. Johnson proceeded with the method of a man born to his trade. His voice was soft and easy, very patient, his hands moving instinctively from one dial to another with perfect familiarity. All the time the monologue continued:

"TSR switch on T for tune; put your anode tuning and aerial matching on ten; now you can switch on your power pack, right?" He pointed to the meter window. "You should get the three-hundred reading, near enough, Fred. Now I'm ready to have a go: I shove my meter selector on three and twiddle the PA tuning till I get my maximum meter reading; now I put her on six—"

"What's PA?"

"Power Amplifier, Fred: didn't you know that?"

"Go on."

"Now I move the anode-tuning knob till I get my minimum value—here you are! She's a hundred with the knob on two, right? Now push your TSR over to S—S for send, Fred—and you're ready to tune the aerial. Here—press the key. That's right, see? You get a bigger reading because you're putting power into the aerial, follow it?"

Silently he performed the brief ritual of tuning the aerial

until the meter obediently dipped to the final reading.

"And Bob's your uncle!" he declared triumphantly. "Now it's Fred's turn. Here, your hand's sweating. You must have had a weekend, your must. Wait a minute, Fred!" He left the room, returning with an oversized white pepperpot, from which he carefully sprinkled French chalk over the black lozenge on the key lever.

"Take my advice," Johnson said, "just leave the girls in peace, see, Fred? Let it grow."

Leiser was looking at his open hand. Particles of sweat had gathered in the grooves. "I couldn't sleep."

"I'll bet you couldn't." He slapped the case affectionately. "From now on you sleep with *her*. She's Mrs. Fred, see, and no one else!" He dismantled the set and waited for Leiser to begin. With childish slowness Leiser painfully reassembled the equipment. It was all so long ago.

Day after day Leiser and Johnson sat at the small table in the bedroom tapping out their messages. Sometimes Johnson would drive away in the van leaving Leiser alone, and they would work back and forth till early morning. Or Leiser and Avery would go—Leiser was not allowed out alone—and from a borrowed house in Fairford they would pass their signals, encoding, sending and receiving *en clair* trivialities disguised as amateur transmissions. Leiser discernibly changed. He became nervy and irritable; he complained to Haldane about the complications of transmitting on a series of frequencies, the difficulty of constant retuning, the shortage of time. His relationship to Johnson was always uneasy. Johnson had arrived late, and for some reason Leiser insisted on treating him as an outsider, not admitting him properly to the companionship which he fancied to exist between Avery, Haldane and himself.

There was a particularly absurd scene one breakfast. Leiser raised the lid of the jam pot, peered inside, and turning to Avery asked, "Is this bee honey?"

Johnson leaned across the table, knife in one hand, bread and butter in the other.

"We don't say that, Fred. We just call it honey."

"That's right, honey. Bee honey."

"Just honey," Johnson repeated. "In England we just call it honey."

Leiser carefully replaced the lid, pale with anger. "Don't you tell me what to say."

Haldane looked up sharply from his paper. "Be quiet, Johnson. Bee honey is perfectly accurate."

Leiser's courtesy had something of the servant, his quarrels with Johnson something of the backstairs.

Despite such incidents as this, like any two men engaged daily upon a single project they came gradually to share their hopes, moods and depressions. If a lesson had gone well, the meal that followed it would be a happy affair. The two of them would exchange esoteric remarks about the state of the ionosphere, the skip distance on a given frequency, or an unnatural meter reading which had occurred during tuning. If badly, they would speak little or not at all, and everyone but Haldane would hasten through his food for want of anything to say. Occasionally Leiser would ask whether he might not take a walk with Avery, but Haldane would shake his head and say there was no time. Avery, a guilty lover, made no move to help.

As the two weeks neared their end, the Mayfly house was several times visited by specialists of one kind or another from London. A photographic instructor came, a tall, hollow-eyed man who demonstrated a sub-miniature camera with interchangeable lenses; there was a doctor, benign and wholly incurious, who listened to Leiser's heart for minutes on end. The Treasury had insisted upon it; there was the question of compensation. Leiser declared he had no dependents, but he was examined all the same to satisfy the Treasury.

With the increase in these activities Leiser came to derive a great comfort from his gun. Avery had given it to him after his weekend's leave. He favored a shoulder holster (the drape of his jackets nicely concealed the bulge) and sometimes at the end of a long day he would draw the gun and finger it, looking down the barrel, raising it and lowering it as he had done on the range. "There isn't a gun to beat it," he would say. "Not for size. You can have your continental types any time. Women's guns, they are, like their cars. Take my advice, John, a three eight's best."

"Nine millimeter they call it now."

His resentment of strangers reached its unexpected climax in the visit of Hyde, a man from the Circus. The morning had gone badly. Leiser had been making a timed run, encoding and transmitting forty groups; his bedroom and Johnson's were now linked on an internal circuit; they played back and forth behind closed doors. Johnson had taught him a number of international code signals: QRJ, your signals are too weak to read: QRW, send faster: QSD, your keying is bad: QSM, repeat the last message: QSZ, send each word twice: QRU, I have nothing for you. As Leiser's transmission became increasingly uneven, Johnson's comments, thus cryptically expressed, added to his confusion, until with a shout of irritation he switched off his set and stalked downstairs to Avery. Johnson followed him.

"It's no good giving up, Fred."

"Leave me alone."

"Look, Fred, you did it all wrong. I *told* you to send the number of groups *before* you send the message. You can't remember a thing, can you—"

"Look, leave me alone, I said!" He was about to add something when the doorbell rang. It was Hyde. He had brought an assistant, a plump man who was sucking something against the weather.

They did not play the tapes at lunch. Their guests sat side by side, eating glumly as if they had the same food every day because of the calories. Hyde was a meager, dark-faced man without a trace of humor who reminded Avery of Sutherland. He had come to give Leiser a new identity. He had papers for him to sign, identity documents, a form of ration card, a driving license, a permit to enter the border zone along a specified area, and an old shirt in a briefcase. After lunch he laid them all out on the drawing room table while the photographer put up his camera.

They dressed Leiser in the shirt and took him full face with both ears showing according to the German regulations, then led him to sign the papers. He seemed nervous.

"We're going to call you Freiser," Hyde said, as if that were an end to the matter.

"Freiser? That's like my own name."

"That's the idea. That's what your people wanted. For signatures and things, so that there's no slip-up. You'd better practice it a bit before you sign."

"I'd rather have it different. Quite different."

"We'll stick to Freiser, I think," said Hyde. "It's been decided at high level." Hyde was a man who leaned heavily upon the Passive Voice.

There was an uncomfortable silence.

"I want it different. I don't like Freiser and I want it different." He didn't like Hyde either, and in half a minute he was going to say so.

Haldane intervened. "You're under instructions. The Department has taken the decision. There is no question of altering it now."

Leiser was very pale.

"Then they can bloody well change the instructions. I want a different name, that's all. Christ, it's only a little thing, isn't it? That's all I'm asking for: another name, a proper one, not a half-cock imitation of my own."

"I don't understand," Hyde said. "It's only training, isn't it?"

"You don't have to understand! Just change it, that's all. Who the hell do you think you are, coming in here and ordering me about?"

"I'll telephone London," Haldane said, and went upstairs. They waited awkwardly until he came down.

"Will you accept Hartbeck?" Haldane inquired. There was a note of sarcasm in his voice.

Leiser smiled. "Hartbeck. That's fine." He spread out his hands in a gesture of apology. "Hartbeck's fine."

Leiser spent ten minutes practicing a signature, then signed the papers with a little flourish each time, as if there was dust on them. Hyde gave them a lecture on the documents. It took a very long time. There were no actual ration cards in East Germany, Hyde said, but there existed a system of registration with food shops, which provided a certificate. He explained the principle of travel permits and the circumstances under which they were granted, he talked at length about the obligation on Leiser to show his identity card, unasked, when he bought a railway ticket or put up at a hotel. Leiser argued with him and Haldane attempted to terminate the meeting. Hyde paid no attention. When he had finished, he nodded and went away with his photographer, folding the old shirt into his briefcase as if it were part of his equipment.

This outburst of Leiser's appeared to cause Haldane

some concern. He telephoned to London and ordered his assistant, Gladstone, to go over Leiser's file for any trace of the name Freiser; he had a search made in all the indices, but without success. When Avery suggested Haldane was making too much of the incident, the other shook his head. "We're waiting for the second vow," he said.

Following upon Hyde's visit, Leiser now received daily briefings about his cover. Stage by stage he, Avery and Haldane constructed in tireless detail the background of the man Hartbeck, establishing him in his work, his tastes and recreations, in his love life and choice of friends. Together, they entered the most obscure corners of the man's conjectured existence, gave him skills and attributes which Leiser himself barely possessed.

Woodford came with news of the Department.

"The Director's putting up a marvelous show." From the way he spoke, Leclerc might have been fighting an illness. "We leave for Lübeck a week from today. Jimmy Gorton's been on to the German frontier people—he says they're pretty reliable. We've got a crossing point lined up and we've taken a farmhouse on the outskirts of the town. He's let it be known that we're a team of academics wanting a quiet time and a bit of fresh air. Woodford looked confidingly at Haldane. "The Department is working wonderfully. As one man. And what a *spirit*, Adrian! No watching the clock these days. And no rank. Dennison, Sandford . . . we're just a single team. You should see the way Clarkie's going for the Ministry about poor Taylor's pension. How's Mayfly bearing up?" he added in a low voice.

"All right. He's doing wireless upstairs."

"Any more signs of nerves? Outbreaks or anything?"

"None so far as I know," Haldane replied, as if he were unlikely to know anyway.

"Is he getting frisky? Sometimes they want a girl about now."

Woodford had brought drawings of Soviet rockets. They had been made by Ministry draughtsmen from photographs held in Research Section, enlarged to about two foot by three, neatly mounted on showcards. Some were stamped with a security classification. Prominent features were marked with arrows and the nomenclature was curiously childish: FIN, CONE, FUEL COMPARTMENT, PAYLOAD. Beside each rocket stood a gay little figure like a penguin in a flying helmet, and printed beneath him: SIZE OF AVERAGE MAN. Woodford arranged them around the room as if they were his own work; Avery and Haldane watched in silence.

"He can look at them after lunch," Haldane said. "Put them together till then."

"I've brought along a film to give him some background. Launchings, transportation, a bit about destructive capacity. The Director said he should have an idea what these things can do. Give him a shot in the arm."

"He doesn't need a shot in the arm," Avery said.

Woodford remembered something. "Oh—and your little Gladstone wants to talk to you. He said it was urgent—didn't know how to get hold of you. I told him you'd give him a ring when you had time. Apparently you asked him to do a job on the Mayfly area. Industry, was it, or maneuvers? He says he's got the answer ready for you in London. He's the best type of N.C.O., that fellow." He glanced at the ceiling. "When's Fred coming down?"

Haldane said abruptly, "I don't want you to meet him, Bruce." It was unusual in Haldane to use a Christian name. "I'm afraid you must take luncheon in the town. Charge it to Accounts."

"Why on earth not?"

"Security. I see no point in his knowing more of us than is strictly necessary. The charts speak for themselves; so, presumably, does the film."

Woodford, profoundly insulted, left.

Avery knew then that Haldane was determined to preserve Leiser in the delusion that the Department housed no posts.

For the last day of the course, Haldane had planned a full-scale exercise to last from ten in the morning until eight in the evening, a combined affair including visual observation in the town, clandestine photography and listening to tapes.

The information which Leiser assembled during the day was to be made into a report, encoded and communicated by wireless to Johnson in the evening. A certain hilarity infected the briefing that morning. Johnson made a joke about not photographing the Oxford Constabulary by mistake; Leiser laughed richly and even Haldane allowed himself a wan smile. It was the end of term; the boys were going home.

The exercise was a success. Johnson was pleased; Avery enthusiastic; Leiser manifestly delighted. They had made two faultless transmissions, Johnson said; Fred was steady as a rock. At eight o'clock they assembled for dinner wearing their best suits. A special menu had been arranged. Haldane had presented the rest of his Burgundy; toasts were made; there was talk of an annual reunion in years to come. Leiser looked very smart in a dark blue suit and a pale tie of watered silk.

Johnson got rather drunk and insisted on bringing down Leiser's wireless set, raising his glass to it repeatedly and calling it Mrs. Hartbeck. Avery and Leiser sat together: the estrangement of the last week was over.

The next day, a Saturday, Avery and Haldane returned to London. Leiser was to remain in Oxford with Johnson until the whole party left for Germany on Monday. On Sunday, an Air Force van would call at the house to collect the suitcase. This would be independently conveyed to Gorton in Hamburg together with Johnson's own base equipment, and thence to the farmhouse near Lübeck from which Operation Mayfly would be launched. Before he left the house Avery took a last look around, partly for reasons of sentiment, and partly because he had signed the lease and was concerned about the inventory.

Haldane was ill at ease on the journey to London. He was still waiting, apparently, for some unknown crisis in Leiser.

15.

IT WAS THE SAME EVENING. Sarah was in bed. Her mother had brought her to London.

"If you ever want me," he said, "I'll come to you, wherever you are."

"You mean when I'm dying." Analyzing, she added, "I'll do the same for you, John. Now can I repeat my question?"

"Monday. There's a group of us going." It was like children: parallel playing.

"Which part of Germany?"

"Just Germany, West Germany. For a conference."

"More bodies?"

"Oh, for God's sake, Sarah, do you think I want to keep it from you?"

"Yes, John, I do," she said simply. "I think if you were allowed to tell me you wouldn't care about the job. You've got a kind of license I can't share."

"I can only tell you it's a big thing . . . a big operation. With agents. I've been training them."

"Who's in charge?"

"Haldane."

"Is that the one who confides in you about his wife? I think he's utterly disgusting."

"No, that's Woodford. This man's quite different. Haldane's odd. Donnish. Very good."

"But they're all good, aren't they? Woodford's good too."

Her mother came in with tea.

"When are you getting up?" he asked.

"Monday, probably. It depends on the doctor."

"She'll need quiet," her mother said, and went out.

"If you believe in it, do it," Sarah said. "But don't—"
She broke off, shook her head, little girl now.

"You're jealous. You're jealous of my job and the secrecy. You don't *want* me to believe in my work!"

"Go on. Believe in it if you can."

For a while they did not look at one another. "If it weren't
for Anthony, I really would leave you," Sarah declared at
last.

"What for?" Avery asked hopelessly, and then, seeing
the opening, "Don't let Anthony stop you."

"You never talk to me—any more than you talk to Anthony. He hardly knows you."

"What is there to talk about?"

"Oh—God."

"I can't talk about my work, you know that. I tell you
more than I should as it is. That's why you're always sneering at the Department, isn't it? You can't understand it,
you don't want to; you don't *like* its being secret but you
despise me when I break the rules."

"Don't go over that again."

"I'm not coming back," Avery said. "I've decided."

"This time, perhaps you'll remember Anthony's present."

"I bought him that milk lorry."

They sat in silence again.

"You ought to meet Leclerc," said Avery. "I think you
ought to talk to him. He keeps suggesting it. Dinner . . . he
might convince you."

"What of?"

She had found a piece of cotton hanging from the seam
of her bedjacket. Sighing, she took a pair of nail scissors
from the drawer in the bedside table and cut it off.

"You should have drawn it through at the back," Avery
said. "You ruin your clothes that way."

"What are they like?" she asked. "The agents? Why do
they do it?"

"For loyalty, partly. Partly money, I suppose."

"You mean you bribe them?"

"Oh shut up!"

"Are they English?"

"One of them is. Don't ask me any more, Sarah; I can't tell you." He advanced his head toward hers. "Don't ask me, sweet." He took her hand; she let him.

"And they're all men?"

"Yes."

Suddenly she said, it was a complete break, no tears, no precision, but quickly, with compassion, as if the speeches were over and this were the choice: "John, I want to know, I've got to know, now, before you go. It's an awful, un-English question, but all the time you've been telling me something, ever since you took this job. You've been telling me people don't matter, that *I* don't, Anthony doesn't; that the agents don't. You've been telling me you've found a vocation. Well, who calls you, that's what I mean: what *sort* of vocation? That's the question you never answer: that's why you hide from me. Are you a martyr, John? Should I admire you for what you're doing? Are you making sacrifices?"

Flatly, avoiding her, Avery replied, "It's nothing like that. I'm doing a job. I'm a technician; part of the machine. You want me to say double-think, don't you? You want to demonstrate the paradox."

"No. You've said what I want you to say. You've got to draw a circle and not go outside it. That's not double-think, it's unthink. It's very humble of you. Do you really believe you're that small?"

"You've made me small. Don't sneer. You're making me small now."

"John, I swear it, I don't mean to. When you came back last night you looked as though you'd fallen in love. The kind of love that gives you comfort. You looked free and at peace. I thought for a moment you'd found a woman. That's why I asked, really it is, whether they're all men. . . . I thought you were in love. Now you tell me you're nothing, and you seem proud of that too."

He waited, then smiling, the smile he gave Leiser, he said, "Sarah, I missed you terribly. When I was in Oxford I went to the house, the house in Chandos Road, remember? It was fun there, wasn't it?" He gave her hand a squeeze. "Real fun. I thought about it, our marriage and you. And Anthony. I love you, Sarah; I love you. For everything . . . the way you bring up our baby." A laugh. "You're both so . . . Sometimes I can hardly tell you apart."

She remained silent, so he continued. "I thought perhaps if we lived in the country, bought a house . . . I'm established now: Leclerc would arrange a loan. Then Anthony could run about more. It's only a matter of increasing our range. Going to the theatre, like we used to at Oxford."

She said absently, "Did we? We can't go to the theatre in the country, can we?"

"The Department gives me something, don't you understand? It's a real job. It's important, Sarah."

She pushed him gently away. "My mother's asked us to Reigate for Christmas."

"That'll be fine. Look . . . about the office. They owe me something now, after all I've done. They accept me on equal terms. As a colleague. I'm one of them."

"Then you're not responsible, are you? Just one of the team. So there's no sacrifice." They were back to the beginning.

Avery, not realizing this, continued softly, "I can tell him, can't I? I can tell him you'll come to dinner?"

"For pity's sake, John," she snapped, "don't try to run me like one of your wretched agents."

Haldane meanwhile sat at his desk, going through Gladstone's report.

There had twice been maneuvers in the Kalkstadt area—in 1952 and 1960. On the second occasion the Russians had staged an infantry attack on Rostock with heavy armored support but no air cover. Little was known of the 1952 exercise, except that a large detachment of troops had occupied the town of Wolken. They were believed to be wearing magenta shoulder-boards. The report was unreliable. On both occasions the area had been declared closed; the restriction had been enforced as far as the northern coast. There followed a long recitation of the principal industries. There was some evidence—it came from the Circus, who refused to release the source—that a new refinery was being constructed on a plateau to the east of Wolken, and that the machinery for it had been transported from Leipzig. It was conceivable (but unlikely) that it had come by rail and had been sent by way of Kalkstadt. There was no evidence of civil or industrial unrest, nor of any incident which could account for a temporary closure of the town.

A note from Registry lay in his in-tray. They had put up the files he had asked for, but some were Subscription Only; he would have to read them in the library.

He went downstairs, opened the combination lock on the steel door of General Registry, groped vainly for the light switch. Finally he made his way in the dark between the shelves to the small, windowless room at the back of the building where documents of special interest or secrecy were kept. It was pitch-dark. He struck a match, put on the light. On the table were two sets of files: MAYFLY, heavily restricted, now in its third volume, with a subscription list pasted on the cover, and DECEPTION *(Soviet and East Germany),* an immaculately kept collection of papers and photographs in hard folders.

After glancing briefly at the Mayfly files he turned his attention to the folders, thumbing his way through the depressing miscellany of rogues, double agents and lunatics who in every conceivable corner of the earth, under every conceivable pretext, had attempted, sometimes successfully, to delude the Western intelligence agencies. There was the boring similarity of technique: the grain of truth carefully reconstructed, culled from newspaper reports and bazaar gossip; the follow-up, less carefully done, betraying the deceiver's contempt for the deceived; and finally the flight of fancy, the stroke of artistic impertinence which wantonly terminated a relationship already under sentence.

On one report he found a flag with Gladstone's initials; written above them in his cautious, rounded hand were the words: *Could be of interest to you.*

It was a refugee report of Soviet tank trials near Gustweiler. It was marked: *Should not issue. Fabrication.* There followed a long justification citing passages in the report which had been abstracted almost verbatim from a 1949 Soviet military manual. The originator appeared to have enlarged every dimension by a third, and added some ingenious flavoring of his own. Attached were six photographs, very blurred, purporting to have been taken from a train with a telephoto lens. On the back of the photographs was written in McCulloch's careful hand: *Claims to have used Exa-two camera, East German manufacture. Cheap housing, Exakta range lens. Low shutter speed. Negatives very blurred owing to camera shake from train. Fishy.* It was all very inconclusive. The same make of camera, that was all. He locked up the registry and went home. Not his duty, Leclerc had said, to prove that Christ was born on Christmas Day; any more, Haldane reflected, than it was his business to prove that Taylor had been murdered.

Woodford's wife added a little soda to her Scotch, a splash: it was habit rather than taste.

"Sleep in the office my foot," she said. "Do you get operational subsistence?"

"Yes, of course."

"Well, it *isn't* a conference then, is it? A conference isn't operational. Not unless," she added with a giggle, "you're having it in the Kremlin."

"All right, it's not a conference. It's an operation. That's why I'm getting subsistence."

She looked at him cruelly. She was a thin, childless woman, her eyes half shut from the smoke of the cigarette in her mouth.

"There's nothing going on at all. You're making it up." She began laughing, a hard false laugh. "You poor sod," she said and laughed again, derisively. "How's little Clarkie? You're all scared of him, aren't you? Why don't you ever say anything against him? Jimmy Gorton used to: *he* saw through him."

"Don't mention Jimmy Gorton to me!"

"Jimmy's *lovely.*"

"Babs, I warn you!"

"Poor Clarkie. Do you remember," his wife asked reflectively, "that nice little dinner he gave us in his club? The time he remembered it was our turn for welfare? Steak and kidney and frozen peas." She sipped her whisky. "And warm gin." Something struck her. "I wonder if he's ever had a woman," she said. "Christ, I wonder why I never thought of that before."

Woodford returned to safer ground.

"All right, so nothing's going on." He got up, a silly grin on his face, collected some matches from the desk.

"You're not smoking that damn pipe in here," she said automatically.

"So nothing's going on," he repeated smugly, and lit his pipe, sucking noisily.

"God, I hate you."

Woodford shook his head, still grinning. "Never mind," he urged, "just never mind. You said it, my dear, I didn't. I'm not sleeping in the office so everything's fine, isn't it? So I didn't go to Oxford either; I didn't even go to the Ministry; I haven't a car to bring me home at night."

She leaned forward, her voice suddenly urgent, dangerous. "What's happening?" she hissed. "I've got a right to know, haven't I? I'm your wife, aren't I? You tell those little tarts in the office, don't you? Well, tell me!"

"We're putting a man over the border," Woodford said. It was his moment of victory. "I'm in charge of the London end. There's a crisis. There could even be a war. It's a damn ticklish thing." The match had gone out, but he was still swinging it up and down with long movements of his arm, watching her with triumph in his eyes.

"You bloody liar," she said. "Don't give me that."

Back in Oxford, the pub at the corner was three-quarters empty. They had the saloon bar to themselves. Leiser sipped a White Lady while the wireless operator drank best bitter at the Department's expense.

"Just take it gently, that's all you got to do, Fred," he urged kindly. "You came up lovely on the last run-through. We'll hear you, don't worry about that—you're only eighty miles from the border. It's a piece of cake as long as you remember your procedure. Take it gently on the tuning or we're all done for."

"I'll remember. Not to worry."

"Don't get all bothered about the Jerries picking it up; you're not sending love letters, just a handful of groups. Then a new call sign and a different frequency. They'll never home on that, not for the time you're there."

"Perhaps they can, these days," Leiser said. "Maybe they got better since the war."

"There'll be all sorts of other traffic getting in their hair; shipping, military, air control, Christ knows what. They're not supermen, Fred; they're like us. A dozy lot. Don't worry."

"I'm not worried. They didn't get me in the war; not for long."

"Now listen, Fred, how about this? One more drink and we'll slip home and just have a nice run-through with Mrs. Hartbeck. No lights, mind. In the dark: she's shy, see? Get it a hundred percent before we turn in. Then tomorrow we'll take it easy. After all, it's Sunday tomorrow, isn't it?" he added solicitously.

"I want to sleep. Can't I sleep a little, Jack?"

"Tomorrow, Fred. Then you can have a nice rest." He nudged Leiser's elbow. "You're married now, Fred. Can't always go to sleep, you know. You've taken the vow, that's what we used to say."

"All right, forget about it, will you?" Leiser sounded on edge. "Just leave it alone, see?"

"Sorry, Fred."

"When do we go to London?"

"Monday, Fred."

"Will John be there?"

"We meet him at the airport. And the Captain. They wanted us to have a bit more practice . . . on the routine and that."

Leiser nodded, drumming his second and third fingers lightly on the table as if he were tapping the key.

"Here—why don't you tell us about one of those girls you had on your weekend in London?" Johnson suggested.

Leiser shook his head.

"Come on then, let's have the other half and you give us a nice game of billiards."

Leiser smiled shyly, his irritation forgotten. "I got a lot more money than you, Jack. White Lady's an expensive drink. Not to worry."

He chalked his cue and put in the sixpence. "I'll play you double or quits; for last night."

"Look, Fred," Johnson pleaded gently. "Don't always go for the big money, see, trying to put the red into the hundred slot. Just take the twenties and fifties—they mount up, you know. Then you'll be home and dry."

Leiser was suddenly angry. He put his cue back in the cradle and took down his camel's hair coat from its peg.

"What's the matter, Fred, what the hell's the matter now?"

"For Christ's sake, let me lose! Stop behaving like a bloody jailer. I'm going on a job, like we all did in the war. I'm not sitting in the hanging cell."

"Don't you be daft," Johnson said gently, taking his coat and putting it back on the peg. "Anyway, we don't say hanging, we say condemned."

Carol put the coffee on the desk in front of Leclerc. He looked up brightly and said thank you, tired but well-drilled, like a child at the end of a party.

"Adrian Haldane's gone home," Carol observed. Leclerc went back to the map. "I looked in his room. He might have said good night."

"He never does," Leclerc said proudly.

"Is there anything I can do?"

"I never remember how you turn yards into meters."

"Neither do I."

"The Circus says this gully is two hundred meters long. That's about two hundred and fifty yards, isn't it?"

"I think so. I'll get the book."

She went to her room and took a ready-reckoner from the bookcase.

"One meter is thirty-nine point three seven inches," she read. "A hundred meters is a hundred and nine yards and thirteen inches."

Leclerc wrote it down.

"I think we should send a confirmatory telegram to Gorton. Have your coffee first, then come in with your pad."

"I don't want any coffee." She fetched her pad.

"Routine Priority will do, we don't want to haul old Jimmy out of bed." He ran his small hand briskly over his hair. "One: advance party, Haldane, Avery, Johnson and Mayfly arrive BEA flight so and so, such and such a time December nine." He glanced up. "Get the details from Administration. Two: all will travel under their own names and proceed by train to Lübeck. For security reasons you will not repeat not meet party at airport but you may discreetly contact Avery by telephone at Lübeck base. We can't put him on to old Adrian," he observed with a short laugh. "The two of them don't hit it off at all." He raised his voice: "Three: party number two consisting of Director only arriving morning flight December ten. You will meet him at airport for short conference before he proceeds to Lübeck. Four: your role is discreetly to provide advice and assistance at all stages in order to bring operation Mayfly to successful conclusion."

She stood up.

"Does John Avery have to go? His poor wife hasn't seen him for weeks."

"Fortunes of war," Leclerc replied without looking at her. "How long does a man take to crawl two hundred and twenty yards?" he muttered. "Oh, Carol—put another sentence onto that telegram: Five: Good Hunting—Old Jimmy likes a bit of encouragement, stuck out there all on his own."

He picked up a file from the in-tray and looked critically at the cover, aware perhaps of Carol's eyes upon him.

"Ah." A controlled smile. "This must be the Hungarian report. Did you ever meet Arthur Fielden in Vienna?"

"No."

"A nice fellow. Rather your type. One of our best chaps . . . knows his way around. Bruce tells me he's done a very good report on unit changes in Budapest. I must get Adrian to look at it. Such a *lot* going on just now." He opened the file and began reading.

Control said, "Did you speak to Hyde?"

"Yes."

"Well, what did he say? What have they got down there?"

Smiley handed him a whisky and soda. They were sitting in Smiley's house in Bywater Street. Control was in the chair he preferred, nearest the fire.

"He said they'd got first-night nerves."

"Hyde said that? Hyde used an expression like that? How extraordinary."

"They've taken over a house in North Oxford. There was just this one agent, a Pole of about forty, and they wanted him documented as a mechanic from Magdeburg, a name like Freiser. They wanted travel papers to Rostock."

"Who else was there?"

"Haldane and that new man, Avery. The one who came to me about the Finnish courier. And a wireless operator, Jack Johnson. We had him in the war. No one else at all. So much for their big team of agents."

"What *are* they up to? And whoever gave them all that money just for *training?* We lent them some equipment, didn't we?"

"Yes, a B2."

"What on earth's that?"

"A wartime set," Smiley replied with irritation. "You said it was all they could have. That and the crystals. Why on earth did you bother with the crystals?"

"Just charity. A B2, was it? Oh well," Control observed with apparent relief, "they wouldn't get far with that, would they?"

"Are you going home tonight?" Smiley asked impatiently.

"I thought you might give me a bed here," Control suggested. "Such a *fag* always traipsing home. It's the people. . . . They seem to get worse every day."

Leiser sat at the table, the taste of the White Ladies still in his mouth. He stared at the luminous dial of his watch, the suitcase open in front of him. It was eleven eighteen; the second hand struggled jerkily toward twelve. He began tapping, JAJ, JAJ—you can remember that, Fred, my name's Jack Johnson, see?—he switched over to receive, and there was Johnson's reply, steady as a rock.

Take your time, Johnson had said, don't rush your fences. We'll be listening all night, there are plenty more schedules. By the beam of a small flashlight he counted the encoded groups. There were thirty-eight. Putting out the flashlight he tapped a three and an eight; numerals were easy but long. His mind was very clear. He could hear Jack's gentle repetitions all the time: You're too quick on your shorts, Fred, a dot is one-third of a dash, see? That's longer than you think. Don't rush the gaps, Fred; five dots between each word, three dots between each letter. Forearm horizontal, in a straight line with the key lever; elbow just clear of the body. It's like knife fighting, he thought with a little smile, and began keying. Fingers loose, Fred, relax, wrist clear of the table. He tapped out the first two groups, slurring a little on the gaps, but not as much as he usually did. Now came the third group: put in the safety signal. He tapped an S, cancelled it and tapped the next ten groups, glancing now and then at the dial of his watch. After two and a half minutes he went off the air, groped for the small capsule which contained the crystal, discovered with the tips of his fingers the twin sockets of the housing, inserted it, and then stage by stage followed the tuning procedure, moving the dials, playing his flashlight on the crescent window to watch the black tongue tremble across it.

He tapped out the second call sign, PRE, PRE, switched quickly to receive and there was Johnson again, QRK 4, your signal readable. For the second time he began transmitting, his hand moving slowly but methodically as his eye followed the meaningless letters, until with a nod of satisfaction he heard Johnson's reply: Signal received. QRU: I have nothing for you.

When they had finished, Leiser insisted on a short walk. It was bitterly cold. They followed Walton Street as far as the main gates of Worcester, thence by way of Banbury Road once more to the respectable sanctuary of their dark North Oxford house.

16.

Takeoff

IT WAS THE SAME WIND. The wind that had tugged at Taylor's frozen body and drove the rain against the blackened walls of Blackfriars Road, the wind that flailed the grass of Port Meadow, now ran headlong against the shutters of the farmhouse.

The farmhouse smelled of cats. There were no carpets. The floors were of stone: nothing would dry them. Johnson lit the tiled oven in the hall as soon as they arrived but the damp still lay on the flagstones, collecting in the cracks like a tired army. They never saw a cat all the time they were there, but they smelled them in every room. Johnson left corned beef on the doorstep: it was gone in ten minutes.

The house was built on one floor with a high granary roof of brick, and it lay against a small coppice beneath a vast Flemish sky, a long, rectangular building with cattle sheds on the sheltered side. It was two miles north of Lübeck. Leclerc had said they were not to enter the town.

A ladder led to the loft, and there Johnson installed his wireless, stretching the aerial between the beams, then through a skylight to an elm tree beside the road. He wore rubber-soled shoes in the house, brown ones of military issue, and a blazer with a squadron crest. Gorton had had food delivered from the Naafi in Celle. It covered the kitchen floor in old cardboard boxes, with an invoice marked *Mr. Gorton's party*. There were two bottles of gin and three of whisky. They had two bedrooms; Gorton had sent army cots, two to each room, and reading lights with standard green shades. Haldane was very angry about the beds. "He must have told every damned department in the area," he complained. "Cheap whisky, Naafi food, army cots. I suppose we shall find he requisitioned the house next. God, what a way to mount an operation."

It was late afternoon when they arrived. Johnson, having put up his set, busied himself in the kitchen. He was a domesticated man; he cooked and washed up without complaint, treading lightly over the flagstones in his neat shoes. He assembled a hash of bully beef and egg, gave them cocoa with a great deal of sugar. They ate in the hall in front of the stove. Johnson did most of the talking; Leiser, very quiet, scarcely touched his food.

"What's the matter, Fred? Not hungry then?"

"Sorry, Jack."

"Too many sweets on the plane, that's your trouble." Johnson winked at Avery. "I saw you giving that air hostess a look. You shouldn't do it, Fred, you know, you'll break her heart." He frowned around the table in mock disapproval. "He really looked her over, you know. A proper tip-to-toe job."

Avery grinned dutifully. Haldane ignored him.

Leiser was concerned about the moon, so after supper they stood at the back door in a small shivering group, staring at the sky. It was strangely light; the clouds drifted like black smoke, so low that they seemed to mingle with the swaying branches of the coppice and half obscure the gray fields beyond.

"It will be darker at the border, Fred," said Avery. "It's higher ground; more hills."

Haldane said they should have an early night; they drank another whisky and at quarter past ten they went to bed, Johnson and Leiser to one room, Avery and Haldane to the other. No one dictated the arrangement. Each knew, apparently, where he belonged.

It was after midnight when Johnson came into their room. Avery was awakened by the squeak of his rubber soles.

"John, are you awake?"

Haldane sat up.

"It's about Fred. He's sitting alone in the hall. I told him to try and sleep, sir; gave him a couple of tablets, the kind my mother takes; he wouldn't even get into bed at first, now he's gone along to the hall."

Haldane said, "Leave him alone. He's all right. None of us can sleep with this damned wind."

Johnson went back to his room. An hour must have passed; there was still no sound from the hall. Haldane said, "You'd better go and see what he's up to."

Avery put on his overcoat and went along the corridor, past tapestries of Biblical quotations and an old print of Lübeck harbor. Leiser was sitting on a chair beside the tiled oven.

"Hello, Fred."

He looked old and tired.

"It's near here, isn't it, where I cross?"

"About five kilometers. The Director will brief us in the morning. They say it's quite an easy run. He'll give you all your papers and that kind of thing. In the afternoon we'll show you the place. They've done a lot of work on it in London."

"In London," Leiser repeated, and suddenly: "I did a job in Holland in the war. The Dutch were good people. We sent a lot of agents to Holland. Women. They were all picked up. You were too young."

"I read about it."

"The Germans caught a radio operator. Our people didn't know. They just went on sending more agents. They said there was nothing else to do." He was talking faster. "I was only a kid then; just a quick job they wanted, in and out. They were short operators. They said it didn't matter me not speaking Dutch, the reception party would meet me at the drop. All I had to do was work the set. There'd be a safe house ready." He was far away. "We fly in and nothing moves, not a shot or a searchlight, and I'm jumping. And when I land, there they are: two men and a woman. We say the words, and they take me to the road to get the bikes. There's no time to bury the parachute—we aren't bothering by then. We find the house and they give me food. After supper we go upstairs where the set is—no schedules, London listened all the time those days. They give the message: I'm sending a call sign—'Come in TYR, come in TYR'—then the message in front of me, twenty-one groups, four-letter."

He stopped.

"Well?"

"They were following the message, you see; they wanted to know where the safety signal came. It was in the ninth letter; a back shift of one. They let me finish the message and then they were on me, one hitting me, men all over the house."

"But *who*, Fred? Who's *they?*"

"You can't talk about it like that: you never know. It's never that easy."

"But for God's sake, whose fault was it? Who did it? Fred!"

"Anyone. You can never tell. You'll learn that." He seemed to have given up.

"You're alone this time. Nobody has been told. Nobody's expecting you."

"No. That's right." His hands were clasped on his lap. He made a hunched figure, small and cold. "In the war it was easier because however bad it got, you thought one day we'd win. Even if you were picked up, you thought, They'll come and get me, they'll drop some men or make a raid. You knew they never would, see, but you could think it. You just wanted to be left alone to think it. But nobody wins this one, do they?"

"It's not the same. But more important."

"What do you do if I'm caught?"

"We'll get you back. Not to worry, eh, Fred?"

"Yes, but how?"

"We're a big outfit, Fred. A lot goes on you don't know about. Contacts here and there. You can't see the whole picture."

"Can you?"

"Not all of it, Fred. Only the Director sees it all. Not even the Captain."

"What's he like, the Director?"

"He's been in it a long time. You'll see him tomorrow. He's a very remarkable man."

"Does the Captain fancy him?"

"Of course."

"He never talks about him," Leiser said.

"None of us talk about him."

"There was this girl I had. She worked in the bank. I told her I was going away. If anything goes wrong I don't want anything said, see. She's just a kid."

"What's her name?"

A moment of mistrust. "Never mind. But if she turns up, just keep it all right with her."

"What do you mean, Fred?"

"Never mind."

Leiser didn't talk after that. When the morning came, Avery returned to his room.

"What's it all about?" Haldane asked.

"He was in some mess in the war, in Holland. He was betrayed."

"But he's giving us a second chance. How nice. Just what they always said." And then: "Leclerc arrives this morning."

His taxi came at eleven. Leclerc was getting out almost before it had pulled up. He was wearing a duffle coat, heavy brown shoes for rough country and a soft cap. He looked very well.

"Where's Mayfly?"

"With Johnson," Haldane said.

"Got a bed for me?"

"You can have Mayfly's when he's gone."

At eleven thirty Leclerc held a briefing: in the afternoon they were to make a tour of the border.

The briefing took place in the hall. Leiser came in last. He stood in the doorway, looking at Leclerc, who smiled at him winningly, as if he liked what he saw. They were about the same height.

Avery said, "Director, this is Mayfly."

His eyes still on Leiser, Leclerc replied, "I think I'm allowed to call him Fred. Hello." He advanced and shook him by the hand, both formal, two weathermen coming out of a box.

"Hello," said Leiser.

"I hope they haven't been working you too hard."

"I'm all right, sir."

"We're all very impressed," Leclerc said. "You've done a grand job." He might have been talking to his constituents.

"I haven't started yet."

"I always feel the training is three-quarters of the battle. Don't you, Adrian?"

"Yes."

They sat down. Leclerc stood a little away from them. He had hung a map on the wall. By some indefinable means—it may have been his maps, it may have been the precision of his language, or it may have been his strict deportment, which so elusively combined purpose with restraint—Leclerc evoked in that hour the same nostalgic, campaigning atmosphere which had informed the briefing in Blackfriars Road a month before. He had the illusionist's gift—whether he spoke of rockets or wireless transmission, of cover or the point at which the border was to be crossed—of implying great familiarity with his subject.

"Your target is Kalkstadt"—a little grin—"hitherto famous only for a remarkably fine fourteenth-century church."

They laughed, Leiser too. It was so good, Leclerc knowing about old churches.

He had brought a diagram of the crossing point, done in different inks, with the border drawn in red. It was all very simple. On the western side, he said, there was a low, wooded hill overgrown with gorse and bracken. This ran parallel to the border until the southern end curved eastward in a narrow arm stopping about two hundred and twenty yards short of the border, directly opposite an observation tower. The tower was set well back from the demarcation line: at its foot ran a fence of barbed wire. It had been observed that this wire was laid out in a single apron and only loosely fixed to its staves. East German guards had been seen to detach it in order to pass through and patrol the undefended strip of territory which lay between the demarcation line and the physical border. That afternoon Leclerc would indicate the precise staves. Mayfly, he said, should not be alarmed at having to pass so close to the tower; experience had shown that the attention of the guards was concentrated on the more distant parts of their area. The night was ideal; a high wind was forecast; there would be no moon. Leclerc had set the crossing time for 0235 hours; the guard changed at midnight, each watch lasted three hours. It was reasonable to suppose that the sentries would not be as alert after two and a half hours on duty as they would be at the start of their watches. The relief guard, which had to approach from a barrack some distance to the north, would not yet be under way.

Much attention had been given, Leclerc continued, to the possibility of mines. They would see from the map—the little forefinger traced the green dotted line from the end of the rise across the border—that there was an old footpath which did indeed follow the very route which Leiser would be taking. The frontier guards had been seen to avoid this path, striking a track of their own some ten yards to the south of it. The assumption was, Leclerc said, that the path was mined, while the area to the side of it had been left clear for the benefit of patrols. Leclerc proposed that Leiser should use the track made by the frontier guards.

Wherever possible over the two hundred odd yards between the foot of the hill and the tower, Leiser should crawl, keeping his head below the level of the bracken. This eliminated the small danger that he would be sighted from the tower. He would be comforted to hear, Leclerc added with a smile, that there was no record of any patrol operating on the western side of the wire during the hours of darkness. The East German guards seemed to fear that one of their own number might slip away unseen.

Once across the border Leiser should keep clear of any path. The country was rough, partly wooded. The going would be hard but all the safer for that; he was to head south. The reason for this was simple. To the south, the border turned westward for some ten kilometers. Thus Leiser, by moving southward, would put himself not two but fifteen kilometers from the border, and more quickly escape the zonal patrols which guarded the eastern approaches. Leclerc would advise him thus—he withdrew one hand casually from the pocket of his duffle coat and lit a cigarette, conscious all the time of their eyes upon him—march east for half an hour, then turn due south, making for Marienhorst Lake. At the eastern end of the lake was a disused boathouse. There he could lie up for an hour and give himself some food. By that time Leiser might care for a drink—relieved laughter—and he would find a little brandy in his rucksack.

Leclerc had a habit, when making a joke, of holding himself at attention and lifting his heels from the ground as if to launch his wit upon the higher air.

"I couldn't have something with gin, could I?" Leiser asked. "White Lady's my drink."

There was a moment's bewildered silence.

"That wouldn't do at all," Leclerc said shortly, Leiser's master.

Having rested, he should walk to the village of Marienhorst and look around for transport to Schwerin. From then on, Leclerc added lightly, he was on his own.

"You have all the papers necesssary for a journey from Magdeburg to Rostock. When you reach Schwerin, you are on the legitimate route. I don't want to say too much about cover because you have been through that with the Captain. Your name is Fred Hartbeck, you are an unmarried mechanic from Magdeburg with an offer of employment at the State Cooperative shipbuilding works at Rostock." He smiled, undeterred. "I am sure you have all been through every detail of this already. Your love life, your pay, medical history, war service and the rest. There is just one thing that *I* might add about cover. Never *volunteer* information. People don't *expect* you to explain yourself. If you are cornered, play it by ear. Stick as closely to the truth as you can. Cover," he declared, stating a favorite maxim, "should never be *fabricated* but only an extension of the truth."

Leiser laughed in a reserved way. It was as if he could have wished Leclerc a taller man.

Johnson brought coffee from the kitchen, and Leclerc said briskly, "Thank you, Jack," as if everything was quite as it should be.

Leclerc now addressed himself to the question of Leiser's target; he gave a résumé of the indicators, implying somehow that they only confirmed suspicions which he himself had long harbored. He employed a tone which Avery had not heard in him before. He sought to imply, as much by omission and inference as by direct allusion, that theirs was a Department of enormous skill and knowledge, enjoying in its access to money, its intercourse with other services and in the unchallenged authority of its judgments an unearthly oracular immunity, so that Leiser might well have wondered why, if all this were so, he need bother to risk his life at all.

"The rockets are in the area now," Leclerc said. "The Captain has told you what signs to look for. We want to know what they look like, where they are and above all who mans them."

"I know."

"You must try the usual tricks. Pub gossip, tracing an old soldier friend, you know the kind of thing. When you find them, come back."

Leiser nodded.

"At Kalkstadt there's a workers' hostel." He unfolded a chart of the town. "Here. Next to the church. Stay there if you can. You may run into people who have actually been engaged . . ."

"I know," Leiser repeated.

Haldane stirred, glanced at him anxiously. "You might even hear something of a man who used to be employed at the station, Fritsche. He gave us some interesting details about the rockets, then disappeared. If you get the chance, that is. You could ask at the station, say you're a friend of his. . . ."

There was a very slight pause.

"Just disappeared," Leclerc repeated—for them, not for himself. His mind was elsewhere. Avery watched him anxiously, waiting for him to go on. At last he said rapidly, "I have deliberately avoided the question of communication," indicating by his tone that they were nearly done. "I imagine you have gone over that enough times already."

"No worries there," Johnson said. "All the schedules are at night. That leaves the frequency range pretty simple. He'll have a clear hand during the day, sir. We've had some very nice dummy runs, haven't we, Fred?"

"Oh yes. Very nice."

"As regards getting back," Leclerc said, "we play the war rules. There are no submarines any more, Fred; not for this kind of thing. When you return, you should report at once to the nearest British Consulate or Embassy, give your proper name and ask to be repatriated. You should represent yourself as a distressed British subject. My instinct would be to advise you to come out the way you went in. If you're in trouble, don't necessarily move west straightaway. Lie up for a bit. You're taking plenty of money."

Avery knew he would never forget that morning, how they had sat at the farmhouse table like sprawling boys at the Nissen hut desks, their strained faces fixed upon Leclerc as in the stillness of a church he read the liturgy of their devotion, moving his little hand across the map like a priest with the taper. All of them in that room—but Avery perhaps best of all—knew the fatal disproportion between the dream and reality, between motive and action. Avery had talked to Taylor's child, stammered out his half-formed lies to Peersen and the Consul: he had heard that dreadful footfall in the hotel, and returned from a nightmare journey to see his own experiences remade into the images of Leclerc's world. Yet Avery, like Haldane and Leiser, listened to Leclerc with the piety of an agnostic, feeling perhaps that this was how, in some clean and magic place, it really ought to be.

"Excuse me," said Leiser. He was looking at the plan of Kalkstadt. He was very much the small man just then. He might have been pointing to a fault in an engine. The station, hostel and church were marked in green; an inset at the bottom left-hand corner depicted the railway warehouses and dumping sheds. At each side, the point of the compass was given adjectivally: WESTERN PROSPECT, NORTHERN PROSPECT.

"What's a prospect, sir?" Leiser inquired.

"A view, an outlook."

"What's it for? What's it for on the map, please?"

Leclerc smiled patiently. "For purposes of orientation, Fred."

Leiser got up and examined the chart closely. "And this is the church?"

"That's right, Fred."

"Why does it face north? Churches go from east to west. You've got the entrance on the eastern side where the altar should be."

Haldane leaned forward, the index finger of his right hand resting on his lip.

"It's only a sketch map," Leclerc said.

Leiser returned to his place and sat to attention, straighter than ever. "I see. Sorry."

When the meeting was over, Leclerc took Avery on one side. "Just one point, John—he's not to take a gun. It's quite out of the question. The Minister was adamant. Perhaps you'll mention it to him."

"No gun?"

"I think we can allow the knife. That could be a general-purpose thing; I mean if anything went wrong we could say it was general purpose."

After lunch they made a tour of the border—Gorton had provided a car. Leclerc brought with him a handful of notes he had made from the Circus frontier report, and these he kept on his knee, together with a folded map.

The extreme northern part of the frontier which divides the two halves of Germany is largely a thing of depressing inconsequence. Those who look eagerly for dragon's teeth and substantial fortifications will be disappointed. It crosses land of considerable variety—gullies and small hills overgrown with bracken and patches of untended forest. Often the Eastern defenses are set so far behind the demarcation line as to be hidden from Western eyes—only a forward pillbox, crumbling roads, a vacated farmhouse or an occasional observation tower excite the imagination.

By way of emphasis the Western side is adorned with the grotesque statuary of political impotence: a plywood model of the Brandenburg Gate, the screws rusting in their sockets, rises absurdly from an untended field; noticeboards, broken by wind and rain, display fifteen-year-old slogans across an empty valley. Only at night, when the beam of a searchlight springs from the darkness and draws its wavering finger across the cold earth, does the heart chill for the captive crouching like a hare in the plow, waiting to break cover and run in terror till he falls.

They followed an unmade road along the top of a hill, and wherever it ran close to the frontier they stopped the car and got out. Leiser was shrouded in a mackintosh and hat. The day was very cold. Leclerc wore his duffle coat and carried a shooting stick—heaven knows where he had found it. The first time they stopped, and the second, and again at the next, Leclerc said quietly, "Not this one." As they got into the car for the fourth time he declared, "The next stop is ours." It was the kind of brave joke favored in battle.

Avery would not have recognized the place from Leclerc's sketch map. The hill was there, certainly, turning inward toward the frontier, then descending sharply to the plain below. But the land beyond it was hilly and partly wooded, its horizon fringed with trees against which, with the aid of glasses, they could discern the brown shape of a wooden tower. "It's the three staves to the left," Leclerc said. As they scanned the ground, Avery could make out here and there the worn mark of the old path.

"It's mined. The path is mined the whole way. Their territory begins at the foot of the hill." Leclerc turned to Leiser. "You start from here." He pointed with his shooting stick. "You proceed to the brow of the hill and lie up till takeoff time. We'll have you here early so that your eyes grow used to the light. I think we should go now. We mustn't attract attention, you know."

As they drove back to the farmhouse the rain came bursting against the windshield, thundering on the roof of the car. Avery, sitting next to Leiser, was sunk in his own thoughts. He realized with what he took to be utter detachment that while his own mission had unfolded as comedy, Leiser was to play the same part as tragedy; that he was witnessing an insane relay race in which each contestant ran faster and longer than the last, arriving nowhere but at his own destruction.

"Incidentally," he said suddenly, addressing himself to Leiser, "hadn't you better do something about your hair? I don't imagine they have much in the way of lotions over there. A thing like that could be insecure."

"He needn't cut it," Haldane observed. "The Germans go in for long hair. Just wash it, that's all that's needed. Get the oil out. A nice point, John. I congratulate you."

17.

THE RAIN HAD STOPPED. The night came slowly, struggling with the wind. They sat at the table in the farm-house, waiting; Leiser was in his bedroom. Johnson made tea and attended to his equipment. No one talked. The pre-tending was over. Not even Leclerc, master of the public school catchword, bothered anymore. He seemed to resent being made to wait, that was all, at the tardy wedding of an unloved friend. They had relapsed into a state of som-nolent fear, like men in a submarine, while the lamp over their heads rocked gently. Now and then Johnson would be sent to the door to look for the moon, and each time he an-nounced that there was none.

"The met reports were pretty good," Leclerc observed, and drifted away to the attic to watch Johnson check his equipment.

Avery, alone with Haldane, said quickly, "He says the Ministry's ruled against the gun. He's not to take it."

"And what bloody fool told him to consult the Ministry in the first place?" Haldane demanded, beside himself with anger. Then: "You'll have to tell him. It depends on you."

"Tell Leclerc?"

"No, you idiot; Leiser."

They had some food and afterward, Avery and Haldane took Leiser to his bedroom.

"We must dress you up," they said.

They made him strip, taking from him piece by piece his warm, expensive clothes: jacket and trousers of matching gray, cream silk shirt, black shoes without toecaps, socks of dark blue nylon. As he loosened the knot of his tartan tie his fingers discovered the gold pin with the horse's head. He unclipped it carefully and held it out to Haldane.

"What about this?"

Haldane had provided envelopes for valuables. Into one of these he slipped the tie-pin, sealed it, wrote on the back, tossed it on the bed.

"You washed your hair?"

"Yes."

"We had difficulty in obtaining East German soap. I'm afraid you'll have to try to get some when you're over there. I understand it's in short supply."

"All right."

He sat on the bed naked except for his watch, crouched forward, his broad arms folded across his hairless thighs, his white skin mottled from the cold. Haldane opened a trunk and extracted a bundle of clothes and half a dozen pairs of shoes.

As Leiser put on each unfamiliar thing—the cheap, baggy trousers of coarse serge, broad at the foot and gathered at the waist; the gray, threadbare jacket with arched pleats; the shoes, brown with a bright, unhealthy finish—he seemed to shrink before their eyes, returning to some former estate which they had only guessed at. His brown hair, free from oil, was streaked with gray and fell undisciplined upon his head. He glanced shyly at them, as if he had revealed a secret; a peasant in the company of his masters.

"How do I look?"

"Fine," Avery said. "You look marvelous, Fred."

"What about a tie?"

"A tie would spoil it."

He tried the shoes one after another, pulling them with difficulty over the coarse woolen socks.

"They're Polish," Haldane said, giving him a second pair. "The Poles export them to East Germany. You'd better take these as well—you don't know how much walking you'll have to do."

Haldane fetched from his own bedroom a heavy cash-box and unlocked it.

First he took a wallet, a shabby brown one with a center compartment of cellophane which held Leiser's identity card, fingered and stamped; it lay open behind its flat frame, so that the photograph of Leiser looked outward, a little prison picture. Beside it was an authority to travel and a written offer of employment from the State Cooperative for shipbuilding in Rostock. Haldane emptied one pocket of the wallet and then replaced the contents paper for paper, describing each in turn.

"Food registration card—driving license—Party Card. How long have you been a Party member?"

"Since forty-nine."

He put in a photograph of a woman and three or four grimy letters, some still in their envelopes.

"Love letters," he explained shortly.

Next came a Union card and a cutting from a Magdeburg newspaper about production figures at a local engineering works; a photograph of the Brandenburg Gate before the war; a tattered testimonial from a former employer.

"That's the wallet, then," Haldane said. "Except for the money. The rest of your equipment is in the rucksack. Provisions and that kind of thing."

He handed Leiser a bundle of bank notes from the box. Leiser stood in the compliant attitude of a man being searched, his arms raised a little from his sides and his feet slightly apart. He would accept whatever Haldane gave him, put it carefully away, then resume the same position. He signed a receipt for the money. Haldane glanced at the signature and put the paper in a black briefcase which he had put separately on a side table.

Next came the odds and ends which Hartbeck would plausibly have about him: a bunch of keys on a chain—the key to the suitcase was among them—a comb, a khaki handkerchief stained with oil and a couple of ounces of substitute coffee in a twist of newspaper; a screwdriver, a length of fine wire and fragments of metal ends newly turned—the meaningless rubble of a workingman's pockets.

"I'm afraid you can't take that watch," Haldane said.

Leiser unbuckled the gold armband and dropped the

watch into Haldane's open palm. They gave him a steel one of eastern manufacture and set it with great precision by Avery's bedside clock.

Haldane stood back. "That will do. Now remain there and go through your pockets. Make sure things are where you would naturally keep them. Don't touch anything else in the room, do you understand?"

"I know the form," said Leiser, glancing at his gold watch on the table. He accepted the knife and hooked the black scabbard into the waistband of his trousers. "What about my gun?"

Haldane guided the steel clip of the briefcase into its housing and it snapped like the latch of a door.

"You don't take one," Avery said.

"No gun?"

"It's not on, Fred. They reckon it's too dangerous."

"Who for?"

"It could lead to a dangerous situation. Politically, I mean. Sending an armed man into East Germany. They're afraid of an incident."

"Afraid?"

For a long time he stared at Avery, his eyes searching the young, unfurrowed face for something that was not there. He turned to Haldane.

"Is that true?"

Haldane nodded.

Suddenly he thrust out his empty hands in front of him, cupped in a terrible gesture of poverty, the fingers crooked and pressed together as if to catch the last water, his shoulders trembling in the cheap jacket, his face drawn, half in supplication, half in panic.

"The gun, John! You can't send a man without a gun! For mercy's sake, let me have the gun!"

"Sorry, Fred."

His hands still extended, he swung around to Haldane. "You don't know what you're doing!"

Leclerc had heard the noise and came to the doorway. Haldane's face was arid as rock; Leiser could have beaten his empty fists upon it for all the charity it held. His voice fell to a whisper. "What are you doing? God Christ, what are you trying to do?" To both of them he cried in revelation, "You hate me, don't you! What have I done to you?

John, what have I done? We were pals, weren't we?"

Leclerc's voice, when at last he spoke, sounded very pure, as if he were deliberately emphasizing the gulf between them.

"What's the trouble?"

"He's worried about the gun," Haldane explained.

"I'm afraid there's nothing we can do. It's out of our hands. You know how we feel about it, Fred. Surely you know that. It's an order, that's all. Have you forgotten how it used to be?" He added stiffly, a man of duty and decision, "I can't question my orders: what do you want me to say?"

Leiser shook his head. His hands fell to his sides. The discipline had gone out of his body.

"Never mind." He was looking at Avery.

"A knife's better in some ways, Fred," Leclerc added consolingly. "Quieter."

"Yes."

Haldane picked up Leiser's spare clothes. "I must put these into the rucksack," he said and, with a sideways glance at Avery, walked quickly from the room, taking Leclerc with him. Leiser and Avery looked at one another in silence. Avery was embarrassed to see him so ugly. At last Leiser spoke.

"It was we three. The Captain, you and me. It was all right, then. Don't worry about the others, John. They don't matter."

"That's right, Fred."

Leiser smiled. "It was the best ever, that week, John. It's funny, isn't it: we spend all our time chasing girls, and it's the men that matter; just the men."

"You're one of us, Fred. You always were; all the time your card was there, you were one of us. We don't forget."

"What does it look like?"

"It's two pinned together. One for then, one for now. It's in the index . . . live agents, we call it. Yours is the first name. You're the best man we've got." He could imagine it now: the index was something they had built together. He could believe in it, like love.

"You said it was alphabetical order," Leiser said sharply. "You said it was a special index for the best."

"Big cases go to the front."

"And men all over the world?"

"Everywhere."

Leiser frowned as if it were a private matter, a decision to be privately taken. He stared slowly around the bare room, then at the cuffs of his coarse jacket, then at Avery, interminably at Avery, until, taking him by the wrist, but lightly, more to touch than to lead, he said under his breath, "Give us something. Give me something to take. From you. Anything."

Avery felt in his pockets, pulling out a handkerchief, some loose change and a twist of thin cardboard, which he opened. It was the photograph of Taylor's little girl.

"Is that your kid?" Leiser looked over the other's shoulder at the small, bespectacled face; his hand closed on Avery's. "I'd like that." Avery nodded. Leiser put it in his wallet, then picked up his watch from the bed. It was gold with a black dial for the phases of the moon. "You have it," he said. "Keep it. I've been trying to remember," he continued, "at home. There was this school. A big court-yard like a barracks with nothing but windows and drain-pipes. We used to bang a ball around after lunch. Then a gate, and a path to the church, and the river on the other side . . ." He was laying out the town with his hands, placing bricks. "We went Sunday, through the side door, the kids last, see?" A smile of success. "That church was facing north," he declared. "Not east at all." Suddenly he asked: "How long; how long have you been in, John?"

"In the outfit?"

"Yes."

"Four years."

"How old were you then?"

"Twenty-eight. It's the youngest they take you."

"You told me you were thirty-four."

"They're waiting for us," Avery said.

In the hall they had the rucksack and the suitcase, green canvas with leather corners. He tried the rucksack on, adjusting the straps until it sat high on his back like a German schoolboy's satchel. He lifted the suitcase and felt the weight of the two things together.

"Not too bad," he muttered.

"It's the minimum," Leclerc said. They had begun to

whisper, though no one could hear. One by one they got into the car.

A hurried handshake and he walked away toward the hill. There were no fine words; not even from Leclerc. It was as if they had all taken leave of Leiser long ago. The last they saw of him was the rucksack gently bobbing as he disappeared into the darkness. There had always been a rhythm about the way he walked.

18.

LEISER LAY in the bracken on the spur of the hill, stared at the luminous dial of his watch. Ten minutes to wait. The key chain was swinging from his belt. He put the keys back in his pocket, and as he drew his hand away he felt the links slip between his thumb and finger like the beads of a rosary. For a moment he let them linger there; there was comfort in their touch; they were where his childhood was. St. Christopher and all his angels, please preserve us from road accidents.

Ahead of him the ground descended sharply, then evened out. He had seen it; he knew. But now, as he looked down, he could make out nothing in the darkness below him. Suppose it was marshland down there? There had been rain; the water had drained into the valley. He saw himself struggling through mud to his waist, carrying the suitcase above his head, the bullets splashing around him.

He tried to discern the tower on the opposite hill, but if it was there it was lost against the blackness of the trees.

Seven minutes. Don't worry about the noise, they said, the wind will carry it south. They'll hear nothing in a wind like this. Run beside the path, on the south side, that means to the right, keep on the new trail through the bracken, it's narrow but clear. If you meet anyone, use your knife, but for the love of heaven don't go near the path.

His rucksack was heavy. Too heavy. So was the case. He'd quarreled about it with Jack. He didn't care for Jack.

"Better be on the safe side, Fred," Jack had explained. "These little sets are sensitive as virgins: all right for fifty miles, dead as mutton on sixty. Better to have the margin, Fred, then we know where we are. They're experts, real experts where this one comes from."

One minute to go. They'd set his watch by Avery's clock.

He was frightened. Suddenly he couldn't keep his mind from it anymore. Perhaps he was too old, too tired, perhaps he'd done enough. Perhaps the training had worn him out. He felt his heart pounding his chest. His body wouldn't stand anymore; he hadn't the strength. He lay there, talking to Haldane: Christ, Captain, can't you see I'm past it? The old body's cracking up. That's what he'd tell them; he would stay there when the minute hand came up, he would stay there too heavy to move. "It's my heart, it's packed in," he'd tell them, "I've had a heart attack, Skipper, didn't tell you about my dickie heart, did I? It just came over me as I lay here in the bracken."

He stood up. Let the dog see the rabbit.

Run down the hill, they'd said; in this wind they won't hear a thing; run down the hill, because that's where they may spot you, they'll be looking at that hillside hoping for a silhouette. Run fast through the moving bracken, keep low and you'll be safe. When you reach level ground, lie up and get your breath back, then begin to crawl.

He was running like a madman. He tripped and the rucksack brought him down, he felt his knee against his chin and the pain as he bit his tongue, then he was up again and the suitcase swung him around. He half fell into the path and waited for the flash of a bursting mine. He was running down the slope, the ground gave way beneath his heels, the suitcase rattling like an old car. Why wouldn't they let him take the gun? The pain rose in his chest like fire, spreading under the bone, burning the lungs: he counted each step, he could feel the thump of each footfall and the slowing drag of the case and rucksack. Avery had lied. Lied all the way. Better watch that cough, Captain; better see a doctor, it's like barbed wire in your guts. The ground leveled out; he fell again and lay still, panting like an animal, feeling nothing but fear and the sweat that drenched his woolen shirt.

He pressed his face to the ground. Arching his body, he slid his hand beneath his belly and tightened the belt of his rucksack.

He began crawling up the hill, dragging himself forward with his elbows and his hands, pushing the suitcase in front of him, conscious all the time of the hump on his back rising above the undergrowth. The water was seeping through his clothes; soon it ran freely over his thighs and knees. The stink of leaf-mold filled his nostrils; twigs tugged at his hair. It was as if all nature conspired to hold him back. He looked up the slope and caught sight of the observation tower against the line of black trees on the horizon. There was no light on the tower.

He lay still. It was too far: he could never crawl so far. It was quarter to three by his watch. The relief guard would be coming from the north. He unbuckled his rucksack, stood up, holding it under his arm like a child. Taking the suitcase in his other hand he began walking cautiously up the rise, keeping the trodden path to his left, his eyes fixed upon the skeleton outline of the tower. Suddenly it rose before him like the dark bones of a monster.

The wind clattered over the brow of the hill. From directly above him he could hear the slats of old timber banging, and the long creak of a casement. It was not a single apron but double; when he pulled, it came away from the staves. He stepped across, reattached the wire and stared into the forest ahead. He felt even in that moment of unspeakable terror, while the sweat blinded him and the throbbing of his temples drowned the rustling of the wind, a full, confiding gratitude toward Avery and Haldane, as if he knew they had deceived him for his own good.

Then he saw the sentry, like the silhouette in the range, not ten yards from him, back turned, standing on the old path, his rifle slung over his shoulder, his bulky body swaying from left to right as he stamped his feet on the sodden ground to keep them from freezing. Leiser could smell tobacco—it was past him in a second—and coffee warm like a blanket. He put down the rucksack and suitcase and moved instinctively toward him; he might have been in the gymnasium at Headington. He felt the haft sharp in his hand, crosshatched to prevent slip. The sentry was quite a young boy under his greatcoat; Leiser was surprised how young. He killed him hurriedly, one blow, as a fleeing man might shoot into a crowd; shortly; not to destroy but to preserve; impatiently, for he had to get along; indifferently because it was a fixture.

"Can you see anything?" Haldane repeated.

"No." Avery handed him the glasses. "He just went into the dark."

"Can you see a light from the watch tower? They'd shine a light if they heard him."

"No, I was looking for Leiser," Avery answered.

"You should have called him Mayfly," Leclerc objected from behind. "Johnson knows his name now."

"I'll forget it, sir."

"He's over, anyway," Leclerc said and walked back to the car.

They drove home in silence.

As they entered the house Avery felt a friendly touch upon his shoulder and turned, expecting to see Johnson; instead he found himself looking into the hollow face of Haldane, but so altered, so manifestly at peace, that it seemed to possess the youthful calm of a man who has survived a long illness; the last pain had gone out of him.

"I am not given to eulogies," Haldane said.

"Do you think he's safely over?"

"You did well." He was smiling.

"We'd have heard, wouldn't we? Heard the shots or seen the lights?"

"He's out of our care. Well done." He yawned. "I propose we go early to bed. There is nothing more for us to do. Until tomorrow night, of course." At the door he stopped, and without turning his head he remarked, "You know, it doesn't seem real. In the war, there was no question. They went or they refused. Why did he go, Avery? Jane Austen said money or love, those were the only two things in the world. Leiser didn't go for money."

"You said one could never know. You said so the night he telephoned."

"He told me it was hate. Hatred for the Germans; and I didn't believe him."

"He went anyway. I thought that was all that mattered to you, you said you didn't trust motive."

"He wouldn't do it for hatred, we know that. What is he
then? We never knew him, did we? He's near the mark,
you know; he's on his deathbed. What does he think of? If
he dies now, tonight, what will be in his mind?"

"You shouldn't speak like that."

"Ah." At last he turned and looked at Avery and the
peace had not left his face. "When we met him, he was a
man without love. Do you know what love is? I'll tell you:
it is whatever you can still betray. We ourselves live without it in our profession. We don't force people to do things
for us. We let them discover love. And of course, Leiser
did, didn't he? He married us for money, so to speak, and
left us for love. He took his second vow. I wonder when."

Avery said quickly, "What do you mean, for money?"

"I mean whatever we gave to him. Love is what he gave
to us. I see you have his watch, incidentally."

"I'm keeping it for him."

"Ah. Good night. Or good morning, I suppose." A little
laugh. "How quickly one loses one's sense of time." Then
he commented, as if to himself: "And the Circus helped us
all the way. It's most strange. I wonder why."

Very carefully Leiser rinsed the knife. The knife was
dirty and must be washed. In the boathouse, he ate the
food and drank the brandy in the flask. "After that," Haldane had said, "you live off the land; you can't run around
with tinned meat and French brandy." He opened the door
and stepped outside to wash his hands and face in the lake.

The water was quite still in the darkness. Its unruffled
surface was like a perfect skin shrouded with floating veils
of gray mist. He could see the reeds along the bank; the
wind, subdued by the approach of dawn, touched them as
it moved across the water. Beyond the lake hung the shadow of low hills. He felt rested and at peace. Until the
memory of the boy passed over him like a shudder.

He threw the empty meat can and the brandy bottle far
out, and as they hit the water a heron rose languidly from
the reeds. Stooping, he picked up a stone and sent it skim-
ming across the lake. He heard it bounce three times before it sank. He threw another but he couldn't beat three.
Returning to the hut, he fetched his rucksack and suitcase.
His right arm was aching painfully, it must have been from

the weight of the case. From somewhere came the bellow of cattle.

He began walking east, along the track which skirted the lake. He wanted to get as far as he could before morning came.

He must have walked through half a dozen villages. Each was empty of life, quieter than the open road because they gave a moment's shelter from the rising wind. There were no signposts and no new buildings, it suddenly occurred to him. That was where the peace came from, it was the peace of no innovation—it might have been fifty years ago, a hundred. There were no streetlights, no gaudy signs on the pubs or shops. It was the darkness of indifference, and it comforted him. He walked into it like a tired man breasting the sea, it cooled and revived him like the wind; until he remembered the boy. He passed a farmhouse. A long drive led to it from the road. He stopped. Halfway up the drive stood a motorbike, an old mackintosh thrown over the saddle. There was no one in sight.

The oven smoked gently.

"When did you say his first schedule was?" Avery asked. He had asked already.

"Johnson said twenty-two twenty. We start scanning an hour before."

"I thought he was on a fixed frequency," Leclerc muttered, but without much interest.

"He may start with the wrong crystal. It's the kind of thing that happens under strain. It's safest for base to scan with so many crystals."

"He must be on the road by now."

"Where's Haldane?"

"Asleep."

"How can anyone sleep at a time like this?"

"It'll be daylight soon."

"Can't you do something about that fire?" Leclerc asked. "It shouldn't smoke like that, I'm sure." He shook his head suddenly, as if shaking off water, and said, "John, there's a most interesting report from Fielden. Troop movements in Budapest. Perhaps when you get back to London . . ." He lost the thread of his sentence and frowned.

"You mentioned it," Avery said softly.

"Yes. Well, you must take a look at it."

"I'd like to. It sounds very interesting."

"It does, doesn't it?"

"Very."

"You know," he said—he seemed to be reminiscing—"they *still* won't give that wretched woman her pension."

He sat very straight on the motorbike, elbows in as if he were at table. It made a terrible noise; it seemed to fill the dawn with sound, echoing across the frosted fields and stirring the roosting poultry. The mackintosh had leather pieces on the shoulders; as he bounced along the unmade road its skirts fluttered behind, rattling against the spokes of the rear wheel. Daylight came.

Soon he would have to eat. He couldn't understand why he was so hungry. Perhaps it was the exercise. Yes, it must be the exercise. He would eat, but not in a town, not yet. Not in a café where strangers came. Not in a café where the boy had been.

He drove on. His hunger taunted him. He could think of nothing else. His hand held down the throttle and drove his ravening body forward. He turned onto a farm track and stopped.

The house was old, falling with neglect; the drive overgrown with grass, pitted with cart tracks. The fences were broken. There was a terraced garden once partly under plow, now left as if it were beyond all use.

A light burned in the kitchen window. Leiser knocked at the door. His hand was trembling from the motorbike. No one came; he knocked again, and the sound of his knocking frightened him. He thought he saw a face, it might have been the shadow of the boy sinking across the window as he fell, or the reflection of a swaying branch.

He returned quickly to his motorbike, realizing with terror that his hunger was not hunger at all but loneliness. He must lie up somewhere and rest. He thought: I've forgotten how it takes you. He drove on until he came to the wood, where he lay down. His face was hot against the bracken.

It was evening; the fields were still light but the wood in which he lay gave itself swiftly to the darkness, so that in a moment the red pines had turned to columns of black.

He picked the leaves from his jacket and laced up his shoes. They pinched badly at the instep. He never had a chance to break them in. He caught himself thinking, It's all right for them; and he remembered that nothing ever bridged the gulf between the man who went and the man who stayed behind, between the living and the dying.

He struggled into the harness of his rucksack and once again felt gratefully the hot, raw pain in his shoulders as the straps found the old bruises. Picking up the suitcase he walked across the field to the road where the motorbike was waiting; five kilometers to Langdorn. He guessed it lay beyond the hill: the first of the three towns. Soon he would meet the roadblock; soon he would have to eat.

He drove slowly, the case across his knees, peering ahead all the time along the wet road, straining his eyes for a line of red lights or a cluster of men and vehicles. He rounded a bend and saw to his left a house with a beer sign propped in the window. He entered the forecourt; the noise of the engine brought an old man to the door. Leiser lifted the bike onto its stand.

"I want a beer," he said, "and some sausage. Have you got that here?"

The old man showed him inside, sat him at a table in the front room from which Leiser could see his motorbike parked in the yard. He brought him a bottle of beer, some sliced sausage and a piece of black bread; then stood at the table watching him eat.

"Where are you making for?" His thin face was shaded with beard.

"North." Leiser knew this game.

"Where are you from?"

Leiser did not reply but asked, "What's the next town?"

"Langdorn."

"Far?"

"Five kilometers."

"Somewhere to stay?"

The old man shrugged. It was a gesture not of indifference nor of refusal, but of negation, as if he rejected everything and everything rejected him.

"What's the road like?" Leiser asked.

"It's all right."

"I heard there was a diversion."

"No diversion," the old man said, as if a diversion were
hope, or comfort, or companionship; anything that might
warm the damp air or lighten the corners of the room.

"You're from the east," the man declared. "One hears it
in the voice."

"My parents," he said. "Any coffee?"

The old man brought him coffee, very black and sour,
tasting of nothing.

"You're from Wilmsdorf," the old man said. "You've
got a Wilmsdorf registration."

"Much business?" Leiser asked, glancing at the door.

The old man shook his head.

"Not a busy road, eh?" Still the old man said nothing.
"I've got a friend near Kalkstadt. Is that far?"

"Not far. Forty kilometers. They killed a boy near
Wilmsdorf."

"He runs a café. On the northern side. The Tom Cat.
Know it at all?"

"No."

Leiser lowered his voice. "They had trouble there. A
fight. Some soldiers from the town. Russians."

"Go away," the old man said.

He tried to pay him but he only had a fifty-mark note.

"Go away," the old man repeated.

Leiser picked up the suitcase and rucksack. "You old
fool," he said roughly, "what do you think I am?"

"You are either good or bad, and both are dangerous.
Go away."

There was no roadblock. Without warning he was in the
center of Langdorn; it was already dark; the only lights in
the main street stole from the shuttered windows, barely
reaching the wet cobbles. There was no traffic. He was
alarmed by the din of his motorbike; it sounded like a
trumpet blast across the market square. In the war, Leiser
thought, they went to bed early to keep warm; perhaps
they still did.

It was time to get rid of the motorbike. He drove
through the town, found a disused church and left it by the
vestry door. Walking back into the town he made for the
railway station. The official wore a uniform.

"Kalkstadt. Single."

The official held out his hand. Leiser took a bank note from his wallet and gave it to him. The official shook it impatiently. For a moment Leiser's mind went blank while he looked stupidly at the flicking fingers in front of him and the suspicious, angry face behind the grille.

Suddenly the official shouted, "Identity card!"

Leiser smiled apologetically. "One forgets," he said, and opened his wallet to show the card in the cellophane window.

"Take it out of the wallet," the official said. Leiser watched him examine it under the light on his desk.

"Travel authority?"

"Yes, of course." Leiser handed him the paper.

"Why do you want to go to Kalkstadt if you are traveling to Rostock?"

"Our cooperative in Magdeburg sent some machinery by rail to Kalkstadt. Heavy turbines and some tooling equipment. It has to be installed."

"How did you come this far?"

"I got a lift."

"The granting of lifts is forbidden."

"One must do what one can these days."

"These days?"

The man pressed his face against the glass, looking down at Leiser's hands.

"What's that you're fiddling with down there?" he demanded roughly.

"A chain; a key chain."

"So the equipment has to be installed. Well? Go on!"

"I can do the job on the way. The people in Kalkstadt have been waiting six weeks already. The consignment was delayed."

"So?"

"We made inquiries . . . of the railway people."

"And?"

"They didn't reply."

"You've got an hour's wait. It leaves at six thirty." A pause. "You heard the news? They've killed a boy at Wilmsdorf," he said. "Swine." He handed him his change.

He had nowhere to go; he dared not deposit his luggage. There was nothing else to do. He walked for half an hour, then returned to the station. The train was late.

"You both deserve great credit," Leclerc said, nodding gratefully at Haldane and Avery. "You too, Johnson. From now on there's nothing any of us can do: it's up to Mayfly." A special smile for Avery: "How about you, John; you've been keeping very quiet. Do you think you've profited from the experience?" He added with a laugh, appealing to the other two, "I do hope we shan't have a divorce on our hands; we must get you home to your wife."

He was sitting at the edge of the table, his small hands folded tidily on his knee. When Avery said nothing he declared brightly, "I had a ticking off from Carol, you know, Adrian; breaking up the young home."

Haldane smiled as if it were an amusing notion. "I'm sure there's no danger of that," he said.

"He made a great hit with Smiley, too: we must see they don't poach him away!"

19.

WHEN THE TRAIN reached Kalkstadt, Leiser waited until the other passengers had left the platform. An elderly guard collected the tickets. He seemed a kindly man.

"I'm looking for a friend," Leiser said. "A man called Fritsche. He used to work here."

The guard frowned.

"Fritsche?"

"Yes."

"What was his first name?"

"I don't know."

"How old then; how old about?"

He guessed: "Forty."

"Fritsche, here, at this station?"

"Yes. He had a small house down by the river; a single man."

"A whole house? And worked at this station?"

"Yes."

The guard shook his head. "Never heard of him." He peered at Leiser. "Are you sure?" he said.

"That's what he told me." Something seemed to come back to him. "He wrote to me in November . . . he complained that Vopos had closed the station."

"You're mad," the guard said. "Good night."

"Good night," Leiser replied; as he walked away he was conscious all the time of the man's gaze upon his back.

There was an inn in the main street called the Old Bell. He waited at the desk in the hall and nobody came. He opened a door and found himself in a big room, dark at the further end. A girl sat at a table in front of an old phonograph. She was slumped forward, her head buried in her arms, listening to the music. A single light burned above her. When the record stopped she played it again, moving the arm of the record player without lifting her head.

"I'm looking for a room," Leiser said. "I've just arrived from Langdorn."

There were stuffed birds around the room: herons, pheasants and a kingfisher. "I'm looking for a room," he repeated. It was dance music, very old.

"Ask at the desk."

"There's no one there."

"They have nothing, anyway. They're not allowed to take you. There's a hostel near the church. You have to stay there."

"Where's the church?"

With an exaggerated sigh she stopped the record, and Leiser knew she was glad to have someone to talk to.

"It was bombed," she declared. "We just talk about it still. There's only the tower left."

Finally he said, "Surely they've got a bed here. It's a big place." He put his rucksack in a corner and sat at the table next to her. He ran a hand through his thick dry hair.

"You look all in," the girl said.

His blue trousers were still caked with mud from the border. "I've been on the road all day. Takes a lot out of you."

She stood up self-consciously and went to the end of the room where a wooden staircase led upward toward a glimmer of light. She called out but no one came.

"Steinhäger?" she asked him from the dark.

"Yes."

She returned with a bottle and a glass. She was wearing a mackintosh, an old brown one of military cut with epaulets and square shoulders.

"Where are you from?" she asked.

"Magdeburg. I'm making north. Got a job in Rostock." How many more times would he say it? "This hostel; do I get a room to myself?"

"If you want one."

The light was so poor that at first he could scarcely

make her out. Gradually she came alive. She was about eighteen and heavily built; quite a pretty face but bad skin. The same age as the boy; older perhaps.

"Who are you?" he asked. She said nothing. "What do you do?"

She took his glass and drank from it, looking at him precociously over the brim as if she were a great beauty. She put it down slowly, still watching him, touched the side of her hair. She seemed to think her gestures mattered. Leiser began again:

"Been here long?"

"Two years."

"What do you do?"

"Whatever you want." Her voice was quite earnest.

"Much going on here?"

"It's dead. Nothing."

"No boys?"

"Sometimes."

"Troops?" A pause.

"Now and then. Don't you know it's forbidden to ask that?"

Leiser helped himself to more Steinhäger from the bottle.

She took his glass, fumbling with his fingers.

"What's wrong with this town?" he asked. "I tried to come here six weeks ago. They wouldn't let me in. Kalkstadt, Langdorn, Wolken, all closed they said. What was going on?"

Her fingertips played over his hand.

"What was up?" he repeated.

"Nothing was closed."

"Come off it," Leiser laughed, "they wouldn't let me near the place, I tell you. Roadblocks here and on the Wolken road." He thought, "It's eight twenty; only two hours till the first schedule."

"Nothing was closed." Suddenly she added, "So you came from the west: you came by road. They're looking for someone like you."

He stood up to go. "I'd better find the hostel." He put some money on the table. The girl whispered, "I've got my own room. In a new flat behind the Friedensplatz. A workers' block. They don't mind. I'll do whatever you want."

Leiser shook his head. He picked up his luggage and went to the door. She was still looking at him and he knew she suspected him.

"Goodbye," he said.

"I won't say anything. Take me with you."

"I had a Steinhäger," Leiser muttered. "We didn't even talk. You played your record all the time." They were both frightened.

The girl said, "Yes. Records all the time."

"It was never closed, you are sure of that? Langdorn, Wolken, Kalkstadt, six weeks ago?"

"What would anyone close this place for?"

"Not even the station?"

She said quickly, "I don't know about the station. The area was closed for three days in November. No one knows why. Russian troops stayed, about fifty. They were billeted in the town. Mid-November."

"Fifty? Any equipment?"

"Lorries. There were maneuvers further north, that's the rumor. Stay with me tonight. Stay with me! Let me come with you. I'll go anywhere."

"What color shoulder-boards?"

"I don't remember."

"Where did they come from?"

"They were new. Some came from Leningrad, two brothers."

"Which way did they go?"

"North. Listen, no one will ever know. I don't talk, I'm not that kind. I'll give it to you, anything you want."

"Toward Rostock?"

"They said they were going to Rostock. They said not to tell. The Party came around to all the houses."

Leiser nodded. He was sweating. "Goodbye," he said.

"What about tomorrow, tomorrow night? I'll do whatever you want."

"Perhaps. Don't tell anyone, do you understand?"

She shook her head. "I won't tell them," she said, "because I don't care. Ask for the Hochhaus behind the Friedensplatz. Apartment nineteen. Come any time. I'll open the door. You give two rings and they know it's for me. You needn't pay. Take care," she said. "There are people everywhere. They've killed a boy in Wilmsdorf. . . ."

He walked to the market square, correct again because everything was closing in, looking for the church tower and the hostel. Huddled figures passed him in the darkness; some wore pieces of uniform; forage caps and the long coats they had in the war. Now and then he would glimpse their faces, catching them in the pale glow of a streetlight, and he would seek in their locked, unseeing features the qualities he hated. He would say to himself, "Hate him— he is old enough," but it did not stir him. They were nothing. Perhaps in some other town, some other place, he would find them and hate them; but not here. These were old and nothing; poor, like him, and alone. The tower was black and empty. It reminded him suddenly of the turret on the border, and the garage after eleven, of the moment when he killed the sentry; just a kid, like himself in the war; even younger than Avery.

"He should be there by now," Avery said.

"That's right, John. He should be there, shouldn't he? One hour to go. One more river to cross." He began singing. No one took him up.

They looked at each other in silence.

"Know the Alias Club at all?" Johnson asked suddenly. "Off Villiers Street? A lot of the old gang meet up there. You ought to come along one evening, when we get home."

"Thanks," Avery replied. "I'd like to."

"It gets nice at Christmastime," he said. "That's when I go. A good crowd. There's even one or two come in uniform."

"It sounds fine."

"They have a mixed do at New Year's. You could take your wife."

"Grand."

Johnson winked. "Or your fancy-girl."

"Sarah's the only girl for me," Avery said.

The telephone was ringing. Leclerc rose to answer it.

20.

Homecoming

HE PUT DOWN the rucksack and the suitcase and looked around the walls. There was an electric outlet beside the window. The door had no lock so he pushed the armchair against it. He took off his shoes and lay on the bed. He thought of the girl's fingers on his hands and the nervous movement of her lips; he remembered her deceitful eyes watching him from the shadows and he wondered how long it would be before she betrayed him.

He remembered Avery: the warmth and English decency of their early companionship; he remembered his young face glistening in the rain, and his shy, dazzled glance as he dried his spectacles, and he thought: He must have said thirty-two all the time. I misheard.

He looked at the ceiling. In an hour he would put up the aerial.

The room was large and bare with a round marble basin in one corner. A single pipe ran from it to the floor and he hoped to God it would do for the earth. He ran some water and to his relief it was cold, because Jack had said a hot pipe was dicey. He drew his knife and carefully scraped the pipe clean on one side. The earth was important; Jack had said so. If you can't do anything else, he'd said, lay your earth wire zigzag fashion under the carpet, the same length as the aerial. But there was no carpet; the pipe would have to do. No carpet, no curtains.

Opposite him stood a heavy wardrobe with bow doors. The place must once have been the main hotel. There was a smell of Turkish tobacco and rank, unscented disinfectant. The walls were of gray plaster; the damp had spread over them in dark shadows, arrested here and there by some mysterious inner property of the house which had dried a path across the ceiling. In some places the plaster had crumbled with the damp, leaving a ragged island of white mildew; in others it had contracted and the plasterer had returned to fill the cavities with paste which described white rivers along the corners of the room. Leiser's eye followed them carefully while he listened for the smallest sound outside.

There was a picture on the wall of workers in a field, leading a horse plow. On the horizon was a tractor. He heard Johnson's benign voice running on about the aerial: "If it's indoors it's a headache, and indoors it'll be. Now listen: zigzag fashion across the room, quarter the length of your wave and one foot below the ceiling. Space them wide as possible, Fred, and not parallel to metal girders, electric wires and that. And don't double her back on herself, Fred, or you'll muck her up properly, see?" Always the joke, the copulative innuendo to aid the memory of simple men.

Leiser thought: I'll take it to the picture frame, then back and forth to the far corner. I can put a nail into that soft plaster; he looked around for a nail or pin, and noticed a bronze hanger on the beading which ran along the ceiling. He got up, unscrewed the handle of his razor. The thread began to the right, it was considered an ingenious detail, so that a suspicious man who gave the handle a casual twist to the left would be going against the thread. From the recess he extracted the knot of silk cloth which he smoothed carefully over his knee with his thick fingers. He found a pencil in his pocket and sharpened it, not moving from the edge of his bed because he did not want to disturb the silk cloth. Twice the point broke; the shavings collected on the floor at his feet. He began writing in the notebook, capital letters, like a prisoner writing to his wife, and every time he made a full stop he drew a ring around it the way he was taught long ago.

The message composed, he drew a line after every two letters, and beneath each compartment he entered the numerical equivalent according to the chart he had memorized: sometimes he had to resort to a mnemonic rhyme in order to recall the numbers; sometimes he remembered wrong and had to rub out and begin again. When he had finished he divided the line of numbers into groups of four and deducted each in turn from the groups on the silk cloth; finally he converted the figures into letters again and wrote out the result, redividing them into groups of four.

Fear like an old pain had again taken hold of his belly so that with every imagined sound he looked sharply toward the door, his hand arrested in the middle of writing. But he heard nothing; just the creaking of an aging house, like the noise of wind in the rigging of a ship.

He looked at the finished message, conscious that it was too long, and that if he were better at that kind of thing, if his mind were quicker, he could reduce it, but just now he couldn't think of a way, and he knew, he had been taught, better put in a word or two too many than make it ambiguous the other end. There were forty-two groups.

He pushed the table away from the window and lifted the suitcase; with the key from his chain he unlocked it, praying all the time that nothing was broken from the journey. He opened the spares box, discovering with his trembling fingers the silk bag of crystals bound with green ribbon at the mouth. Loosening the ribbon, he shook the crystals onto the coarse blanket which covered the bed. Each was labeled in Johnson's handwriting, first the frequency and below it a single figure denoting the place where it came in the signal plan. He arranged them in line, pressing them into the blanket so that they lay flat. The crystals were the easiest part. He tested the door against the armchair. The handle slipped in his palm. The chair provided no protection. In the war, he remembered, they had given him steel wedges. Returning to the suitcase he connected the transmitter and receiver to the power pack, plugged in the earphones and unscrewed the Morse key from the lid of the spares box. Then he saw it.

Mounted inside the suitcase lid was a piece of adhesive paper with half a dozen groups of letters and beside each its Morse equivalent; they were the international code for standard phrases, the ones he could never remember.

When he saw those letters, drawn out in Jack's neat, postoffice hand, tears of gratitude started to his eyes. He never told me, he thought, he never told me he'd done it. Jack was all right after all. Jack, the Captain and young John; what a team to work for, he thought; a man could go through life and never meet a set of blokes like that. He steadied himself, pressing his hands sharply on the table. He was trembling a little, perhaps from the cold; his damp shirt clung to his shoulder-blades; but he was happy. He glanced at the chair in front of the door and thought: When I've got the headphones on I shan't hear them coming, the way the boy didn't hear me because of the wind.

Next he attached aerial and earth to their terminals, led the earth wire to the water pipe and fastened the two strands to the cleaned surface with tabs of adhesive plaster. Standing on the bed, he stretched the aerial across the ceiling in eight lengths, zigzag as Johnson had instructed, fixing it as best he could to the curtain rail or plaster on either side. This done, he returned to the set and adjusted the wave-bank switch to the fourth position, because he knew that all the frequencies were in the three-megacycle range. He took from the bed the first crystal in the line, plugged it into the far left-hand corner of the set, and settled down to tune the transmitter, muttering gently as he performed each movement. Adjust crystal selector to "Fundamental all crystals," plug the coil; anode tuning and aerial matching controls to ten.

He hesitated, trying to remember what happened next. A block was forming in his mind. "PA—don't you know what PA stands for?" He set the meter switch to three to read the Power Amplifier grid current . . . TSR switch to T for tuning. It was coming back to him. Meter switch to six to ascertain total current . . . anode tuning for minimum reading.

Now he turned the TSR switch to S for send, pressed the key briefly, took a reading, manipulated the aerial matching control so that the meter reading rose slightly; hastily readjusted the anode tuning. He repeated the procedure until to his profound relief he saw the finger dip against the white background of the kidney-shaped dial and knew that the transmitter and aerial were correctly tuned, and that he could talk to John and Jack.

He sat back with a grunt of satisfaction, lit a cigarette, wished it were an English one because if they came in now they wouldn't have to bother about the brand of cigarette he was smoking. He looked at his watch, turning the winder until it was stiff, terrified lest it run down; it was matched with Avery's and in a simple way this gave him comfort. Like divided lovers, they were looking at the same star.

He had killed that boy.

Three minutes to schedule. He had unscrewed the Morse key from the spares box because he couldn't manage it properly while it was on that lid. Jack had said it was all right; he said it didn't matter. He had to hold the key base with his left hand so that it didn't slide about, but Jack said every operator had his quirks. He was sure it was smaller than the one they gave him in the war; he was sure of it. Traces of French chalk clung to the lever. He drew in his elbows and straightened his back. The third finger of his right hand crooked over the key. JAJ's my first call sign, he thought, Johnson's my name, they call me Jack, that's easy enough to remember. JA, John Avery; JJ, Jack Johnson. Then he was tapping it out. A dot and three dashes, dot dash, a dot and three dashes, and he kept thinking: It's like the house in Holland, but there's no one with me.

Say it twice, Fred, then get off the air. He switched over to receive, pushed the sheet of paper further toward the middle of the table and suddenly realized he had nothing to write with when Jack came through.

He stood up and looked around for his notebook and pencil, the sweat breaking out on his back. They were nowhere to be seen. Dropping hastily to his hands and knees he felt in the thick dust under the bed, found the pencil, groped vainly for his notebook. As he was getting up he heard a crackle from the earphones. He ran to the table, pressed one phone to his ear, at the same time trying to hold still the sheet of paper so that he could write in a corner of it beside his own message.

"QSA3: hearing you well enough," that's all they were saying. "Steady, boy, steady," he muttered. He settled into the chair, switched to transmit, looked at his own encoded message and tapped out four-two because there were forty-two groups. His hand was coated with dust and sweat, his right arm ached, perhaps from carrying the suitcase. Or struggling with the boy.

You've got all the time in the world, Johnson had said. We'll be listening: you're not passing an exam. He took his handkerchief from his pocket and wiped away the grime from his hands. He was terribly tired; the tiredness was like a physical despair, like the moment of guilt before making love. Groups of four letters, Johnson had said, think of four-letter words, eh Fred? You don't need to do it all at once, Fred, have a little stop in the middle if you like; two and a half minutes on the first frequency, two and a half on the second, that's the way we go; Mrs. Hartbeck will wait, I'm sure. With his pencil he drew a heavy line under the ninth letter because that was where the safety device came. That was something he dared think of only in passing.

He put his face in his hands, summoning the last of his concentration, then reached for the key and began tapping. Keep the hand loose, first and second fingers on top of the key, thumb beneath the edge, no, putting the wrist on the table, Fred. Breathe regular, Fred, you'll find it helps you to relax.

God, why were his hands so slow? Once he took his fingers from the key and stared impotently at his open palm; once he ran his left hand across his forehead to keep the sweat from his eyes, and he felt the key drifting across the table. His wrist was too stiff: the hand he killed the boy with. All the time he was saying it over to himself—dot, dot, dash, then a K, he always knew that one. A dot between two dashes—his lips were spelling out the letters, but his hand wouldn't follow, it was a kind of stammer that got worse the more he spoke, and always the boy in his mind, only the boy. Perhaps he was quicker than he thought. He lost all notion of time; the sweat was running into his eyes, he couldn't stop it anymore. He kept mouthing the dots and dashes, and he knew that Johnson would be angry because he shouldn't be thinking in dots and dashes at all but musically, de-dah dah, the way the professionals did, but Johnson hadn't killed the boy. The pounding of his heart outran the weary tapping of the key; his hand seemed to grow heavier and still he went on signaling because it was the only thing left to do, the only thing to hold on to while his body gave way. He was waiting for them now, wishing they'd come—take me, take it all—longing for the footsteps. Give us your hand, John; give us a hand.

When at last he had finished, he went back to the bed. Almost with detachment he caught sight of the line of crystals on the blanket, untouched, still and ready, dressed by the left and numbered, flat on their backs like dead sentries.

Avery looked at his watch. It was quarter past ten. "He should come on in five minutes," he said.

Leclerc announced suddenly: "That was Gorton on the telephone. He's received a telegram from the Ministry. They have some news for us apparently. They're sending out a courier."

"What could that be?" Avery asked.

"I expect it's the Hungarian thing. Fielden's report. I may have to go back to London." A satisfied smile. "But I think you people can get along without me."

Johnson was wearing earphones, sitting forward on a high-backed wooden chair carried up from the kitchen. The dark green receiver hummed gently from the mains transformer; the tuning dial, illuminated from within, glowed palely in the half light of the attic.

Haldane and Avery sat uncomfortably on a bench. Johnson had a pad and pencil in front of him. He lifted the phones above his ears and said to Leclerc who stood beside him, "I shall take him straight through the routine, sir; I'll do my best to tell you what's going on. I'm recording too, mind, for safety's sake."

"I understand."

They waited in silence. Suddenly—it was their moment of utter magic—Johnson had sat bolt upright, nodded sharply to them, switched on the tape recorder. He smiled, quickly turned to transmission and was tapping. "Come in, Fred," he said out loud. "Hearing you nicely."

"He's made it!" Leclerc hissed. "He's on target now!" His eyes were bright with excitement. "Do you hear that, John? Do you hear?"

"Shall we be quiet?" Haldane suggested.

"Here he comes," Johnson said. His voice was level, controlled. "Forty-two groups."

"Forty-two!" Leclerc repeated.

Johnson's body was motionless, his head inclined a little

to one side, his whole concentration given to the earphones, his face impassive in the pale light.

"I'd like silence now, please."

For perhaps two minutes his careful hand moved briskly across the pad. Now and then he muttered inaudibly, whispered a letter or shook his head, until the message seemed to come more slowly, his pencil pausing while he listened, until it was tracing out each letter singly with agonizing care. He glanced at the clock.

"Come on, Fred," he urged, "come on, change over, that's nearly three minutes." But still the message was coming through, letter by letter, and Johnson's simple face assumed an expression of alarm.

"What's going on?" Leclerc demanded. "Why hasn't he changed his frequency?"

But Johnson only said, "Get off the air, for Christ's sake, Fred, get off the air."

Leclerc touched him impatiently on the arm. Johnson raised one earphone.

"Why's he not changed frequency? Why's he still talking?"

"He must have forgotten! He never forgot on training. I *know* he's slow, but Christ!" He was still writing automatically. "Five minutes," he muttered. "Five bloody minutes. Change the bloody crystal!"

"Can't you tell him?" Leclerc cried.

"Of course I can't. How can I? He can't receive and send at the same time!"

They sat or stood in dreadful fascination. Johnson had turned to them, his voice beseeching. "I told him; if I told him once I told him a dozen times. It's bloody suicide, what he's doing!" He looked at his watch. "He's been on damn near six minutes. Bloody, bloody, *bloody* fool."

"What will they do?" said Haldane.

"If they pick up the signal? Call in another station, take a fix. Then it's simple trigonometry when he's on this long." He banged his open hands helplessly on the table, indicated the set as if it were an affront. "A kid could do it. Do it with a pair of compasses. Christ Almighty! Come on, Fred, for Jesus' sake, come on!" He wrote down a handful of letters, then threw his pencil aside. "It's on tape, anyway," he said.

Leclerc turned to Haldane. "Surely there's something we can do!"

"Be quiet," Haldane said.

The message stopped. Johnson tapped an acknowledgment fast, a stab of hatred. He wound back the tape recorder and began transcribing. Putting the coding sheet in front of him he worked without interruption for perhaps a quarter of an hour, occasionally making simple sums on the rough paper at his elbow. No one spoke. When he had finished he stood up, a half-forgotten gesture of respect. "Message reads: Area Kalkstadt closed three days mid-November when fifty unidentified Soviet troops seen in town. No special equipment. Rumors of Soviet maneuvers farther north. Troops believed moved to Rostock. Fritsche not repeat not known Kalkstadt railway station. No road check on Kalkstadt road." He tossed the paper on to the desk. "There are fifteen groups after that which I can't unbutton. I think he's muddled his coding."

The Vopo sergeant in Rostock picked up the telephone; he was an elderly man, graying and thoughtful. He listened for a moment, then began dialing on another line. "It must be a child," he said, still dialing. "What frequency did you say?" He put the other telephone to his ear and spoke into it fast, repeating the frequency three times. He walked into the adjoining hut. "Witmar will be through in a minute," he said. "They're taking a fix. Are you still hearing him?" The corporal nodded. The sergeant held a spare headphone to his ear.

"It couldn't be an amateur," he muttered. "Breaking the regulations. But what is it? No agent in his right mind would put out a signal like that. What are the neighboring frequencies? Military or civilian?"

"It's near the military. Very near."

"That's odd," the sergeant said. "That would fit, wouldn't it? That's what they did in the war."

The corporal was staring at the tapes slowly revolving on their spindles. "He's still transmitting. Groups of four."

"Four?" The sergeant was searching in his memory for something that had happened long ago.

"Let me hear again. Listen, listen to the fool! He's as slow as a child."

The sound struck some chord in his memory—the slurred gaps, the dots so short as to be little more than clicks. He could swear he knew that hand . . . from the war, in Norway . . . but not so slow: nothing had ever been as slow as this. Not Norway . . . France. Perhaps it was only imagination. Yes, it was imagination.

"Or an old man," the corporal said.

The telephone rang. The sergeant listened for a moment, then ran, ran as fast as he could, through the hut to the officers' mess across the tarmac path.

The Russian captain was drinking beer; his jacket was slung over the back of his chair and he looked very bored. "You wanted something, Sergeant?" He affected the languid style.

"He's come. The man they told us about. The one who killed the boy."

The captain put down his beer quickly.

"You heard him?"

"We've taken a fix. With Witmar. Groups of four. A slow hand. Area Kalkstadt. Close to one of our own frequencies. Sommer recorded the transmission."

"Christ," he said quietly. The sergeant frowned.

"What's he looking for? Why should they send him here?" the sergeant asked.

The captain was buttoning his jacket. "Ask them in Leipzig. Perhaps they know that too."

21.

IT WAS VERY LATE.

The fire in Control's grate was burning nicely, but he poked at it with effeminate discontent. He hated working at night.

"They want you at the Ministry," he said irritably. "Now, of all hours. It really is too bad. Why does everyone get so agitato on a Thursday? It will *ruin* the weekend." He put down the poker and returned to his desk. "They're in a dreadful state. Some idiot talking about ripples in a pond. It's extraordinary what the night does to people. I do *detest* the telephone." There were several in front of him.

Smiley offered him a cigarette and he took one without looking at it, as if he could not be held responsible for the actions of his limbs.

"What Ministry?" Smiley asked.

"Leclerc's. Have you *any* idea what's going on?"

Smiley said. "Yes. Haven't you?"

"Leclerc's so *vulgar*. I admit, I find him vulgar. He thinks we compete. What on earth would *I* do with his dreadful militia? Scouring Europe for mobile laundries. He thinks I want to gobble him up."

"Well don't you? Why *did* we cancel that passport?"

"What a *silly* man. A silly, vulgar man. However did Haldane fall for it?"

"He had a conscience once. He's like all of us. He's learnt to live with it."

"Oh dear. Is that a dig at me?"

"What does the Ministry want?" Smiley asked sharply.

Control held up some papers, flapping them. "You've seen these from Berlin?"

"They came in an hour ago. The Americans have taken a fix. Groups of four; a primitive letter code. They say it comes from the Kalkstadt area."

"Where on *earth's* that?"

"South of Rostock. The message ran six minutes on the same frequency. They said it sounded like an amateur on a first runthrough. One of the old wartime sets: they wanted to know if it was ours."

"And you replied?" Control asked quickly.

"I said no."

"So I should hope. Good Lord."

"You don't seem very concerned," Smiley said.

Control seemed to remember something from long ago. "I hear Leclerc's in Lübeck. Now *there's* a pretty town. I adore Lübeck. The Ministry wants you immediately. I said you'd go. Some meeting." He added in apparent earnest, "You must, George. We've been the most awful fools. It's in every East German newspaper; they're screaming about peace conferences and sabotage." He prodded at a telephone. "So is the Ministry. God, how I loathe Civil Servants."

Smiley watched him with skepticism. "We could have stopped them," he said. "We knew enough."

"Of course we could," Control said blandly. "Do you know why we didn't? Plain, idiot Christian charity. We let them have their war game. You'd better go now. And Smiley . . ."

"Yes?"

"Be gentle." And in his silly voice: "I do envy them Lübeck all the same. There's that restaurant, isn't there; what do they call it? Where Thomas Mann used to eat. So interesting."

"He never did," Smiley said. "The place you're thinking of was bombed."

Smiley still did not go. "I wonder," he said. "You'll never tell me, will you? I just wonder." He was not looking at Control.

"My dear George, what *has* come over you?"

"We handed it to them. The passport that was canceled

. . . a courier service they never needed . . . a clapped-out wireless set . . . papers, frontier reports . . . who told Berlin to listen for him? Who told them what frequencies? We even gave Leclerc the crystals, didn't we? Was that just Christian charity too? Plain, idiot Christian charity?"

Control was shocked.

"What *are* you suggesting? How *very* distasteful. Who-ever would do a thing like that?"

Smiley was putting on his coat.

"Good night, George," Control said; and fiercely, as if he were tired of sensibility: "Run along. And preserve the difference between us: your country needs you. It's not *my* fault they've taken so long to die."

The dawn came and Leiser had not slept. He wanted to wash but dared not go into the corridor. He dared not move. If they were looking for him, he knew he must leave normally, not bolt from the hostel before the morning came. Never run, they used to say: walk like the crowd. He could go at six: that was late enough. He rubbed his chin against the back of his hand: it was sharp and rough, marking the brown skin.

He was hungry and no longer knew what to do, but he would not run.

He half turned on the bed, pulled the knife from inside the waistband of his trousers and held it before his eyes. He was shivering. He could feel across his brow the un-natural heat of incipient fever. He looked at the knife, and remembered the clean, friendly way they had talked: thumb on top, blade parallel to the ground, forearm stiff. "Go away," the old man had said. "You are either good or bad and both are dangerous." How should he hold the knife when people spoke to him like that? The way he held it for the boy?

It was six o'clock. He stood up. His legs were heavy and stiff. His shoulders still ached from carrying the rucksack. His clothes, he noticed, smelled of pine and leaf-mold. He picked the half-dried mud from his trousers and put on his second pair of shoes.

He went downstairs, looking for someone to pay, the new shoes squeaking on the wooden steps. There was an old woman in white overalls sorting lentils into a bowl, talking to a cat.

"What do I owe?"

"You fill in the form," she said sourly. "That's the first thing you owe. You should have done it when you came."

"I'm sorry."

She rounded on him, muttering but not daring to raise her voice. "Don't you know it's forbidden, staying in town and not reporting your presence to the police?" She looked at his new shoes. "Or are you so rich that you think you need not trouble?"

"I'm sorry," Leiser said again. "Give me the form and I'll sign it now. I'm not rich."

The woman fell silent, picking studiously among the lentils.

"Where do you come from?" she asked.

"East," Leiser said. He meant south, from Magdeburg, or west from Wilmsdorf.

"You should have reported last night. It's too late now."

"What do I pay?"

"You can't," the woman replied. "Never mind. You haven't filled in the form. What will you say if they catch you?"

"I'll say I slept with a girl."

"It's snowing outside," the woman said. "Mind your nice shoes."

Grains of hard snow drifted forlornly in the wind, collecting in the cracks between the black cobbles, lingering on the stucco of the houses. A drab, useless snow, dwindling where it fell.

He crossed the Friedensplatz and saw a new, yellow building, six or seven stories high, standing on a patch of wasteland beside a new estate. There was washing hanging on the balconies, touched with snow. The staircase smelled of food and Russian petrol. The flat was on the third floor. He could hear a child crying and a wireless playing. For a moment he thought he should turn and go away, because he was dangerous for them. He pressed the bell twice, as the girl had told him. She opened the door; she was half asleep. She had put on her mackintosh over the cotton nightdress and she held it at the neck because of the freez-

ing cold. When she saw him she hesitated, not knowing
what to do, as if he had brought bad news. He said
nothing, just stood there with the suitcase swinging gently
at his side. She beckoned with her head; he followed her
across the corridor to her room, put the suitcase and
rucksack in the corner. There were travel posters on the
walls, pictures of desert, palm trees and the moon over a
tropical sea. They got into bed and she covered him with
her heavy body, trembling a little because she was afraid.

"I want to sleep," he said. "Let me sleep first."

The Russian captain said, "He stole a motorbike at
Wilmsdorf and asked for Fritsche at the station. What will
he do now?"

"He'll have another schedule. Tonight," the sergeant replied. "If he's got anything to say."

"At the same time?"

"Of course not. Nor the same frequency. Nor from the
same place. He may go to Witmar or Langdorn or Wolken;
he may even go to Rostock. Or he may stay in town but go
to another house. Or he may not send at all."

"House? Who would harbor a spy?"

The sergeant shrugged as if to say he might himself.
Stung, the captain asked, "How do you know he's sending
from a house? Why not a wood or a field? How can you be
so sure?"

"It's a very strong signal. A powerful set. He couldn't
get a signal like that from a battery, not a battery you
could carry around alone. He's using the mains."

"Put a cordon around the town," the captain said.
"Search every house."

"We want him alive." The sergeant was looking at his
hands. "You want him alive."

"Then tell me what we should do?" the captain insisted.

"Make sure he transmits. That's the first thing. And
make him stay in town. That is the second."

"Well?"

"We would have to act quickly," the sergeant observed.

"Well?"

"Bring some troops into town. Anything you can find.
As soon as possible. Armor, infantry, it doesn't matter.

Create some movement. Make him pay attention. But be quick!"

"I'll go soon," Leiser said. "Don't let me stay. Give me coffee and I'll go."

"Coffee?"

"I've got money," Leiser said, as if it were the only thing he had. "Here." He climbed out of bed, fetched the wallet from his jacket and drew a hundred-mark note from the wad.

"Keep it."

She took the wallet and with a little laugh emptied it out on the bed. She had a ponderous, kittenish way which was not quite sane; and the quick instinct of an illiterate. He watched her indifferently, running his fingers along the line of her naked shoulder. She held up a photograph of a woman; a blond, round head.

"Who is she? What is her name?"

"She doesn't exist," he said.

She found the letters and read one aloud, laughing at the affectionate passages. "Who is she?" she kept taunting him. "Who is she?"

"I tell you, she doesn't exist."

"Then I can tear them up?" She held a letter before him with both hands, teasing him, waiting for him to protest. Leiser said nothing. She made a little tear, still watching him, then tore it completely, and a second and a third.

She found a picture of a child, a girl in spectacles, eight or nine years old perhaps, and again she asked, "Who is it? Is it your child? Does *she* exist?"

"Nobody. Nobody's kid. Just a photograph." She tore that too, scattering the pieces dramatically over the bed, then fell on him, kissing him on the face and neck. "Who are you? What is your name?"

He wanted to tell her when she pushed him away.

"No!" she cried. "No!" She lowered her voice. "I want you with nothing. Alone from it all. You and me alone. We'll make our own names, our own rules. Nobody, no one at all, no father, no mother. We'll print our own newspapers, passes, ration cards; make our own people." She was whispering, her eyes shining.

"You're a spy," she said, her lips in his ear. "A secret agent. You've got a gun."

"A knife is quieter," he said. She laughed, on and on, until she noticed the bruises on his shoulders. She touched them curiously, with respect, as a child might touch a dead thing.

She went out carrying a shopping basket, still clutching the mackintosh at her neck. Leiser dressed, shaving in cold water, staring at his lined face in the distorted mirror above the basin. When she returned it was nearly midday and she looked worried.

"The town's full of soldiers. And Army trucks. What do they want here?"

"Perhaps they are looking for someone."

"They are just sitting about, drinking."

"What kind of soldiers?"

"I don't know what kind. Russian . . . How can I tell?"

He went to the door. "I'll come back in an hour."

She said, "You're trying to get away from me." She held his arm, looking up at him, wanting to make a scene.

"I'll come back. Maybe not till later. Maybe this evening. But if I do . . ."

"Yes?"

"It will be dangerous. I shall have to . . . do something here. Something dangerous."

She kissed him, a light, silly kiss. "I like danger," she said.

"Four hours," Johnson said. "If he's still alive."

"Of course he's alive," Avery said angrily. "Why do you talk like that?"

Haldane interrupted. "Don't be an ass, Avery. It's a technical term. Dead or live agents. It has nothing to do with his physical condition."

Leclerc was drumming his fingers lightly on the table.

"He'll be all right," he said. "Fred's a hard man to kill. He's an old hand." The daylight had revived him apparently. He glanced at his watch. "What the devil's happened to that courier, I wonder?"

Leiser blinked at the soldiers like a man emerging from the dark. They filled the cafés, gazed into shopwindows, looked at the girls. Trucks were parked in the square, their wheels thick with red mud, a thin surface of snow on their hoods. He counted them and there were nine. Some had heavy couplings at the rear for pulling trailers; some a line of Cyrillic script on their battered doors, or the imprint of unit insignia and a number. He noted the emblems of the drivers' uniforms, the color of their shoulder-boards; they came, he realized, from a variety of units.

Walking back to the main street he pushed his way into a café and ordered a drink. Half a dozen soldiers sat disconsolately at a table, sharing three bottles of beer. Leiser grinned at them; it was like the encouragement of a tired whore. He lifted his fist in a Soviet salute and they watched him as if he were mad. He left his drink and made his way back to the square; a group of children had gathered around the trucks, and the drivers kept telling them to go away.

He made a tour of the town, went into a dozen cafés, but no one would talk to him because he was a stranger. Everywhere the soldiers sat or stood in groups, aggrieved and bewildered, as if they had been roused to no purpose.

He ate some sausage and drank a Steinhäger, walked to the station to see if anything was going on. The same man was there, watching him, this time without suspicion, from behind his little window; and somehow Leiser knew, though it made no difference, that the man had told the police.

Returning from the station, he passed a cinema. A group of girls had gathered around the photographs and he stood with them, pretending to look. Then the noise came, a metallic, irregular drone, filling the street with the piping rattling of engines, metal and war. He drew back into the cover of the foyer, saw the girls turn and the ticket seller stand up in her box. An old man crossed himself; he had lost one eye, and wore his hat at an angle. The tanks rolled through the town; they carried troops with rifles. The gun barrels were too long, marked white with snow. He watched them pass, then made his way across the square quickly.

She smiled as he came in; he was out of breath.

"What are they doing?" she asked. She caught sight of his face. "You're afraid," she whispered, but he shook his head. "You're afraid," she repeated.

"I killed the boy," he said.

He went to the basin, examined his face with the great care of a man under sentence. She followed him, clasped him around the chest, pressing herself against his back. He turned and seized her, wild, held her without skill, forced her across the room. She fought him with the rage of a daughter, calling some name, hating someone, cursing him, taking him, the world burning and only they alive; they were weeping, laughing together, falling, clumsy lovers clumsily triumphant, recognizing nothing but each himself, each for that moment completing lives half-lived, and for that moment the whole damned dark forgotten.

Johnson leaned out of the window and gently drew on the aerial to make sure it was still fast, then began looking over his receiver like a racing driver before the start, needlessly touching terminals and adjusting dials. Leclerc watched him admiringly.

"Johnson, that was nobly done last time. Nobly done. We owe you a vote of thanks." Leclerc's face was shiny, as if he had only recently shaved. He looked oddly fragile in the pale light. "I propose to hear one more schedule and get back to London." He laughed. "We've work to do, you know. This isn't the season for continental holidays."

Johnson might not have heard. He held up his hand. "Thirty minutes," he said. "I shall be asking you for a little hush soon, gentlemen." He was like a conjurer at a children's party. "Fred's a devil for punctuality," he observed loudly.

Leclerc addressed himself to Avery. "You're one of those lucky people, John, who have seen action in peacetime." He seemed anxious to talk.

"Yes. I'm very grateful."

"You don't have to be. You've done a good job, and we recognize that. There's no question of *gratitude*. You've achieved something very rare in our work. I wonder if you know what it is?"

Avery said he did not.

"You've induced an agent to *like* you. In the ordinary way—Adrian will bear me out—the relationship between an agent and his controllers is clouded with suspicion. He resents them, that's the first thing, for not doing the job themselves. He suspects them of ulterior motives, ineptitude, duplicity. But we're not the Circus, John: that's not the way we do things."

Avery nodded. "No, quite."

"You've done something else, you and Adrian. I would like to feel that if a similar need arose in the future we could use the same technique, the same facilities, the same *expertise*—that means the Avery-Haldane combination. What I'm trying to say is"—Leclerc raised one hand and with his forefinger and thumb lightly touched the bridge of his nose in an unusual gesture of English diffidence—"the experience you've made is to our mutual advantage. Thank you."

Haldane moved to the stove and began warming his hands, rubbing them gently as if he were separating wheat.

"That Budapest thing," Leclerc continued, raising his voice, partly in enthusiasm and partly perhaps to dispel the atmosphere of intimacy which suddenly threatened them: "It's a complete reorganization. Nothing less. They're moving their armor to the border, do you see. The Ministry is talking about forward strategy. They're really most interested."

Avery said, "More interested than in the Mayfly area?"

"No, no," Leclerc protested lightly. "It's all part of the same complex—they think very big over there, you know —a move here and a move there—it all has to be pieced together."

"Of course," Avery said gently. "We can't see it ourselves, can we? We can't see the whole picture." He was trying to make it better for Leclerc. "We haven't the perspective."

"When we get back to London," Leclerc proposed, "you must come and dine with me, John: you and your wife; both come. I've been meaning to suggest it for some time. We'll go to my club. They do a rather good dinner in the ladies' dining room; your wife would enjoy it."

"You mentioned it. I asked Sarah. We'd love to. My mother-in-law's with us just now. She could baby-sit."

"How nice. Don't forget."

"We're looking forward to it."

"Am I not invited?" Haldane asked coyly.

"Why of course, Adrian. Then we shall be four. Excellent." His voice changed. "Incidentally, the landlords have complained about the house in Oxford. They say we left it in a poor state."

"Poor state?" Haldane echoed angrily.

"It appears we have been overloading the electrical circuit. Parts of it are quite burnt out. I told Woodford to cope with it."

"We should have our own place," said Avery. "Then we wouldn't have to worry."

"I agree. I spoke to the Minister about it. A training center is what we need. He was enthusiastic. He's keen on this kind of thing, now, you know. They have a new phrase for it over there. They are speaking of ICOs—Immediate Clarification Operations. He suggests we find a place and take it for six months. He proposes to speak to the Treasury about a lease."

"That's terrific," Avery said.

"It could be very useful. We must be sure not to abuse our trust."

"Of course."

There was a draft, followed by the sound of someone cautiously ascending the stairs. A figure appeared in the attic doorway. He wore an expensive overcoat of brown tweed, a little too long in the sleeve. It was Smiley.

22.

SMILEY PEERED around the room, at Johnson, now in earphones, busy with the controls of his set, at Avery staring over Haldane's shoulder at the signal plan, at Leclerc who stood like a soldier, who alone had noticed him, whose face, though turned to him, was empty and far away.

"What do you want here?" Leclerc said at last. "What do you want with me?"

"I'm sorry. I was sent."

"So were we all," Haldane said, not moving.

A note of warning entered Leclerc's voice. "This is my operation, Smiley. We've no room for your people here."

There was nothing in Smiley's face but compassion, nothing in his voice but that dreadful patience with which we speak to the insane.

"It wasn't Control who sent me," he said. "It was the Ministry. They asked for me, you see, and Control let me go. The Ministry laid on a plane."

"Why?" Haldane inquired. He seemed almost amused.

One by one they stirred, waking from a single dream. Johnson laid his earphones carefully on the table.

"Well?" Leclerc asked. "Why did they send you?"

"They called me around last night." He managed to indicate that he was as bewildered as they. "I had to admire the operation, the way you'd conducted it; you and Haldane. All done from nothing. They showed me the files. Scrupulously kept . . . Library Copy, Operational Copy,

sealed minutes: just like in the war. I congratulate you
. . . I really do."

"They showed you the files? *Our* files?" Leclerc repeated. "That's a breach of security: interconsciousness
between Departments. You've committed an offense, Smiley.
They must be mad! Adrian, do you hear what Smiley has
told me?"

Smiley said, "Is there a schedule tonight, Johnson?"

"Yes, sir. Twenty-one hundred."

"I was surprised, Adrian, that you felt the indicators
were strong enough for such a *big* operation."

"Haldane was not responsible," Leclerc said crisply.
"The decision was a collective one: ourselves on the one
side, the Ministry on the other." His voice changed key.
"When the schedule is finished I shall want to know, Smiley,
I have a right to know, how you came to see those
files." It was his committee voice, powerful and fluent; for
the first time it had the ring of dignity.

Smiley moved toward the center of the room. "Something's happened; something you couldn't know about.
Leiser killed a man on the border. Killed him with a knife
as he went over, two miles from here, at the crossing
point."

Haldane said, "That's absurd. It needn't be Leiser. It
could have been a refugee coming west. It could have been
anyone."

"They found tracks leading east. Traces of blood in the
hut by the lake. It's in all the East German papers. They've
been putting it over the wireless since midday yesterday—"

Leclerc criied, "I don't believe it. I don't believe he did
it. It's some trick of Control's."

"No," Smiley replied gently. "You've got to believe me.
It's true."

"They killed Taylor," Leclerc said. "Have you forgotten
that?"

"No, of course not. But we shall never know, shall we?
How he died, I mean. Whether he was murdered
. . ." Hurriedly he continued, "Your Ministry informed the
Foreign Office yesterday afternoon. The Germans are
bound to catch him, you see; we have to assume that. His
transmissions are slow . . . very slow. Every policeman,
every soldier, is after him. They want him alive. We think

they're going to stage a show trial, extract a public confession, display the equipment. It could be very embarrassing. You don't have to be a politician to sympathize with the Minister. So there's the question of what to do."

Leclerc said, "Johnson, keep an eye on the clock." Johnson put on his earphones, but without conviction.

Smiley appeared to want someone else to speak, but no one did, so he repeated ponderously, "It's a question of what to do. As I say, we're not politicians, but one can see the dangers. A party of Englishmen in a farmhouse two miles from where the body was found, posing as academics, stores from the Naafi and a house full of radio equipment. You see what I mean? Making your transmissions," he went on, "on a single frequency . . . the frequency Leiser receives on. . . . There could be a very big scandal indeed. One can imagine even the West Germans getting awfully angry."

Haldane spoke first again: "What are you trying to say?"

"There's a military plane waiting at Hamburg. You fly in two hours; all of you. A truck will collect the equipment. You're to leave nothing behind, not even a pin. Those are my instructions."

Leclerc said, "What about the target? Have they forgotten why we're here? They're asking a lot, you know, Smiley: a great lot."

"Yes, the target," Smiley conceded. "We'll have a conference in London. Perhaps we could do a joint operation."

"It's a military target. I shall want my Ministry represented. No monolith: it's a policy decision, you know."

"Of course. And it'll be your show."

"I suggest the product go out under our joint title: my Ministry could retain autonomy in the matter of distribution. I imagine that would meet their more obvious objections. How about your people?"

"Yes, I think Control would accept that."

Leclerc said casually, everyone watching, "And the schedule? Who takes care of that? We've an agent in the field, you know." It was only a small point.

"He'll have to manage by himself."

"The war rules," Leclerc spoke proudly, "we play the

war rules. He knew that. He was well trained." He seemed reconciled; the thing was dismissed.

Avery spoke for the first time. "You can't leave him out there alone." His voice was flat.

Leclerc intervened: "You know Avery, my aide?" This time no one came to his rescue. Smiley, ignoring him, observed, "The man's probably been caught already. It's only a matter of hours."

"You're leaving him there to die!" Avery was gathering courage.

"We're disowning him. It's never a pretty process. He's as good as caught already, don't you see?"

"You can't do it," he shouted. "You can't just leave him there for some squalid diplomatic reason!"

Now Haldane swung around on Avery, furious. "You of all people should not complain! You wanted a faith, didn't you? You wanted an eleventh Commandment that would match your rare soul!" He indicated Smiley and Leclerc. "Well, here you have it: here is the law you were looking for. Congratulate yourself; you found it. We sent him because we needed to; we abandon him because we must. That is the discipline you admired." He turned to Smiley. "You too: I find you contemptible. You shoot us, then preach to the dying. Go away. We're technicians, not poets. Go away!"

Smiley said, "Yes. You're a very good technician, Adrian. There's no pain in you anymore. You've made technique a way of life . . . like a whore . . . technique replacing love." He hesitated. "Little flags . . . the old war piping in the new. There was all that, wasn't there? And then the man . . . he must have been heady wine. Comfort yourself, Adrian, you weren't fit."

He straightened his back, making a statement. "A British-naturalized Pole with a criminal record escapes across the border to East Germany. There is no extradition treaty. The Germans will say he is a spy and produce the equipment; we shall say they planted it and point out that it's twenty-five years old. I understand he put out a cover story that he was attending a course in Coventry. That is easily disproved: there is no such course. The conclusion is that he proposed to flee the country; and we shall imply that he owed money. He was keeping some young girl, you know; she worked in a bank. That ties in quite nicely. I mean with the criminal record, since we have to make one up. . . ." He nodded to himself. "As I say, it's not an attractive process. By then we shall all be in London."

"And he'll be transmitting," Avery said, "and no one will listen!"

"To the contrary," Smiley retorted bitterly. "They'll be listening."

Haldane asked: "Control too, no doubt. Isn't that right?"

"Stop!" Avery shouted suddenly, "Stop for God's sake! If anything matters, if anything is real, we've got to hear him now! For the sake of . . ."

"Well?" Haldane inquired with a sneer.

"Love. Yes, love! Not yours, Haldane, mine. Smiley's right! You made me do it for you, made me love him! It wasn't in you anymore! I brought him to you, I kept him in your house, made him dance to the music of your bloody war! I piped for him, but there's no breath in me now. He's Peter Pan's last victim, Haldane, the last one, the last love; the last music gone."

Haldane was looking at Smiley: "My congratulations to Control," he said. "Thank him, will you? Thank him for the help, the *technical* help, Smiley; for the encouragement, thank him for the rope. For the kind words too: for lending you to bring the flowers. So nicely done."

But Leclerc seemed impressed by the neatness of it.

"Let's not be hard on Smiley, Adrian. He's only doing his job. We must all get back to London. There's the Fielden report . . . I'd like to show you that, Smiley. Troop dispositions in Hungary: something new."

"And I'd like to see it," Smiley replied politely.

"He's right, you know, Avery," Leclerc repeated. His voice was quite eager. "Be a soldier. Fortunes of war; keep to the rules! We play the war rules in this game. Smiley, I owe you an apology. And Control too, I fear. I had thought the old rivalry was still awake. I'm wrong." He inclined his head. "You must dine with me in London. My club is not your mark, I know, but it's quiet there; a good set. Very good. Haldane must come. Adrian, I invite you!"

Avery had buried his face in his hands.

"There's something else I want to discuss with you, Adrian—Smiley, you won't mind this I'm sure, you're practically one of the family—the question of Registry. The system of library files is really out of date. Bruce was on me about it just before I left. Poor Miss Courtney can hardly keep pace. I fear the answer is more copies . . . top copy to the case officer, carbons for information. There's a new machine on the market, cheap photostats, threepence halfpenny a copy, that seems quite reasonable in these dog days. . . . I must speak to the people about it . . . the Ministry . . . they know a good thing when they see one. Perhaps—" He broke off. "Johnson, I could wish you made less noise, we're still operational, you know." He spoke like a man intent upon appearances, conscious of tradition.

Johnson had gone to the window. Leaning on the sill he reached outside and with his customary precision began winding in the aerial. He held a spool in his left hand like a bobbin. As he gathered in the wire he gently turned it as an old woman spins her thread. Avery was sobbing like a child. No one heeded him.

23.

THE GREEN VAN MOVED slowly down the road, crossed the Station Square where the empty fountain stood. On its roof the small loop aerial turned this way and that like a hand feeling for the wind. Behind it, well back, were two trucks. The snow was settling at last. They drove on sidelights, twenty yards apart, following each other's tire marks.

The captain sat in the back of the van with a microphone for speaking to the driver, and beside him the sergeant, lost in private memories. The corporal crouched at his receiver, his hand constantly turning the dial as he watched the line tremble in the small screen.

"The transmission's stopped," he said suddenly.

"How many groups have you recorded?" the sergeant asked.

"A dozen. The call sign over and over again, then part of a message. I don't think he's getting any reply."

"Five letters or four?"

"Still four."

"Did he sign off?"

"No."

"What frequency was he using?"

"Three six five zero."

"Keep scanning across it. Two hundred either side."

"There's nothing there."

"Keep searching," he said sharply. "Right across the

band. He's changed the crystal. He'll take a few minutes to tune up."

The operator began spinning the large dial, slowly, watching the eye of green light in the center of the set which opened and closed as he crossed one station after another. "Here he is. Three eight seven zero. Different call sign but the same handwriting. Quicker than yesterday: better."

The tape recorder wound monotonously at his elbow. "He's working on alternating crystals," the sergeant said. "Like they did in the war. It's the same trick." He was embarrassed, an elderly man confronted with his past.

The corporal slowly raised his head. "This is it," he said. "Zero. We're right on top of him."

Quietly the two men dismounted from the van. "Wait here," the sergeant told the corporal. "Keep listening. If the signal breaks, even for a moment, tell the driver to flash the headlights, do you understand?"

"I'll tell him." The corporal looked frightened.

"If it stops altogether, keep searching and let me know."

"Pay attention," the captain warned as he dismounted. The sergeant was waiting impatiently; behind him, a tall building standing on wasteland.

In the distance, half hidden in the falling snow, lay row after row of small houses. No sound came.

"What do they call this place?" the captain asked.

"A block of flats; workers' flats. They haven't named it yet."

"No, beyond."

"Nothing. Follow me," the sergeant said. Pale lights shone in almost every window; six floors. Stone steps thick with leaves led to the cellar. The sergeant went first, shining his flashlight ahead of them on to the shoddy walls. The captain nearly fell. The first room was large and airless, half of brick and half unrendered plaster. At the far end were two steel doors. On the ceiling a single bulb burned behind a wire cage. The sergeant's flashlight was still on; he shone it needlessly into the corners.

"What are you looking for?" the captain asked.

The steel doors were locked.

"Find the janitor," the sergeant ordered, "quickly."

The captain ran up the stairs and returned with an old

man, unshaven, gently grumbling; he held a bunch of long keys on a chain. Some were rusty.

"The switches," said the sergeant. "For the building. Where are they?"

The old man sorted through the keys. He pushed one into the lock and it would not fit, he tried another and a third.

"Quick, you fool!" the captain shouted.

"Don't fuss him," said the sergeant.

The door opened. They pushed into the corridor, their flashlights playing over the whitewash. The janitor was holding up a key, grinning. "Always the last one," he said. The sergeant found what he was looking for, hidden on the wall behind the door; a box with a glass front. The captain put his hand to the main lever, had half pulled it when the other struck him roughly away.

"No! Go to the top of the stairs; tell me when the driver flashes his headlights."

"Who's in charge here?" the captain complained.

"Do as I ask." He had opened the box and was tugging gently at the first fuse, blinking through his gold-rimmed spectacles; a benign man.

With diligent, surgical fingers the sergeant drew out the fuse, cautiously, as if he were expecting an electric shock, then immediately replaced it, his eyes turning toward the figure at the top of the steps; then a second and still the captain said nothing. Outside the motionless soldiers watched the windows of the block, saw how floor by floor the lights went out, then quickly on again. The sergeant tried another and a fourth and this time he heard an excited cry from above him: "The headlights! The headlights have gone out."

"Quiet! Go and ask the driver which floor. But *quietly*."

"They'll never hear us in this wind," the captain said irritably, and a moment later: "The driver says third floor. The third floor light went out and the transmission stopped at the same time. It's starting again now."

"Put the men around the building," the sergeant said. "And pick five men to come with us. He's on the third floor."

Softly, like animals, the Vopos dismounted from the two trucks, their carbines held loosely in their hands, advancing

in a ragged line, plowing the thin snow, turning it to
nothing; some to the foot of the building, some standing
off, staring at the windows. A few wore helmets, and their
square silhouette was redolent of the war. From here and
there came a click as the first bullet was sprung gently into
the breech; the sound rose to a faint hail and died away.

Leiser unhooked the aerial and wound it back on the
reel, screwed the Morse key into the lid, replaced the earphones in the spares box and folded the silk cloth into the
handle of the razor.

"Twenty years," he protested, holding up the razor,
"and they still haven't found a better place."

"Why do you do it?"

She was sitting contentedly on the bed in her nightdress,
wrapped in the mackintosh as if it gave her company.

"Who do you talk to?" she asked again.

"No one. No one heard."

"Why do you do it, then?"

He had to say something so he said, "For peace."

He put on his jacket, went to the window and peered
outside. Snow lay on the houses. The wind blew angrily
across them. He glanced into the courtyard below, where
the silhouettes were waiting.

"Whose peace?" she asked.

"The light went out, didn't it, while I was working the
set?"

"Did it?"

"A short break, a second or two, like a power cut?"

"Yes."

"Put it out again now." He was very still. "Put the light
out."

"Why?"

"I like to look at the snow."

She put the light out and he drew the threadbare curtains. Outside the snow reflected a pale glow into the sky.
They were in half darkness.

"You said we'd love now," she complained.

"Listen; what's your name?"

He heard the rustle of her raincoat.

"What is it?" His voice was rough.

"Anna."

"Listen, Anna." He went to the bed. "I want to marry you," he said. "When I met you, in that inn, when I saw you sitting there, listening to the records, I fell in love with you, do you understand? I'm an engineer from Magdeburg, that's what I said; are you listening?"

He seized her arms and shook her. His voice was urgent.

"Take me away," she said.

"That's right! I said I'd make love to you, take you away to all the places you dreamed of, do you understand?" He pointed to the posters on the wall. "To islands, sunny places—"

"Why?" she whispered.

"I brought you back here. You thought it was to make love, but I drew this knife and threatened you. I said if you made a sound, I'd kill you with the knife, like I—I told you I'd killed the boy and I'd kill you."

"Why?"

"I had to use the wireless. I needed a house, see? Somewhere to work the wireless. I'd nowhere to go so I picked you up and used you. Listen: if they ask you, that's what you must say."

She laughed. She was afraid. She lay back uncertainly on her bed, inviting him to take her, as if that was what he wanted.

"If they ask, remember what I said."

"Make me happy. I love you."

She put out her arms and pulled his head toward her. Her lips were cold and damp, too thin against her sharp teeth. He drew away but she still held him. He strained his ears for any sound above the wind, but there was none.

"Let's talk a bit," he said. "Are you lonely, Anna? Who've you got?"

"What do you mean?"

"Parents, boy friend. Anyone."

She shook her head in the darkness. "Just you."

"Listen; here, let's button your coat up. I like to talk first. I'll tell you about London. You want to hear about London, I'll bet. I went for a walk, once, it was raining and there was this man by the river, drawing on the pavement in the rain. Fancy that! Drawing with chalk in the rain, and the rain just washing it away."

"Come now. Come."

"Do you know what he was drawing? Just dogs, cottages and that. And the people, Anna—listen to this!—standing in the rain, watching him."

"I want you. Hold me. I'm frightened."

"Listen! Do you know why I went for a walk? They wanted me to make love to a girl. They sent me to London and I went for this walk instead."

He could make her out as she watched him, judging him according to some instinct he did not understand.

"Are you alone too?"

"Yes."

"Why did you come?"

"They're crazy people the English! That old fellow by the river: they think the Thames is the biggest river in the world, you know that? And it's nothing! Just a little brown stream, you could nearly jump across it some places!"

"What's that noise?" she said suddenly. "I know that noise! It was a gun; the cocking of a gun!"

He held her tightly to stop her trembling.

"It was just a door," he said, "the latch of a door. This place is made of paper. How could you hear anything in such a wind?"

There was a footfall in the corridor. She struck at him in terror, the raincoat swinging around her. As they came in he was standing away from her, the knife at her throat, his thumb uppermost, the blade parallel to the ground. His back was very straight and his small face was turned to her, empty, held by some private discipline, a man once more intent upon appearances, conscious of tradition.

The farmhouse lay in darkness, blind and not hearing, motionless against the swaying larches and the running sky.

They had left a shutter open and it banged slowly without rhythm, according to the strength of the storm. Snow gathered like ash and was dispersed. They had gone, leaving nothing behind them but tire tracks in the hardening mud, a twist of wire, and the sleepless tapping of the north wind.